An Old-Fashioned MURDER

Also by Carol Miller

Murder and Moonshine

A Nip of Murder

An Old-Fashioned MURDER

CAROL MILLER

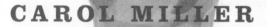

MINOTAUR BOOKS

A THOMAS DUNNE BOOK

NEW YORK

A THOMAS DUNNE BOOK FOR MINOTAUR BOOKS.
An imprint of St. Martin's Publishing Group.

www.thomasdunnebooks.com
www.minotaurbooks.com

Designed by Omar Chapa

Library of Congress Cataloging-in-Publication Data

Names: Miller, Carol, 1972– author.
Title: An old-fashioned murder : a moonshine mystery / Carol Miller.
Description: First edition. | New York : Minotaur Books, 2016. |
    Series: Moonshine mystery series ; 3 | "A Thomas Dunne book."
Identifiers: LCCN 2015049040 | ISBN 9781250077257 (hardcover) |
    ISBN 9781466889156 (e-book)
Subjects: LCSH: Waitresses—Virginia—Fiction. | Women detectives—
    Virginia—Fiction. | Murder—Investigation—Fiction. | BISAC:
    FICTION / Mystery & Detective / Women Sleuths. | GSAFD: Mystery
    fiction.
Classification: LCC PS3613.I53277 O43 2016 | DDC 813/.6—dc23
LC record available at http://lccn.loc.gov/2015049040

Our books may be purchased in bulk for promotional, educational, or business use. Please contact your local bookseller or the Macmillan Corporate and Premium Sales Department at 1-800-221-7945, extension 5442, or by e-mail at MacmillanSpecialMarkets@macmillan.com.

First Edition: May 2016

10 9 8 7 6 5 4 3 2 1

For my family,
who's weathered many a storm

An Old-Fashioned MURDER

CHAPTER
1

"Any sign of the truck yet, Ducky?"

"Not since the last time you asked, which was about two minutes ago."

"You're sure?" Aunt Emily called.

Daisy restrained a smile. "I'm standing at the window, looking straight out at the driveway and the road. I couldn't possibly miss it."

There was a momentary silence, then a set of loudly clicking heels headed down the entrance hall of the Tosh Inn. Daisy turned from the tall casement window just as the heels rounded the corner of the parlor. She met Aunt Emily's blue eyes. Ordinarily they were shrewd—too shrewd for comfort, on occasion—but today they were more anxious than anything else.

"They should be here by now," Aunt Emily warbled in an equally anxious tone.

"The delivery was scheduled for three o'clock," Daisy reminded her. "It's only a little bit after—"

The clock on the marble mantle chimed the half-hour.

"They're late!" Aunt Emily knit her freshly manicured fingers together. "What if there's been a mix-up about the day?"

"There couldn't have been a mix-up," Daisy replied patiently. "You confirmed the date with the shop at least half a dozen times over the past week. I did it twice myself."

"But what if there's been some sort of a problem with the loading, or the truck broke down, or there's been an accident—"

It was a rare spate of fretfulness from Aunt Emily, who was the proprietor of the inn and not in fact Daisy's—or anyone else's, for that matter—aunt. She was usually a tough old biddy, a very apt expression that she was fond of using to describe herself. Although she was closing in on seventy, advancing age had dampened neither Emily Tosh's beauty nor her considerable wit. Silver hair and a smattering of laugh lines and wrinkles merely complemented her invariably fashionable appearance and razor-sharp mind. She did tend to dance to the beat of her own drum, however, which sometimes gave the impression of her being a tad eccentric, not to mention a few apples short of a bushel.

"If they don't come soon," Aunt Emily pressed together the nervous raspberry lips that matched her nails, "the guests will begin arriving, and there will be no furniture for them."

"There's plenty of furniture," Daisy countered, gesturing around the room. "Armchairs and settees, tea tables and coffee tables. Everyone will have a place to sit and," she added with a slight chuckle, "a place to set their drink."

Aunt Emily nodded earnestly in agreement. "Thank heavens for that, at least."

Daisy shivered.

"Are you cold, Ducky? Should we turn up the heat?"

"No." She took a step back from the window. "I just got a chill. The wind must be picking up outside, because I felt a gust come through."

"The price of being an old Southern house, I'm afraid. Paper-thin walls and windows that never close quite right."

"I do wish that you could have replaced them, Aunt Emily. They're so drafty this time of year."

"The insurance simply wouldn't cover it," she responded regretfully. "The moldy rugs and draperies, yes. The stained and broken furniture, also yes. But the windows were fine and still plenty usable, according to the adjusters. Nothing that a little bleach and paint couldn't fix, they kept telling me."

"Well, bleach and paint sure don't fix the bugs and humidity that creep in during the summer or the cold breezes that whip around from corner to corner in the winter," Daisy returned dryly.

Aunt Emily nodded again. "But I think it came out all right in the end, don't you, Ducky? The parlor looks nice after the repairs, doesn't it?"

"Very nice! Especially when you consider what a complete mess it was only a couple of months ago."

It had been four months, to be exact. In October, the inn's well had gone wonky and ended up bursting into a geyser on the side lawn—flooding the parking lot, several of the outbuildings, and a portion of the grand Victorian behemoth in the process. The wraparound front porch and the stately parlor with its plethora of antique furnishings had sadly taken the brunt of the damage.

After weighing their collective options, Aunt Emily and the rest of the inn's regular inhabitants—Daisy and her sickly mama included—had determined to rally together and loyally stayed put. They didn't, in truth, have much of a choice. For a variety of reasons, they were all at the inn because they were otherwise without a home. But they resolved to make the best of the unfortunate situation— sharing rooms when necessary, helping with the dismal ensuing cleanup, and using whatever talents or abilities they possessed to assist with the lengthy list of repairs.

The work was finally completed in early February, and the Tosh Inn stood once again in all of its majestic, yellow-gabled glory. Aunt Emily had wasted no time in organizing a reopening celebration. The inn had never officially been closed, but that made not the slightest difference to her. She was an extremely social creature by nature and never missed an opportunity to play the role of hostess, which she always did with great skill and flair. A small weekend party for a select group of friends and neighbors was the perfect way to show off the inn's renovations. The only hiccup in the plan was that some of the new—albeit antique— furniture that had been purchased as part of the parlor redecoration was now tardy in its arrival.

"Is that the delivery truck?" Aunt Emily said hopefully.

Daisy looked out the window. A vehicle had turned off the main road onto the long driveway leading up to the inn. It was a rusty old pickup.

"Wait a minute." Aunt Emily squinted at it. "Doesn't that belong to—"

"Rick," Daisy answered.

Aunt Emily glanced at her questioningly. "What's he doing here?"

"I have no idea."

The pickup halted in the middle of the driveway, at the far end of the front walk.

"Oh, he can't park there!" Aunt Emily protested. "It'll interfere with the delivery."

She hurried from the parlor into the hall, and a moment later, the front door of the inn swung open with a heralding squeak.

Trailing after her, Daisy shook her head. "I don't know how you managed it, Aunt Emily. The whole entrance was fixed from top to bottom, but somehow that door still squeaks like a screechy cat toy."

"It works much better than any fancy, overpriced alarm system," she replied gravely.

Daisy didn't argue, knowing full well that Aunt Emily could—and would—go on at length about the numerous safety and snooping benefits of squeaky doors and creaky steps, another one of her perennially favorite topics. Even though the front porch steps of the inn had also been repaired after the flood damage, somehow they still creaked, too. It was Daisy's guess that at the conclusion of the renovations, the amply skilled carpenters had departed with several gratis jars of Aunt Emily's highly coveted gooseberry brandy in their deliberately creak-and-squeak-producing hands.

Together they watched Rick as he sprang from his truck and walked with long, lean strides toward the porch. He was wearing worn jeans and construction boots, with a navy wool shirt over a white T-shirt. His hair was dark and tousled. When he saw them standing at the open door waiting for him, he laughed. It was an arch, mocking sort of laugh, perfectly in keeping with his personality.

Richard Balsam was an exceedingly clever and incorrigible country boy, fond of guns, blueticks, and corn whiskey. A childhood friend of Daisy, he was an inveterate snake charmer, with lots of money from his extensive illegal moonshine enterprises. As part of his likker empire, Rick owned Daisy's ancestral home, which was a continual source of irritation to her, along with his tendency to appear—and then just as unexpectedly, disappear—at the most inopportune moments. Rick could be loyal. He also had a capricious temper.

"Hello, ladies," he drawled. "You look lovely today, Aunt Emily. As always."

As always when Rick flattered her, Aunt Emily blushed. "Why, thank you, Rick. You're so kind. Isn't he kind, Ducky?"

Daisy rolled her eyes.

"Now don't be jealous, darlin'," Rick chastised her. "You know I've got a soft spot for Aunt Emily."

"Only because she's got a soft spot for your sweet talk," Daisy retorted.

Rick grinned. "I'd talk plenty sweet to you, if you'd let me."

She rolled her eyes again, but she couldn't refrain from smiling a little, too. The man really was incorrigible.

With a wink, Rick changed the subject. "I heard that you were having some furniture delivered this afternoon," he said to Aunt Emily. "I thought I'd come by and see if you needed any help."

"Yes, we are expecting a delivery," Aunt Emily acknowledged, with some surprise. "How did you know?"

He shrugged. "I have my sources."

Daisy knew what that meant. "Let me guess," she responded wryly. "One of the furniture deliverymen moonlights for you? Hauling antiques during the day and then bootlegging 'shine at night?"

"People tell me things," Rick answered, not elaborating further. He dropped his voice to a more intimate tone and locked his dark eyes onto her. "I wish you wanted to tell me more things, Daisy."

Like the inescapable gravitational pull of a planet, his bewitching gaze drew her in. Then she reminded herself that she had to be careful. Rick might seem as cool as the moon, but he could burn her just as brutally as the sun. With effort, Daisy blinked and turned away.

"I tell you plenty of things," she said lightly, pretending that she hadn't understood him. "So does Aunt Emily. But we didn't tell you about the inn's new furniture, because we don't need any help with it."

"But we very much appreciate the offer," Aunt Emily added graciously. "We're having a little party to celebrate the redecoration. If you'd like to join us, Rick, you're more than welcome."

Daisy frowned at her.

"You're more than welcome," Aunt Emily repeated, ignoring Daisy's displeasure. "However, you will have to move your truck for the furniture to arrive."

Although she could feel Rick looking at her, this time Daisy refused to meet his gaze. Her eyes went to the thick gray clouds that were gathering on the horizon, inching their way toward the weak winter sun.

Rick watched her for a moment longer, then he said, "You know how much I enjoy your parties, Aunt Emily. They're always chock-full of surprises. But I'm afraid I can't stay." He motioned toward the sky. "There's a storm coming. By the looks of it, it could be a big one. I have to check on a few things. Batten down some hatches, just in case."

Daisy breathed an inaudible sigh of relief. To her chagrin, Aunt Emily proceeded to leave the invitation open.

"Well, you know where we are, Rick, if you change your mind."

"I might just do that," he replied. And with a parting nod, he turned toward his truck. When he reached it, he paused for a minute and glanced back at the inn. Finding Daisy still standing on the porch, Rick cocked his head at her, and his lips twitched with a hint of a grin. Then he jumped in and drove away.

As he disappeared down the road, Aunt Emily clucked her tongue. "I hope you know what you're doing with that one, Ducky."

Daisy's brow furrowed.

Aunt Emily gave a sudden shout of excitement and pointed. "Look, it's them! They're finally here!"

A new vehicle had pulled into the driveway, a small delivery truck. A tiny white hatchback preceded it, and a big black pickup traveled after it. They were all driving slowly and close together, like three odd-size geese waddling awkwardly in a row.

"It's no wonder that they're late," Daisy said, chuckling. "They probably left the shop well over an hour ago, but with the Fowler sisters in the lead, they never got faster than a crawl, even on the highway."

For the last thirty years—which was three years longer than Daisy had been alive—Edna and May Fowler had owned a little antiques shop in a nearly invisible dot on the map called Motley. It was Aunt Emily's favorite antiques shop not only in Pittsylvania County but also in all of southwestern Virginia, which was quite an accomplishment. Aunt Emily went crazy for old folk art, so she made a point of visiting every store, shack, and tumbledown shed in the area that sold anything remotely resembling an antique, no matter how broken or rusted.

"Go check the parlor for me, please, Ducky," Aunt Emily directed eagerly. "We have to make sure there's nothing in their way when they bring in the furniture. Quickly now!"

Daisy was tempted to respond that there was no need to hurry. Based on the current snail's pace at which the procession of vehicles was moving up the driveway, it would take a while before they reached the parking lot, stopped and organized themselves, and began unloading. But she didn't want to dampen Aunt Emily's enthusiasm, so she headed dutifully inside and surveyed the room.

The edges of the floral-patterned Persian carpets were all flat. No stray magazines or throw pillows were lying on the ground. The path to the empty spot between the two casement windows was clear, earmarked for the new long-case clock. Likewise, the path to the empty spot next to the marble mantel was also clear. The barrister bookcase was slated to go there. There were additionally two tip-top candle stands on the delivery list. Aunt Emily was constantly changing her mind about where she wanted them, but they were comparatively small and easy to move, so it didn't really matter where they were initially placed.

"Looks good!" Daisy reported. "No curled rug corners or odd bits on the floor for anybody to trip over."

"Who does that black pickup driving behind the delivery truck belong to?" Aunt Emily asked from the entrance hall.

"Drew," she answered.

Aunt Emily appeared instantly in the parlor. This time when Daisy met her blue eyes there was no anxiety in them. With the arrival of the furniture, it had been replaced by their usual shrewdness.

"He's very prompt," Aunt Emily remarked.

It was meant as a compliment. Aunt Emily didn't approve of folks being fashionably late. On the contrary, she firmly believed that it was only good manners to be punctual, particularly for events that she hosted.

"He certainly must be keen to see *someone*," Aunt Emily continued, with a sly smile. "Otherwise he wouldn't be the first guest for the party. The first official guest," she amended, no doubt thinking of Rick.

"Drew's not the first guest," Daisy corrected her matter-of-factly. "The Fowler sisters were invited, too, and their car is in front of the others."

"True," Aunt Emily conceded. "But Edna and May don't ogle your behind every time you saunter out of the room, Ducky."

Daisy's cheeks went a bit pink.

The sly smile grew. "Just so you know, I put Drew in the Stonewall Jackson room for the weekend. Not that I expect him to actually spend the night there."

"Oh, Aunt Emily—"

"You've been dating the man since last fall, more or less," Aunt Emily cut her off briskly, "so there's no need to get all bashful about it. You're a married woman, not a child."

That was precisely the problem, in Daisy's mind. She was still a married woman, and it bothered her. Only, she couldn't seem to get around to doing anything about it.

Matt McGovern was gone. There was no question about that. He had driven off one morning nearly five years ago and never come home again. The man had been an ardent gambler, a far too heavy drinker, and his choice in friends—Rick Balsam included—hadn't helped the situation any. But even with all that, he was still her husband, and Daisy was by nature loyal.

Drew Alcott, a bat conservationist whom she had met in the nearby mountains just prior to the inn calamity, had been remarkably understanding. When Daisy had told him about her estranged husband, Drew had called Matt several choice names and then let the subject drop, which had been just fine with her. They were both very busy. Drew traveled a lot for his job, and Daisy struggled on a daily basis to keep her little bakery, Sweetie Pies, afloat. That had kept their relationship on the lighter side. But Daisy realized that the time was slowly coming when she would have to make some sort of a decision about which direction she wanted to head in with him. Eventually she was either going to have to fish or cut bait, so to speak. She figured that the party—their first overnight weekend together—was the perfect opportunity to better test the water.

Aunt Emily's tone softened. "I just want you to be happy, Ducky. Your mama does, too. Sometimes we worry that you're waiting for—"

A loud crash from the direction of the kitchen interrupted her.

"Oh, for criminy sake!" Aunt Emily's raspberry lips tightened in irritation. "Georgia?" she called.

"Sorry," came a plaintive voice in reply.

"That girl is going to be the death of me," Aunt Emily groused. "Or at least the death of all my dishes."

Although Daisy nodded in sympathy, at the same time she said a silent word of thanks. Georgia's clumsiness had saved her from having to participate further in a conversation that she really preferred to avoid. It had nothing to do with bashfulness. Rather, Daisy found it so difficult to explain her continually varying and conflicting feelings regarding her marriage and the men in her life to herself that she couldn't possibly begin to explain them to anyone else, not even dear and well-meaning Aunt Emily.

"I better see what it was this time." Aunt Emily sighed. "Hopefully not any more of the stemware. She broke two goblets yesterday alone." She lowered her voice discreetly. "I'm starting to wonder if hiring her was such a good idea."

"Georgia's a hard worker," Daisy said.

"She's also a hard dropper."

Daisy couldn't refute that.

"I fear it may be a bad omen for the weekend," Aunt Emily mused mournfully.

"Nonsense!" Daisy exclaimed. "It's going to be a perfectly lovely weekend."

Aunt Emily sighed again.

In an effort to bolster her sagging spirits, Daisy added, "While you're in the kitchen, I'll go check on the furniture. They must be about ready to bring it in. I'm sure that it will look great when it's all in its proper place."

With a mumble of gratitude and another grumble about her stemware, Aunt Emily headed down the hall. Daisy, in turn, headed toward the front door.

Stepping onto the porch, she looked over at the parking lot. The crawling convoy had finally reached its destination. Two suitably burly chaps were arranging a pair of dollies and climbing into the back of the delivery truck. The Fowler sisters appeared to be helping someone out of the rear seat of their hatchback. And Drew was waving at her while pulling an overnight bag from the bed of his pickup. Just as Daisy was about to wave back, a cold gust of wind hit her. Rick was right. A storm was coming.

CHAPTER
2

"Careful with those legs, young man! That's not a bunch of last season's kindling you're holding. It's two-hundred-year-old rosewood."

The burly delivery chap with the tip-top candle stand in his hands looked slightly askance at Henry Brent but said nothing.

"Set it down there in the corner. That's the right spot. Gentle, now. Gentle! Pretend it's a nice full crate of beer. You wouldn't want to break a bottle, would you?"

When the candle stand with its delicate cabriole legs was safely on the ground next to the potted dwarf Meyer lemon tree, Henry Brent heaved a great sigh of relief. Then he promptly instructed the delivery chap on how best to proceed with the second candle stand, which was still waiting in the truck.

"Should I go with him?" he mused aloud, half to himself and half to Daisy. "Check that he's carrying it properly?"

"I'm sure that he'll do it all right," Daisy answered, smiling. "It's very kind of you to help with the delivery, but you really shouldn't go outside again, Mr. Brent. The air is getting awfully chilly."

He acquiesced with a nod. "When one starts getting up in years, Ducky, one does have to be more cautious about these things."

More cautious or not, at ninety-four, Henry Brent was still plenty spry. If everyone could have retained their faculties as well as he had, no one would have ever feared aging. He was well read, frequently droll, and all-around impossible not to like, except perhaps by delivery chaps who had been chastised for their rough handling of antiques.

Aunt Emily called him the dapper clacker, which fit the man perfectly. Henry Brent had proudly spent his life being dapper, and today was no exception. He wore a burgundy-striped seersucker suit, followed by scuffed white buck wingtips. His matching burgundy and white polka dot clip-on bow tie gave him the appearance of Clarence Darrow—albeit a slightly more Southern version—confidently marching up the courthouse steps for the start of a new and important trial.

"It's a rotten thing," Henry Brent's dentures clacked, hence the second part of Aunt Emily's affectionate appellation, "always having to consider the weather before poking your head an inch outdoors. It's like being a durn rabbit checking for a coyote skulking at the edge of your hole. But I'm afraid that at my age even the smallest sniffle can easily turn into pneumonia."

Daisy nodded back at him. "When we saw the forecast, we were worried that you might not come."

"Edna and May thought the same thing, so they decided to bring me with them. I couldn't very well say no, especially not with the surprise I have planned."

"A surprise? What surprise?"

The dapper clacker chortled and clacked with glee. "If I told you that, Ducky, then it wouldn't be a surprise no more."

"No, I suppose it wouldn't." Daisy chuckled at his gusto. "But I know that Aunt Emily will be thrilled to see you."

Henry Brent looked around the parlor. "Where is the grande dame?"

"She'll be here in a minute. She's in the kitchen with Georgia."

"Georgia?" He frowned. "I don't recall a Georgia. Don't tell me the ol' noodle is beginning to go at last?"

"The ol' noodle is just fine. Georgia's new," Daisy explained. "She showed up at the inn one day a couple of weeks ago, looking for a job and a place to stay. Aunt Emily felt sorry for her, so she hired her to help with the cleaning and cooking and such." She added silently, *And now the grande dame is feeling rather sorry for herself.*

"Has she got kin in these parts?"

"I'm not sure, but I don't believe so. She hasn't mentioned any, and as far as I know, nobody's ever called or come by asking for her." Daisy glanced at the Fowler sisters, who were debating vigorously between themselves and the other delivery chap whether it was too warm next to the mantel for the barrister bookcase. Edna and May were both excellent gossips, and Daisy dropped her voice accordingly. "I think Georgia's pretty down on her luck, but she doesn't like to talk about it."

"Well, that's certainly understandable," Henry Brent said. "Nobody wants to share bad stories about themselves, especially not when life's taken a turn for the worse. But it's good of Emily to give her a chance."

Daisy didn't tell him that the chance might not last much longer if Georgia couldn't stop dropping things, particularly the stemware.

"She's always had a kind heart. Speaking of kind hearts," he looked around the parlor again, "where is your lovely mama?"

"Upstairs in bed, I'm sorry to report."

Henry Brent responded with a concerned double clack. "Oh, dear. Nothing too serious, I hope?"

She shook her head. "It's just a bad cold, but the doctor gave her strict instructions to stay in her room. No exceptions allowed. Her lungs are already so weak from all of her other problems, and he's worried about her cough. It's been getting steadily worse over the last few days. We don't want it to become bronchitis."

"From your mouth to God's ear, Ducky."

"I should bring her some tea." Daisy checked her watch. "She was napping earlier, but she's probably awake by now."

"Tea!" Henry Brent exclaimed in protest. "Tea won't do your mama a lick of good. What she needs is a hot toddy. 'In damp or wet,' my meemaw always said. And for flus and colds, an extra shot in the cup. Rum and rye are good, but corn whiskey is best."

Daisy couldn't help thinking that if his meemaw were still on this earth, she and Aunt Emily would have gotten along swimmingly. Aunt Emily equated moonshine with medicine, too. Scientifically proven or not, she was convinced that her gooseberry brandy had the miraculous ability to cure a wide assortment of ailments.

A throat cleared gruffly next to them. The delivery chap was back from the truck with the second candle stand.

"So," he asked a bit sharply, "where do you want it?"

With an equally sharp clack in reply, Henry Brent directed him to the opposite end of the room, next to the well-stocked liquor cart. It was not one of the spots that Aunt Emily had originally selected, but Daisy knew when she saw it that she would be in full agreement. With the top tipped up, the candle stand was just the right height and offered just the right amount of space to serve as an overflow for an extra stack of cocktail napkins, another ice bucket, and an additional decanter or two.

As Henry Brent shifted his—and the delivery chap's—attention to the unwieldy longcase clock that was next on the list, Daisy felt a hand on her shoulder.

"Hey there, beautiful."

It was Drew. She started to turn, but was stopped by his arms wrapping around her from behind.

"I sure am glad to see you." Pulling her toward him, Drew's face sunk into her hair. "You smell nice—cinnamon and vanilla."

"I should." Daisy smiled. "I work in a bakery, after all."

"Mmm." His breath was warm on her cheek.

Closing her eyes, she relaxed against him.

"I bet you taste nice, too." Drew's lips traveled down her neck.

It felt good—really good. She pressed into his body.

"I don't suppose," the lips worked back up along her jaw, "that we could disappear for a little while—"

A stern *tsk-tsk* interrupted the enticing proposition. "I did not expect this sort of behavior from you, Daisy Mc-Govern. What in heaven's name would your mama say if she saw you making such a public spectacle?"

"She'd say," a voice, followed by a jovial laugh, answered, "that they ought to go somewhere and get a room."

"Parker!"

"Oh, wait." The laugh became an uproarious cackle. "They already are somewhere with rooms. They're at an inn!"

Daisy's first thought was a combination of regret and annoyance at having her pleasant interlude with Drew brought to such an abrupt end. Her second thought went to Aunt Emily's earlier remark about bad omens for the weekend.

The stern *tsk-tsk* repeated itself. "My goodness, Daisy. If Matt were here—"

That was enough to elevate Daisy's annoyance to anger. Detaching herself from Drew, she spun around on her heel. "Well, he's not here, Lillian. He hasn't been here for a very long time, as you well know."

Lillian Barker responded with a characteristically sour lemon face.

"She has a point, Lill—"

The sour lemon face turned immediately to her still-chortling husband, Parker, effectively silencing him.

Not wanting to blow the matter out of proportion, Daisy took a deep breath. Lillian Barker hadn't always been such a sour lemon, or at least not quite so sour. She did by nature have the rather disagreeable tendency to be both pessimistic and exceedingly critical. To her, the glass was habitually half empty. Decent civilization was continually on the brink of collapse. And everything was much better in the good old days, even though the woman was barely fifty, so the good old days weren't all that far back.

While Lillian's personality could never have been considered really warm, there was a time when Daisy would have called her a friend. They had occasionally spent an

afternoon together shopping in Lynchburg or sharing a plate
of barbecue at the local diner where Daisy had been a waitress before its conversion to the bakery. Lillian was Matt's
paternal aunt, and when her brother—Matt's daddy—had
died unexpectedly in a propane tank explosion along with
Daisy's daddy a few years back, it had hit her just as hard as
everybody else. She had slowly started to come to terms
with the shock and the grief the same as Daisy and her
mama, but then Matt had decided to run off shortly thereafter. The sudden departure of her beloved nephew was
more than Lillian could bear, and instead of gradually heal-
ing, she had grown progressively bitter.

Unlike Aunt Emily and the rest of their mutual acquain-
tances, Lillian didn't want Daisy to move on. On the contrary, she believed that Daisy should spend the remainder
of her life in solemn and solitary contemplation, patiently
waiting for Matt's return. It didn't seem to occur to her that
there was not the slightest indication that he would ever
return. At first, Daisy had been sympathetic, thinking that
Lillian was simply trying to turn back the clock to happier
times. But as the weeks and months and years rolled by, and
Lillian became increasingly strident in her views, Daisy
found it tougher to swallow. After working so hard to come
to grips with her loss and inch her way forward, she didn't
appreciate Lillian insisting that she stay permanently sad
and alone.

In a more densely populated area, it might have been
easier to avoid the Barkers. Not so in rural Pittsylvania
County, where Lillian and Parker were not only in-laws but
also neighbors. Thankfully their farmhouse was a good mile
up the road from the inn, which meant that they weren't
strolling by too often, especially not in winter.

"We were anxious to see the renovations," Parker announced amiably, clearly making an effort to offset his wife.

Although he was the same age as Lillian, Parker had the entirely opposite disposition. He loved to joke and laugh, had a cheerful round face, and possessed an even rounder body, remarkably resembling a cantaloupe. In contrast, Lillian was a stiff and chewy string bean—topped with a sour lemon face.

"Good of you to come, Dog. Good of you to come!" Henry Brent turned momentarily away from the tricky maneuvering of the longcase clock to shake Parker's hand.

"His name is Parker," Lillian snapped.

"Parker 'Dog' Barker," Henry Brent responded with a woof, not the least bit deterred by her imperious attitude.

Lillian's lemon mouth puckered.

"Now, my dear," Parker said, his soothing tone barely concealing a chuckle. "You know Henry's called me that since I was a wee shaver. Everyone has—"

"Well, you're not a wee shaver anymore," she retorted brusquely.

"No, he certainly isn't," Henry Brent concurred, gesturing toward Parker's cantaloupe belly.

The two men laughed heartily, and Lillian's pucker tightened.

"Uh, excuse me," one of the delivery chaps interjected, as he struggled to maintain his hold on the base of the clock.

"It ain't gettin' any lighter," the other delivery chap added peevishly.

Seeing the latter's fingers dig into the clock's intricately carved hood, Henry Brent jumped in alarm and redirected his focus to the furniture. Always helpful—and smart enough after so many years of marriage to recognize an easy avenue of escape—Parker inquired whether he could be of any assistance and promptly waddled off with the group, leaving his wife glaring after them.

"How's everything coming?" Aunt Emily said, appearing at Daisy's side. "I could hear the laughter all the way in the kitchen, so it must be good . . ."

Her words trailed away as she met Daisy's grim gaze.

"I can't believe that you invited the Barkers," Daisy muttered.

"The Barkers?" Aunt Emily echoed in surprise. "No, I didn't. Of course I wouldn't. Not when—" Noticing Lillian, who was still glaring at her husband and Henry Brent, she broke off abruptly. "Oh, Lord help us."

Daisy couldn't have said it any better herself.

An instant later, Aunt Emily assumed the serene expression of the consummate hostess. "Lillian, such a pleasure!"

Turning to her, Lillian offered a polite and mildly warm smile. "Hello, Emily. Thank you for having us."

"And Parker? Is he . . ." Aunt Emily spotted him tripping over the delivery chaps and the clock. "Helping Henry with the furniture, I see."

"I assume the Robinsons told you that we were coming in their stead?" Lillian asked.

"Ah, the Robinsons." A sudden light of understanding shone in Aunt Emily's eyes. "They did telephone this morning to let me know about their last-minute change in plans." She looked at Daisy. "You remember the Robinsons' daughter—the one in Savannah—who's expecting?"

Daisy nodded.

"Well, apparently she went into labor early, so they had to dash off lickety-split to be with her."

"I like the Robinsons," Daisy replied wistfully, making an involuntary mental comparison.

"So do I, Ducky. So do I."

"I happened to be driving by their house when they were packing up the car," Lillian explained. "And they told me how sorry they were about having to miss your little get-together this weekend. When I said I hadn't heard of it, they mentioned how tight you were for space. Then it occurred to me that with them not coming, you'd have a room free. Parker really was anxious to see the renovations, and Daisy and I haven't had a good chance lately to sit down for a serious chat—"

Daisy swallowed a groan.

"—so Parker and I decided to take the Robinsons' place," Lillian concluded. "I hope that's all right." Her brisk tone made it more of a pronouncement than a query.

"Of course," Aunt Emily responded lightly. "The more, the merrier. You're always welcome."

"Now that's settled, I should have Parker bring in our bags." Lillian glanced around in search of her husband. "Sooner rather than later. I think the weather is about to turn."

And as she said it, the sky obediently darkened, and the parlor fell into gloom.

CHAPTER
3

"Those nice boys did such a good job of bringing in the furniture—" May began.

"—and setting it all up," Edna agreed.

"The candle stand with the mahogany inlay looks lovely —" May continued.

"—although the oak bookcase is very handsome, too," Edna added.

Drew leaned against the scuffed leather smoking chair in which Daisy was sitting. It was her favorite seat in the parlor, and she claimed it whenever she could. Somehow the chair had managed to weather the flood, and as a result, Daisy felt an odd sense of solidarity with it. A pair of scrappy survivors.

"Do the two of them always—" Drew began.

"—finish each other's sentences?" Daisy cut him off, with a smile. "Oh, yes. It can drive you a little crazy at first, but they're both so awfully sweet that you just get used to it after a while."

"You drove me a little crazy at first," he said, smiling back at her.

"And you got used to it?"

"No, now you drive me a lot crazy."

Daisy laughed. "Believe it or not, you aren't the only person to have told me that."

"Oh, I believe it." Drew settled himself on the wide arm of the chair. "So which is Edna, and which is May?"

"Edna is the one wearing the navy skirt and has the curls. May is in the taupe skirt and has the bangs."

He studied the two women. "I can't decide if they look alike or not."

"It's the white hair with the matching sweater sets and pearls," Daisy told him. "It's misleading. Once you get to know them better, you'll see the differences."

Edna Fowler was the elder sister by a year, had a cleft chin, a slightly stockier build, and tended to be the sentence finisher. She was also the more business-minded of the pair, organizing the inventory for the antiques shop and negotiating the prices. May, on the other hand, was the artist in the family. She dealt primarily with the pottery and the paintings and would occasionally wax poetic about ethereal sunrises and the beauty of morning dew. It didn't seem to bother her that she frequently didn't get beyond the first half of a sentence. Her double dimples merely smiled as she started a new one.

Although Daisy didn't know exactly how old the sisters were, her best guess was somewhere in their late fifties or early sixties. They were a bit tricky with age. Their hair had not a tinge of color left in it, and they could be doting and grandmotherly, but they also operated the store full-time with no outside help, and they did it with a good deal of spunk.

"Now tell us honestly—" May began.

"—what do you think?" Edna concluded.

Aunt Emily's gaze traveled slowly around the parlor, first to the barrister bookcase next to the mantel, then to the two tip-top candle stands in their respective corners, and finally to the longcase clock in between the windows.

"It's all wonderful!" she proclaimed at last, beaming. "I couldn't possibly pick a favorite piece."

"Everything looks good," Henry Brent agreed. "Nothing broken or banged about too badly in the delivery."

"It almost makes me glad that we had the flood," Aunt Emily said, as she hugged each sister in turn. "Such beautiful new—well, old—furniture to enjoy."

"We're so happy—"

"—that you're so happy."

"But there's still more to be happy about!" Henry Brent gave an excited double clack. "There's a surprise, isn't there, Ducky?"

The group turned expectantly toward Daisy.

"A surprise?" Lillian echoed from the edge of the parlor. Parker had just collected their bags from the car, and she was in the process of directing him upstairs. "Oh, Daisy! Is it Matt? Is Matt the surprise?"

Daisy stared at her.

"You should have told me that he was back!" she went on breathlessly. "I would have prepared. We would have thrown a party."

There was a moment of stunned silence all around. Daisy's mouth opened, but not a syllable emerged.

"We *are* throwing a party," Aunt Emily reminded Lillian crisply after a minute, "and I can assure you that Matt McGovern is not in any way involved."

Lillian's face fell.

With his own face hidden behind a humongous paisley

carpet bag, Parker said, "Which room was it again, my dear?"

"The James Longstreet," Aunt Emily answered. "Third floor. First door on your right. The key will be in the lock."

Henry Brent gave an amused clack. "Very appropriate choice in rooms, I'd say," he commented to Drew.

Drew looked at Daisy quizzically. History was not his forte.

"All of the inn's rooms are named after Confederate generals," she explained briefly. "Longstreet isn't considered the most popular. He befriended Grant after the war—"

"—and lost Gettysburg," Edna finished for her, with a distinct hint of pique.

"Yes, indeed," Henry Brent chimed in. "Edna is the president-elect of our local chapter of the Daughters of the Confederacy. If there's anything that you want to know about the war, she's the one to go to."

Edna's back straightened proudly. Both she and her sister were loyal, longtime members of the organization. Edna had been diligently working her way up the rungs of the officer ladder for many years. When finally selected as president, she had proclaimed to everybody who would listen that it was the happiest day of her life.

"What room am I in?" Henry Brent asked Daisy.

"The Jubal Early, I believe."

He nodded approvingly.

"It's on this floor, on the other side of the dining room," Daisy told him.

"We didn't want you to have to climb up and down the stairs all weekend, Henry," Aunt Emily added.

"But climbing is evidently just fine for us," Lillian remarked acidly.

Aunt Emily turned to respond, but she and Parker had already started down the hall toward the stairs.

"That woman is going to be a headache, isn't she?" Drew said in a low tone that only Daisy could hear.

"*Headache* isn't a strong enough word," she replied with a sigh.

His brow furrowed. "Should I try talking to her?"

Daisy shook her head. "It won't do any good."

"But maybe if she got to know me a little better, then she wouldn't be quite so stuck on your ex."

"It's a nice idea," Daisy put her hand on his appreciatively, "except Lillian will always be stuck on Matt. Somewhere along the line she decided that her darling nephew could neither be blamed for anything nor do anything wrong. And she's getting worse about it, not better. Talking to her will only provoke her. It's like waving a hunk of fresh hamburger in front of an ornery badger."

"Well, I'm not just going to sit by and let her ruin the whole weekend for you," Drew said.

"She's not going to ruin anything." Daisy gave his fingers an affectionate squeeze.

He responded with a rakish grin. "Good, because I have no intention of being separated from you for the next two days."

"Only the days?" Daisy returned, with her own grin. "Not the nights?"

Her flirtations were cut short by Aunt Emily.

"Now, about this surprise?" Aunt Emily chirped, looking back and forth between Daisy and Henry Brent.

Daisy could only shrug. "I know nothing about it, other than there is one."

Henry Brent gurgled mischievously. He might as well have been a seven-year-old hiding a stash of gum balls.

"It must be a good surprise," Aunt Emily prodded him eagerly.

He gurgled some more.

May started to speak, but the squeaky front door interrupted her.

"The rain has arrived," a booming voice announced.

"Rain!" Henry Brent hiccupped in distress.

"Give it another couple of minutes," the voice continued, "and it should be a real downpour."

"Oh, then I must hurry!" And without hesitation, Henry Brent set off in a full sprint for the entrance hall.

"Mr. Brent," Daisy called after him, remembering how cold the wind had been. "You're not going outside, are you? Because I don't think—"

She began to rise from her chair to follow him, but Drew stopped her.

"I'll go," he volunteered. "He may need help anyway, with whatever his surprise is."

Daisy nodded gratefully, and Drew trotted after him. There was a loud bustle in the entrance hall as folks came in and folks went out. The weather prognosticator appeared a moment later.

"Those are some mighty black clouds rolling in." His voice boomed just as loudly in the parlor as it had from the front door. "I predict one heck of a deluge."

"Then we're glad to have you back before it hits," Aunt Emily answered with all the courtesy of the good innkeeper. "Is your wife with you, Mr. Lunt?"

"Kenneth. I keep telling you to call me Kenneth," he corrected her in an affable but firm tone. "And yes, Sarah's right behind me."

Sarah Lunt stepped out of her husband's sizable shadow and murmured a faint greeting. She was a tiny woman, barely five feet tall with an equally petite frame. She reminded Daisy of a skittish field mouse. Her thin hair was a mousy brown, her darting eyes were the same drab shade, and her pointed little chin quivered whenever anyone spoke to her—or even looked at her—a smidge too hard. She couldn't have been older than thirty-five, yet she moved haltingly, as if weighed down by an oppressive burden.

What that burden might have been, Daisy didn't know. Kenneth Lunt was a boisterous and assertive sort of person who expressed his thoughts freely, but he didn't give any indication of being mean or aggressive toward his wife. If she was a field mouse, then he was a noisy blue jay. In his upper thirties, he had black hair that was beginning to gray at the sideburns and a bulky upper body that didn't match his angular legs.

"The Lunts have been staying at the inn while house-hunting in the area," Aunt Emily explained to the rest of the group. "You sure did get an early start today," she said to the couple in a polite way of making conversation. "We missed you at breakfast."

"It wasn't as early of a start as hers," Kenneth replied, motioning toward Daisy. "Are you always out the door at such an ungodly hour?"

Daisy responded with a small smile. "It's the curse of working in bakeries and diners, unfortunately—up before the rooster. But I am sorry if I woke you. I do try hard to be quiet, and I'm usually pretty good at it. I've lived here long enough to know where all the creaky old floorboards are, so I manage to avoid most of them. The stairs can get a bit tricky, though, especially this time of year when the wood is drier and more prone to squeaks."

"No worries," Kenneth told her. "I tend to be a light

sleeper away from home. Every strange tick and click wakes me, even the quiet ones."

Aunt Emily frowned at the newly delivered longcase clock. "Then perhaps we better not set that one while you're here. They can take some getting used to, and if you're already restless during the night, all those gongs every hour could be frustrating."

"No worries," Kenneth repeated. "I heard the clock over there on the mantel chime each half-hour, and it didn't bother me."

Daisy blinked at him in surprise. "The chimes from that little clock are really light. You must have exceptionally good hearing."

"He does," his wife confirmed softly.

Aunt Emily's frown deepened. "I do wish that you would have mentioned this earlier. I could have moved you to a different room when there were still more options available. Let me think for a moment. You're in the George Pickett. That's directly at the top of the stairs on the second floor—"

"We would be happy to switch," Lillian proposed, as she and Parker reappeared in the parlor.

She spoke the words with such a complete lack of expression that Daisy couldn't tell if the offer was one of genuine kindness or simply another complaint about having to climb to the third floor.

"That's generous of you, Lillian," Aunt Emily replied. "But your room is directly at the top of the stairs, too, only slightly higher. I don't believe that's going to help much with noises echoing up the steps."

"Sarah and I don't need to move," Kenneth said.

"There is an empty room further down the hall on the

third floor," Aunt Emily told him. "It's rather small, though, because it tucks up into the attic, so I'm not sure how comfortable the two of you would be."

"We're fine where we are," he answered.

Aunt Emily didn't press the point further. He was the customer, after all. If he didn't have a problem with the location of his room, then neither did she. A somewhat awkward pause followed, during which Lillian and Parker deposited themselves on the gold-brocaded settee across from the Fowler sisters, who were seated on the emerald-brocaded settee.

"If you decide to set both clocks," May observed after a moment to no one in particular, "you should check that they have the same time—"

"—or you'll have dueling chimes," Edna concurred.

Although Parker wheezed in amusement, somehow the remark made the pause even more awkward. Daisy tried a new subject.

"Did you have any luck with the house-hunting today?" she asked Sarah, hoping to draw the woman—who was still standing half hidden in the shadow of her husband—out of her shell.

"There was one brick ranch," Sarah began timidly. She looked at Kenneth for corroboration.

"We talked about this already." He used the same tone that he had earlier with Aunt Emily—affable but firm. "It's not big enough."

"But the garden was terribly pretty."

Kenneth gave his wife an almost pitying glance. "It's the middle of winter. The garden was bare dirt with a few matted leaves in the corners."

Sarah sniffled.

"Now, the garden here," he went on, "that's an entirely different matter." He turned to Aunt Emily. "I've seen those azaleas that you have along the eastern side of the house. They're so big, they must be ancient."

Aunt Emily nodded with pride. "They were planted before I was born. We were very lucky not to lose them in the flood."

Kenneth nodded back at her. "I bet they put on a fantastic show in the spring." He turned again to his wife. "Wouldn't you like to have that for a garden?"

Sarah's drab eyes flashed with the barest hint of a spark. "Oh, I would."

He smiled down at her. "That settles it then." With a broad, sweeping gesture of his arm and an almost thunderous voice, he declared, "We've decided to buy the inn."

CHAPTER
4

Daisy's instinctive reaction was that Kenneth Lunt must be joking, but he wasn't laughing.

"Buy the inn?" Aunt Emily echoed slowly.

"Buy the inn," Kenneth confirmed.

The smile to his wife had been replaced by rigid lips and a jaw set in sober determination. The man definitely wasn't joking.

"I'm not . . ." Aunt Emily hesitated.

Her brow was furrowed, and her lips became rigid, too. She seemed confused, which in turn confused Daisy. Aunt Emily was the last surviving member of the oldest family in Pittsylvania County. Her kinfolk had originally settled the area, and the venerable Victorian was the final vestige of the once glorious Tosh tobacco empire, which had long ago crumbled into dust. The house had survived fires, earthquakes, tornadoes, and most recently, the flood. It was not only Aunt Emily's ancestral home, it was also her heritage. She wouldn't ever give it up—or so Daisy had always been led to believe.

"You'll be well compensated," Kenneth said. "Taking into consideration all the work you've had done recently, of course. I will need some more information on the plumbing and electrical updates. And," he made another sweeping gesture with his arm, "we'll take it fully furnished."

"What a generous offer," Lillian remarked.

Except it sounded much more like a demand than an offer. Or if not an actual demand, then at the very least an assumption that the matter was already a done deal. Ironing out a specific moving day and perhaps negotiating the disposition of a favorite knickknack was all that seemed to remain. Based on Kenneth Lunt's assured demeanor, the inn and its contents were practically signed, sealed, and as good as delivered to him and his wife.

Sufficient minutes had now passed that Daisy expected Aunt Emily to have overcome her initial shock and respond with a decisive rejection, but she didn't. Instead she appeared earnest and thoughtful, as though the idea required serious contemplation.

"Sell the inn." Parker shook his head. "I didn't think I would ever see the day."

"Time marches on," Lillian replied casually.

Daisy shot her an irritated glance. Apparently it only marched on when it was convenient and agreeable to Lillian.

"But what would happen to my girls?" Aunt Emily mused, more to herself than to the rest of the group.

That was precisely Daisy's question. There was not the slightest doubt about the inn belonging to Aunt Emily and her having every right to do with it as she chose, but it was also the place where Daisy and her mama lived. Without it, they'd be out on the street—or more accurately, setting up cots and sleeping bags on the floor of the bakery—along with Daisy's best friend, Beulah, who likewise called the inn her home. In addition, Beulah's popular little hair salon occupied a former potting shed on one corner of the inn's property. She was working there right now, Friday afternoon being among her busiest times. Daisy could only imagine how horrified Beulah would be at the prospect of losing her business.

May drew a white lace handkerchief from the pocket of her skirt and pressed it between her palms. "Such a shame—" she began.

It was Aunt Emily and not her sister who interrupted her.

"No," Aunt Emily said. "I couldn't possibly sell."

Kenneth's mouth twitched in evident surprise. "Of course you can."

"No." This time Aunt Emily included a resolute nod. "I can't sell the inn."

The twitch repeated itself. "If it's a matter of money . . ."

"Money?" Aunt Emily gave a little chuckle. "If I spent my days worrying about money—or rather, my lack of it—I would have been in the ground twenty years ago."

That answer clearly did not please Kenneth Lunt, because his whole body visibly stiffened.

"I'm so glad that you like the house." Aunt Emily used her most soothing tone—the patient nursery maid placating a disappointed toddler blended with the savvy business owner flattering a valuable client. "And we very much enjoy having you here, but the inn isn't for sale."

"Why not?" Kenneth retorted.

The words were spoken so sharply that both Edna and May shifted uncomfortably on their settee.

It's the timing," Aunt Emily told him. "The timing simply doesn't work."

Daisy found it an odd thing for her to say. She didn't see how timing played any part in it. This wasn't a case of Aunt Emily at long last reaching retirement age and deciding to move to a vacation spot at the sunny seaside or downsizing to be nearer to the grandchildren. Either she wanted to remain in the house where she had been born and spent her entire life, or she didn't.

"Then maybe we need to fix the timing," Kenneth growled.

Sarah placed a gentle hand on his arm. "I don't think—"

"Do you want the place or not?" he cut her off.

"Yes, but—"

"Then we're getting it!"

"Now see here." Parker straightened up in his seat. "There's no need to start shouting. If Emily doesn't want to sell, then she doesn't have to sell."

Kenneth turned to him with a narrow gaze.

Parker shifted uncomfortably on the settee, just as Edna and May had done a few moments earlier. "It's supposed to be a jolly party," he muttered.

"Jolly indeed," Daisy agreed under her breath. So far there had been a lot more bickering and bad omens than merriment.

"Drinks!" Aunt Emily proclaimed. "Drinks for everyone!"

There was an audible sigh of relief from Edna and May, and Parker instantly brightened at the idea.

Aunt Emily looked at Daisy. "Ducky—"

"Right." She nodded. "I'm on it."

After so many years of being the local diner waitress, Daisy was frequently called upon to act as the barmaid of the inn. There were plenty of occasions when she grumbled about it, but today she was happy to try to break the growing tension in the room. A nip all around might be just the ticket.

Rising from her chair, she headed toward the liquor cart. Her first thought as she picked up one of the crystal decanters was that she didn't have enough glasses. Aunt Emily preempted her.

"Georgia," she called toward the kitchen. "Could you bring some extra glasses into the parlor, please?"

Daisy smiled. "You're awfully daring."

Aunt Emily spread her hands ruefully. "I figure that it's a question of odds. How many more could she really break today?"

"You don't actually want me to answer that, do you?"

There was a flurry of activity at the front door—loud thumping and bumping accompanied by one or two profane grunts.

"Dang, this thing is heavy."

"You ain't kiddin'."

"Watch the corner. Watch the corner!" Henry Brent interjected in warning.

"I am watchin' the corner!"

"Better watch that you don't drop the dang thing on our feet!"

The group in the parlor collectively turned toward the entrance hall as the pair of burly delivery chaps—assisted by Drew and directed by Henry Brent—inched their way into the inn. The three younger men struggled with a large rectangular object that was covered by a cotton sheet.

"Oh, it's a furniture surprise!" Aunt Emily exclaimed. "Henry, you shouldn't have!"

"I thought the boys had gone," Edna said, glancing around the room at the new furniture. "I thought it had all been delivered."

"There's something extra," May told her. "Henry was just waiting for the right moment to bring it inside."

Edna looked perplexed.

"Henry wanted a gift for Emily," May explained. "He came by the shop yesterday when you were at the salon getting your hair done. He found the perfect piece in the back room, and the boys added it to the truck this morning."

"They did? I didn't notice that. Which piece in the back room?"

"You'll see in a minute. It wouldn't be fair for me to give it away now."

"No previews!" Henry Brent hollered, as both Aunt Emily and Edna started, curious, toward the hall. "You'll have to wait until we've got it set up."

Aunt Emily slowed but didn't stop. "Where are you putting it?" she asked excitedly.

"In the nook off the dining room," he answered. "It's the best spot."

"But then you should come through the parlor. It's much easier this way."

"And then you'd peek!"

"She's trying to peek now," Lillian informed him. "Edna, too."

"Tattler," Edna said, sticking out her tongue at Lillian.

Lillian gasped. "Parker! Did you see what she did?"

"By golly," Parker chortled, "I believe this party is beginning to pick up."

"Just wait until we get a little liquor in everybody," Daisy murmured.

"Start with my wife, would you?" he murmured back at her.

"My pleasure." Daisy took one of the etched crystal tumblers that matched the decanter already in her hand and filled it with a generous two-finger pour. "Here's your drink, Lillian. You don't like ice, if I recall correctly?"

In fact, Daisy recalled quite clearly—as she did automatically with all food and drink preferences after having served countless plates, mugs, and bowls to friends and strangers alike—that Lillian didn't have a preference one way or the other regarding ice. But she figured that no ice equalled a stronger beverage, which in turn would hopefully equal a little less potent Lillian.

"Thank you, Daisy." Accepting the proffered glass, Lillian took a small sip. She must have liked the sample, because she promptly followed it with a hearty gulp.

Daisy and Parker exchanged a discreet smile.

"What's the drink for today?" May asked. "It's Thursday—no, Friday—so that would make it—"

"—rye," Edna answered.

"Oh, I like rye." May carefully smoothed her handkerchief and returned it to her skirt pocket. "But I thought Saturday was—"

"—bourbon," Edna said.

"Saturday is bourbon?" Parker leaned toward the sisters with interest. "Well, that's certainly something to look forward to tomorrow. Although I'm awfully fond of rye, too."

"Rye on Friday and bourbon on Saturday?" Kenneth squinted at them. "What is that—some sort of nutty local superstition?"

Parker tittered. "Hear that, Emily? You're a superstitious nut."

"No doubt about it," she replied matter-of-factly. "I don't think there's a person in the county who'd disagree."

And as if to prove the point, Aunt Emily danced a little jig while bending and stretching in every direction in an effort to catch a better glimpse of her furniture surprise as it moved down the hallway under its protective sheet.

"You're going to hurt yourself," Daisy said. "Or make the boys lose their hold because they're laughing so hard, which might end up hurting one of them—and that includes Drew. Just be patient a moment and have a seat. I'll pour you a drink."

Daisy started dropping cubes from the ice bucket into a tumbler, but Aunt Emily was far too energized to sit down.

"Georgia," she called again, "we're going to need those glasses!"

"Ice?" Daisy asked Kenneth Lunt.

He was still squinting. "What exactly are my options?"

"Ice or no ice. Rye or no rye." Daisy smiled as she added, "Or any other drink that you want, but then you'll have to wait a minute while I hunt down the right bottle in another room. Aunt Emily is a bit like the Royal Navy. They have a different toast every day, and she serves a different liquor every day."

Kenneth's mouth sagged open with all the grace of a gasping bass. Daisy had to smother a laugh. The man was obviously not the type to be often at a loss for words, but Aunt Emily's peculiar eccentricities had the impressive ability to render even the most self-assured person speechless on occasion.

Sarah took a small shuffling step forward. "I wouldn't mind trying the rye," she squeaked. "Unless it's terribly strong," she amended hastily.

"I'll add a little water," Daisy told her, as she proceeded to fill and serve the remaining empty tumblers.

"Georgia!" Aunt Emily's tone rose impatiently.

Georgia neither responded nor appeared with the requested glasses.

"What can that girl possibly be—" Aunt Emily began, but she was distracted an instant later by the arrival of her furniture surprise in the dining room.

"That's the spot," Henry Brent said to Drew and the delivery chaps, pointing at their final destination. "Over there, next to the doors. In the nook."

The parlor and dining room were separated by a set of beautiful antique French doors. Each door had eight panels of glass that were placed in pairs starting at the top of the door and reaching to within a foot of the bottom. The final foot was solid wood, which had been painted an almost yellow ivory with a lovely depiction of pea-green English ivy vines that appeared to be crawling upward. The nook was immediately adjacent to the doors on the dining room side. It was a relatively narrow recess that fit a buffet perfectly, although there was nothing there now, because after the flood, Aunt Emily had decided to move the china cabinet to the opposite end of the room.

"Right up against the wall," Henry Brent instructed the three men. "As close as you can get to the molding."

They heaved and hauled and pushed.

"Be mindful of the floor!" he cautioned them as they labored, clacking his dentures anxiously. "It'll scratch if you drag instead of lift."

There was some low grumbling and an exasperated glance from one of the delivery chaps, but they didn't argue as they had before. They looked simply too tired.

While the mysterious object was being painstakingly positioned, Aunt Emily, Edna, and Lillian all took turns guessing its identity. Far too tall for a sideboard, observed Aunt Emily. Not nearly wide enough for the old farm cupboard that had been in the back room of the shop, remarked Edna. Much heavier than a decorative credenza, commented Lillian.

Finally the piece was in its assigned place. The group in the parlor flocked forward eagerly for the unveiling. Daisy pushed back the French doors as far as they would go to give everybody enough space. And with a double clack of supreme satisfaction, Henry Brent reached for the sheet.

In the same moment that he pulled it off, Georgia appeared in the dining room through the kitchen doorway, carrying a silver serving tray loaded with glasses. She took one look at the crowd standing before her, and the tray crashed to the ground.

CHAPTER
5

Everybody's head immediately snapped from the unveiling in the nook to the shattered glasses on the dining room floor. Everybody's except for Daisy's. Her eyes were on Georgia. Unlike all the others, Georgia wasn't looking at the mess that she had made or even at the new piece of furniture. She was still looking at the group. More accurately, she was staring at the group. And if Daisy wasn't much mistaken, Georgia seemed to be staring at one person in particular.

Who that person was, Daisy couldn't tell. She was standing slightly behind and to the side of the group—closest still to the parlor—so her view was partially blocked. She could see Georgia's pixie cut of strawberry blond hair, the thick sprinkling of sunny freckles across her cheeks and nose, and most significant, her wide gray eyes that were focused unblinkingly on some person in front of her. Daisy took a quick survey. No one was staring back, or at least no one appeared to be staring back. They were all standing and looking awkward, as though nobody quite knew what to say or do.

The stolid hostess broke the silence first.

"Georgia," Aunt Emily said calmly, showing not the slightest anger or even agitation over the loss of yet more glasses, perhaps because these were inexpensive water glasses instead of her heirloom crystal stemware, "please get the broom and dustpan from the closet. We need to make sure that every last shard is cleaned up. We don't want anyone to cut themselves."

There was a brief moment of hesitation, then in one ungainly movement, Georgia dropped her head, wheeled around, and lurched through the kitchen doorway.

"So that's Georgia," Henry Brent said, nodding first at Daisy and then at Aunt Emily. "Good of you to take her on, Emily."

Aunt Emily responded by clucking her tongue, after which she also wheeled around, albeit in a much more graceful manner than Georgia. Instead of heading toward the kitchen, however, her attention returned to the nook and her furniture surprise.

"Oh, Henry." Aunt Emily sighed. "It's spectacular."

It wasn't necessary to be an antiques connoisseur to understand her admiration. Henry Brent's gift was a stunning tiger maple Chippendale secretary with a slant-front desk. The lower portion of the piece consisted of four graduated drawers set on bracket feet. The upper portion contained a carved bookcase covered by two paneled doors. The finish was markedly old, with a warm, almost glowing gold tone. The brass pulls were old, too.

Even with Daisy's limited knowledge of period furniture, she could tell that regardless of its placement in the back room of the Fowler sisters' shop, the secretary must have been one of their priciest and most valuable pieces.

Had it been displayed in a fancy urban New England boutique rather than tucked away in tiny rural Motley, Virginia, it would have no doubt commanded a lordly sum.

"Oh, Henry." Aunt Emily sighed again. "You really shouldn't have. It's absolutely magnificent, of course. But it's far too much."

"Rubbish!" Henry Brent straightened his bow tie proudly. "I'm not in the poorhouse or taking alms. I had a little money saved."

"Even so . . . ," Aunt Emily protested.

"Being as ancient as I am," he gave a lively clack, "I don't have many rainy days left, so there's no need for me to be hoarding my pennies."

"You can't take 'em with you," Parker chimed in cheerfully.

"Don't be morbid, Parker," Lillian chastised him.

"But he's right," Henry Brent countered. "It can't be avoided. One day we all take the long dirt nap." He and his dentures grinned. "Even you, Lillian."

She flushed. "Yes, well, that hardly makes it an appropriate topic of conversation for—"

"Then it's just you and the earthworms!" Parker wheezed in amusement.

His wife's face turned plum purple.

"Ain't that the truth, Dog!" Henry Brent wheezed and woofed back at him.

"His name is Parker!" Lillian hollered.

Ignoring the digression, Aunt Emily said sweetly to May, "Thank you for organizing the delivery of such a wonderful gift. And, Henry," she turned to face him, "I hardly know what to say. Thanking you doesn't seem at all sufficient."

He straightened his bow tie again, this time a bit sheep-ishly.

"I really feel as though I must do something in return," Aunt Emily went on. "I'm trying to think of what I could possibly—"

"You've already done it," he interrupted her. His laugh-ter at Lillian and the earthworms had been replaced by a grave sincerity. "When my dear Agnes got ill, you were so kind to her, Emily. I'll never forget it."

May sniffled.

"And after she passed," Henry Brent continued, "you always checked on me. You made sure that my belly was full and I was getting out of bed each day."

Edna gurgled.

"I've always wanted to find some way to repay you. To give you a token of my tremendous appreciation. And," he swallowed with difficulty, "I hope that I finally have."

Aunt Emily blinked hard, sniffled hard, and threw her arms around the man in a heartfelt embrace. After a moment, she reached out and pulled Edna and May over to join them. There was a good deal of hugging, blubbering, and kissing among the four.

"My gracious," Aunt Emily said, wiping her cheeks and blowing her nose when they at last separated. "We must stop being so maudlin, or the young folks will start rolling their eyes and muttering about the old wrinklies' reunion."

A crunching noise caught Daisy's attention. She glanced over and saw Georgia sweeping together the broken glass.

Lillian sucked on her teeth disapprovingly. "That isn't the proper way of doing it. First you collect the big pieces, then you brush up the little bits."

"Otherwise you're just spreading slivers of glass all over the place," Kenneth Lunt concurred sternly.

"You really should be more careful," Lillian admonished.

Georgia's shoulders tightened, but she didn't look up or reply. She simply kept on sweeping—improperly, as it were.

"Those two have an opinion on just about everything, don't they?" Drew remarked in a low tone as he came over to stand next to Daisy.

"Always. And they always think they know everything better, or at least Lillian does." Daisy made a show of taking Drew's hand. "That should distract her."

"Hey, I like this strategy." Drew moved closer to her. "So are we trying to annoy Lillian or help Georgia?"

Daisy smiled. "Both would be nice."

It worked, too. Lillian's critical gaze immediately switched from the glass on the floor to Drew and Daisy's entwined fingers. Daisy had to restrain a grin.

"Before I forget," she said to Drew, "thanks for helping to bring in the secretary. I hope it wasn't too heavy."

He groaned. "Heavy doesn't begin to cover it. That thing weighs a ton! It may not look like it, but it does."

She nodded sympathetically. "I've been to enough antique stores with Aunt Emily to know that some of those old pieces of furniture made with solid wood might as well be solid rocks."

"My aching back won't argue with that."

"Poor baby. How about if I give you a little massage later?"

It was Drew's turn to grin. "Promise?"

Like a volcano on the verge of eruption, there was a deep rumbling from the direction of Lillian. Thankfully she was distracted once more before she could blow, this time by Henry Brent.

"A real beauty, isn't she?" he proclaimed loudly, as he stepped back to admire the secretary.

"She certainly is," May agreed.

Edna shook her head. "I had no idea that you sold it."

"It was so exciting when Henry wanted it!" May told her. "We've had it in the back room forever—twenty years at least, maybe more. I don't even remember how it ended up there. Why didn't we ever move it out to the front for more people to see?"

Edna went on shaking her head.

"Tippy," Lillian said abruptly.

"Tippy?" Aunt Emily asked.

Lillian pointed.

Daisy followed her outstretched finger to the nook. As handsome as the secretary was, it was also very large. Seven feet high, nearly four feet wide, and two feet deep. It fit in the nook, but just barely.

"She's right," Sarah Lunt commented softly. "It's tippy."

Drew frowned. "A bit too tippy."

Releasing Daisy's hand, he walked over to the secretary for a closer look. Kenneth, Parker, and Henry Brent all joined him. They crowded around the piece like a group of mechanics examining an engine for an oil leak.

"Maybe it's too close to the molding," Parker said.

"That doesn't make it tippy," Kenneth informed him. "That just keeps it from sitting flush against the wall."

"But maybe if it were flush against the wall . . . ," Parker returned.

Moving to one side, Drew studied the secretary's profile. "It can't sit flush against the wall, molding or no molding," he determined. "The back of the bookcase extends beyond the back of the desk."

"It does?" Parker and Kenneth said in unison.

Henry Brent nodded. "There was a time when a good many secretaries—and a lot of other cabinets, too—were built that way. It's designed to accommodate a chair rail, back in the days when most of the nicer houses still had chair rails."

"The staircase here has a chair rail," Aunt Emily reminded him. "And so do all of the bedrooms."

"You could always move it to one of them," Lillian suggested.

"Should we try to catch the delivery boys—" May began anxiously.

"—before they drive off?" Edna finished.

"Those two are long gone," Drew replied. "They skedaddled the instant they got paid. And, no," he added hastily, "I can't move the monster all by myself."

"No one would ever ask you to," Daisy said, just to staunch the possibility of anybody even considering it.

"Frankly," Drew continued, "I don't think an army of professional movers could get that secretary up the stairs. Ignoring the weight, it's too big to maneuver around the turns and through those narrow doorways."

"I was about to say the same thing myself," Kenneth agreed.

"Well, I don't want to move it," Aunt Emily said. "Not unless we really have to." She turned questioningly to Henry Brent.

He appeared entirely unconcerned. "She looks fine to me."

"It never fell over—" May said.

"—at the shop."

"We never worried about it—"

"—or even paid any attention," Edna concluded.

Henry Brent clacked in accord with the sisters. "She's been standing that way for a couple hundred years, and I'd wager she'll keep standing that way for another couple hundred more."

That was apparently enough to reassure Aunt Emily, because after one last happy glance at the secretary, she turned from it and began herding her guests back toward the parlor. Thirsty and tired of being on their feet, the group complied without dispute. There was a general mumbling about who had been seated where and which half-empty glass belonged to whom.

"I still think it's tippy," Drew said, partially to himself and partially to Daisy as the others moved out of the dining room.

"They won't listen," Georgia responded tersely.

Daisy glanced at her in surprise. She hadn't heard Georgia take a sharp tone before, even slightly.

"They *never* listen," she added with emphasis.

Georgia's gray eyes were once again focused on someone in the group, except this time her gaze was narrow and almost as sharp as her tongue. Daisy still couldn't tell who the person was, and that piqued her interest. It also made her realize just how little she actually knew about Georgia.

She was eighteen years old. Her last name was Ross. And with her pixie cut and carpet of freckles, she was almost adorably cute. Georgia was also far from lazy, regrettably clumsy, and she always tried hard to please Aunt Emily. But that was it. Aside from those few passing observations, Daisy knew nothing else. Not a lick about Georgia's family, her friends, where she had been raised or why she wasn't there any longer, barely even anything about her most basic likes and dislikes, such as her favorite color or her least favorite flavor of ice cream. Granted, Georgia had only been at the inn for a couple of weeks, and Daisy worked long hours at the bakery, so they hadn't spent very much time together. Except that made Daisy all the more curious now.

Drew was evidently curious, too. "Who doesn't listen?" he asked Georgia.

"Everybody," she answered flatly.

There was an almost childish sullenness to her voice, but the intensity with which she continued to gaze at the unidentified person in the parlor wasn't childish in the least. Georgia wasn't just idly looking at them. She was watching them, studying them, it seemed.

"Anyone in particular?" Drew pressed her.

The gray eyes clouded. Georgia hesitated just as she had earlier when Aunt Emily had asked her to get the broom and dustpan from the closet. She seemed to be debating how—or even if—she should respond.

Daisy thought she understood. Georgia must not have expected to see the person standing in the dining room of the inn, and she had dropped the tray with the glasses in surprise. But now that she had recovered from her initial shock, she either realized that the person wasn't in fact who she had originally taken them to be, or she seriously didn't like the person—both of which would explain her hard and studious gaze.

"Well, Daisy is an excellent listener," Drew said after a moment, trying to make Georgia feel more at ease. "She lets me whine about all my problems at work. So I'm sure she'd be great at listening to whatever you—"

He didn't finish the sentence. Georgia shot him a deeply troubled look, hurriedly scooped up the broom and dustpan filled with broken glass, and lurched once more through the kitchen doorway.

"That girl," Drew murmured after her, echoing Daisy's own thoughts, "has got some secrets."

CHAPTER
6

Secrets or no, Georgia didn't return to the dining room. Daisy wondered if her and Drew's instincts were right, or if they were overthinking it all, and Georgia was just being shy. The group could certainly be overwhelming, especially for a young woman who might not be used to such an eclectic, opinionated, and voluble collection of folks. Their lively conversation in the parlor could be heard throughout the inn.

Henry Brent and Parker were drinking and woofing merrily. Lillian was complaining about the woofing and about the potential dust from the new furniture. Kenneth Lunt and Edna Fowler were vigorously debating the fluctuating prices in the antiques market. May Fowler had somehow succeeded in getting Sarah Lunt to talk about gardening. And Aunt Emily was dashing among them all like a circus ringmaster simultaneously directing flying trapeze, clown car, and fire juggling performances.

Daisy watched them from the edge of the dining room and sighed. Drew put a comforting hand on her back.

"Tired?" he asked. "How was business at the bakery today?"

"A little chaotic this morning," she said. "It was weather paranoia, I think. Everybody seemed to be worried about the rain coming and wanted to stock up for the weekend. The bread and rolls flew out the door."

"When we brought in the secretary, it was starting to mist, but with the temperature falling like it is, there's probably a good chance for sleet."

Aunt Emily temporarily stopped dashing and turned toward Drew. "Did I hear you say *sleet*?"

He nodded. "If it keeps up, there could be some snow later on."

She nodded back at him, then at Daisy. "I do hope that Brenda gets here soon, Ducky. You know how nervous she is about driving in bad weather. And she's even worse when it's dark out."

Brenda was a longtime friend of Aunt Emily's, a fellow former waitress from Daisy's days at the diner, and now her trusty business partner at Sweetie Pies.

"Didn't I tell you?" Daisy said. "Brenda isn't coming this evening. She volunteered to handle the bakery alone tomorrow, so I could stay here and sleep in." She smiled at Drew. "But since she has to be up so early, Brenda figured that she'd be better off at home in her own bed tonight. She'll head over as soon as she closes up, which will probably be around noon, or maybe earlier if the weather really does get bad and the place is empty."

"Oh, that's right." Aunt Emily nodded again. "You did tell me. I remember now. Too many lists bumping around in my head, I guess." And she promptly dashed off once more, this time to the far end of the parlor where Lillian,

Parker, and Henry Brent were engaged in a spirited dialogue regarding the merits of placing a candle stand next to a dwarf Meyer lemon tree.

"That stand looks ridiculous where it is!" Lillian snapped like an irate alligator. "The tree should be there alone. It's much too fine a plant—"

"Naturally *you* would take the lemon's side," Henry Brent interjected with a laugh and a clack.

Parker laughed, too. Lillian's sour lips puckered.

"Of course you're right, my dear," Parker said hastily, trying to be conciliatory. "It's a mighty fine plant. But I don't see what difference it makes where the candle stand—"

"It makes a difference," she cut him off indignantly, "because the stand detracts from the tree."

Daisy rolled her eyes. Of all the silly things to get indignant about. It was a mystery to her how Lillian managed to get out of bed each morning, considering the degree to which she was continually offended by everything and everyone. It was also a mystery why Parker hadn't packed a bag long ago and moved to the inn permanently.

"The candle stand should be in the other corner," Lillian went on with her usual high-handedness. "Next to the tea table, where it could—"

"Tea!" Daisy exclaimed to herself. "I forgot all about my mama's tea."

With a peck on Drew's cheek—which unsurprisingly elicited a severe glance from Lillian, although it didn't stop her from continuing her lemon tree tirade—Daisy hurried out of the dining room. The afternoon was quickly fading to evening. Surely her mama would be up from her nap by now. She was probably waiting for her. She had probably been waiting for quite some time, not that her mama would ever complain about her tardiness.

While Lillian took umbrage at almost everything, Daisy's mama—Lucy Berger Hale—was the exact opposite and took umbrage at nearly nothing. She had always been a very patient and gentle person, the kind who rescued baby birds after a windstorm when they had fallen out of their nest and who never failed to scrape an extra dollar or two out of her already meager purse for the sad soul with an empty stomach huddled around the side of the supermarket. Then life took a hard turn, and Lucy lost her husband, her home, and her health all in rapid succession. But instead of growing nasty and resentful, she became so accommodating and unfalteringly sweet-tempered that it was actually a cause for concern to her daughter at times. Daisy worried that one day her mama might be taken advantage of, that a not-so-sweet person would come along and exploit her boundless trust and kindness.

As she entered the kitchen to make the overdue tea, Daisy found Georgia sitting on the floor on a throw rug at the edge of the hearth. Her knees were drawn up to her chest, and she was leaning against the wrought iron log holder, which was stacked with wood.

"Hey there," Daisy said, mildly surprised. She had never seen Georgia curled up in the corner before.

Georgia responded with a faint noise that sounded like the mewing of a lost kitten.

For a moment, Daisy considered sitting down next to her and trying to find out what—or who—was troubling her, but then she thought better of it. She didn't want to overstep. Secrets were secrets for a reason, after all, and Georgia was certainly entitled to keep hers private. Daisy picked up the kettle and filled it with fresh water.

"You okay?" she asked, deliberately keeping her tone casual.

The mewing repeated itself.

While she organized a cup and saucer and waited for the water to heat, Daisy glanced at Georgia as surreptitiously as she could. She wasn't crying, sulking, or hiding her face as one might have expected from her location and deportment. On the contrary, Georgia's chin was propped up on her knees, and her eyes were open and clear. But she wasn't looking back at Daisy. Her face was turned to the side, and she appeared to be looking over her shoulder at something above her head.

Daisy followed her gaze. There was no mistaking what Georgia was looking at. She was sitting alongside the old stone fireplace, and there was only one thing above her head. Aunt Emily's shotgun.

The Remington was a double-barreled 20-gauge, and it was nearly the same age as Aunt Emily herself. For as long as Daisy could remember, the gun had been kept on two wooden pegs on the kitchen chimney. An out-of-town guest—who apparently wasn't used to firearms sitting around in the open—had once asked Aunt Emily whether it wouldn't be better if the shotgun were stored elsewhere, presumably someplace more private and under lock and key. She had replied that if the wooden pegs and kitchen chimney were good enough for her grandpappy, then they were good enough for her.

For safety purposes—considering that there were visitors and children regularly roaming about the inn—the Remington was kept unloaded. But the shotgun shells were invariably close at hand. They were stored in Aunt Emily's needlepoint bag, a fact that she was careful not to publicly announce. Daisy's gaze went to the wall directly behind the log holder. The needlepoint bag was hanging from its usual hook, raggedy and bulging with shell boxes, although none was visible. Aunt Emily was careful about that, too.

Daisy's eyes returned to Georgia, and she frowned. There was something about the way Georgia was looking at the shotgun that made her a bit uncomfortable. She wasn't quite sure why. Georgia had been in the kitchen every day since her arrival at the inn, which meant that she must have seen the gun on its pegs at least a hundred times over the past few weeks. There wasn't anything new or suddenly startling about it now. Except Daisy had never seen Georgia staring at the Remington before, and she had just seen her staring at somebody in the dining room and the parlor with the same puzzling intensity.

"Georgia . . ."

Daisy didn't continue. She felt as though she should ask her something, but she didn't know what.

"Are you making tea for your mama?" Georgia said, abruptly snapping her head forward like she had just awoken from a trance. "I put those favorite bags of hers in the Rhett Butler cookie jar."

"Did you? I was wondering where they went."

"I figured it might be a good idea to separate them from the rest. That way if we run out of the others—some of the guests can get a little piggy—we'll still have plenty left over for your mama."

"Thank you, Georgia. That was very thoughtful."

It was so thoughtful, in fact, and seemingly mature that it made Daisy begin to doubt whether Georgia would have raced out of the dining room due to youthful shyness.

"Your water is boiling," she said.

"Right." Daisy removed the kettle from the heat and reached for Clark Gable's ceramic head.

Over the years, Aunt Emily had amassed an extensive and unusual collection of cookie jars. They varied widely in age and condition, and ranged from animals and cartoon characters to movie stars and historical figures. Somehow word had gotten out that Aunt Emily had an affinity for them, and ever since, they kept appearing with wearisome regularity on all birthdays, holidays, and as hostess gifts. The funny thing was that Aunt Emily didn't actually like cookie jars. She didn't think that they kept cookies particularly fresh, and she was annoyed at always having to make space for the new ones, some of which could only be described as bizarre, such as an abominable snowman wearing spurs and a cowboy hat.

The Clark Gable as Rhett Butler cookie jar was considerably more attractive than most of the others, although Clark's lips were such a neon shade of purple that it looked like he had been frozen in time sucking on a grape lollipop. It sat just about in the middle of the line of cookie jars, with a grinning pink hippopotamus on one side and a slightly lewd dancing girl on the other. The cookie jar shelf was on the wall above the old farm double sink. Without the aid of a stepladder, Daisy could reach it only by standing on her tiptoes. She stretched a hand blindly into Clark's cutaway and pulled out one of her mama's tea bags.

"I could barely reach it, too," Georgia told her. "But I figured the bags would be safer that way. Less chance of pilfering guests poking their sticky fingers where they don't belong."

Daisy raised a curious eyebrow. Georgia was apparently not only thoughtful but also somewhat cunning, at least when it came to choosing hiding places.

"I hate sticky fingers." Her voice cracked, then rose. "You shouldn't take what isn't yours! It isn't right!"

The eyebrow went higher, although Georgia couldn't see it, because Daisy had her back to her while she steeped the tea. Daisy agreed with her in principle, of course, but the moral outrage seemed a tad excessive.

"Are we still talking about tea bags?" Daisy said, having the distinct impression that they weren't.

There was a momentary hesitation on Georgia's part. Daisy turned around to look at her. The gray eyes were locked on the steaming cup and saucer. Daisy couldn't tell if Georgia was thinking hard or hardly thinking. After a minute, she rubbed her freckled arms and jumped up from the floor.

"We don't have enough potatoes for dinner," she declared, a bit too chirpily.

"Georgia—"

"And we wouldn't want anyone to go hungry," she added with equal blitheness, spinning on her heel toward the cellar door.

The stairway leading down to the cellar was on the opposite side of the kitchen chimney. It was a true old-time country cellar, rather than a modern concrete or cinder block basement. The narrow stairs were steep and rickety. The walls were mortar and stone. And the ground was bare dirt. There was absolutely nothing decorative or finished about it. But it held all the inn's essentials—baskets of onions and potatoes; jars of jams, jellies, and assorted pickled products; oil lanterns with gallon bottles of the necessary fuel; and a veritable stockpile of rusted gardening implements and cast-iron cookware.

Georgia tugged at the glass knob on the cellar door. Over the years, the door had warped, so it tended to stick in the frame and was difficult to open. Nevertheless, the door was always kept closed. Otherwise in winter, the drafts from the cellar made the kitchen too cold, and in summer, they made it too damp.

"Georgia—" Daisy began once more.

She stopped tugging.

"What Drew said earlier . . . I really am a good listener . . ."

Her brow furrowed, and she rubbed her arms again, harder this time.

"If you ever feel like chatting or whatever," Daisy went on lightly. She could see from the way Georgia had tensed—both earlier with Drew and now with her—that although she was clearly unsettled by something, she also wasn't comfortable discussing it. "If not, that's okay, too. No pressure. Just thought I'd mention it."

Georgia's mouth opened. She started to respond but then evidently thought better of it, and her lips clamped shut.

"Well, I'm here if you change your mind," Daisy concluded with a shrug.

Meeting her gaze, Georgia shrugged back at her. It seemed like a shrug of futility—an aged, world-weary futility—and in that moment, Georgia looked exhausted and many decades beyond her years. A second later, she gave the cellar door a determined yank. It wrenched open, and she inelegantly went half skipping, half skidding down the steps, suddenly not so mature, after all.

CHAPTER 7

"It's late. I know. I'm sorry."

Balancing the teacup and saucer in one hand and a plate stacked with a generous serving of shortbread in the other, Daisy pushed open the slightly ajar door to her mama's room with her shoulder.

"Hi, honey." Lucy Hale smiled warmly at her daughter from the bed. She was lying under a large patchwork quilt, her neck and shoulders propped up by a quartet of thick feather pillows. "There's no need to apologize. I woke up just a little while ago, and Beulah's been keeping me company."

Beulah greeted her from the yellow painted rocking chair at the side of the bed, her stocking feet propped up on the edge of the mattress after a long day of cuts and colors. "You need any help?"

"I'm good. Thanks." Daisy had not the least difficulty walking, talking, and carrying hot beverages all at the same time. Once a waitress, forever a waitress. "But I am surprised to see you up here. How did you manage to sneak into the inn past the lovely group in the parlor?"

Tucking an unruly red curl behind her ear, Beulah grinned. "No sneaking necessary. I came in the front, and the door squeaked like it always does. Except Lillian Barker was, well, barking so loud that no one heard it. I was going to stop and be all polite, but then I realized that no one heard me either. Lillian and Henry Brent were too busy sniping at each other like a couple of wet ferrets." The grin grew. "I figured they didn't need me interfering in their business, so I went right by and came upstairs."

"Smart girl," Daisy complimented her.

"Lillian's here?" Lucy asked, astonished.

Daisy grimaced in affirmation.

"Oh, dear." Lucy looked at her daughter with concern. "I assume that she's her usual charming self? Has she said anything about—"

"About Matt?" Daisy supplied, when her mama hesitated. "First words out of Lillian's mouth, practically. She was even delusional enough to think that he might be coming to the party this weekend. And she keeps trying to stare down Drew, as though he were committing some mortal sin just by standing next to me. I should really go and rescue him, but . . ."

She let the sentence trail away with a sigh.

"Drew will be just fine without you for a few minutes," Beulah assured her. "From what I saw, he was entertaining the Fowler sisters quite nicely. I don't think they've had that much attention from a man—let alone a young and handsome man—for a good many years."

Lucy chuckled. "You're probably right about that, Beulah." As her daughter neared the nightstand that served double duty as a small eating table, she raised her head to get a better look at the contents of the plate in Daisy's hand. "Shortbread! My favorite. Thank you, honey."

"And also your favorite tea." Daisy set down the dishes. "Henry Brent said that I should make it a hot toddy instead."

She chuckled some more. "Let me guess—he suggested corn whiskey?"

"Of course, with rum and rye as suitable alternatives. Well-established advice from his meemaw, apparently."

"I shouldn't laugh, really," Lucy said. "If I recall correctly, his meemaw was only two days shy of her one hundred and second birthday when she passed. And Henry isn't too far away from that. So it could very well be excellent advice that I should be heeding."

"But not with the cough medicine that you're taking," Daisy reminded her.

As if on cue, Lucy coughed. It was a deep, rasping cough, and her face contorted with pain.

"Isn't it getting any better?" Daisy asked anxiously, when her mama had regained her breath. "Is the medicine not working at all?"

"The doctor said that it might seem like it's getting worse before it gets better."

Daisy frowned doubtfully.

"He did," Lucy insisted. "And it happened like that before. Do you remember when I had that terrible cold a year ago Christmas? It was awful—and it kept getting worse—and then all of a sudden, it got better. It went away almost overnight."

The frown remained. "I don't care about before, Mama. I care about you getting well now."

Lucy reached out a thin hand from under the quilt and patted Daisy's arm. "Don't worry, honey. I am getting well now."

As much as Daisy wanted to believe that, her mama's

appearance told a different story. It wasn't just her hand that was thin. It was her entire body. She was gaunt and frail. Her skeletal neck and shoulders seemed to disappear into the downy pillows. And everything about her was pale. Her skin, her hair, even her teeth and eyes had a ghostly, almost otherworldly translucence about them.

Seeing the distress in her daughter's face, Lucy patted Daisy's arm once more and deftly changed the subject. "So tell me all the gossip from downstairs. Who's there, and what's happening?"

"Well . . ." Although Daisy was still uneasy about the cough, she played along. Belaboring her mama's ill health wasn't going to do either of them any good. "Kenneth Lunt wants to buy the inn."

"What!" Beulah exclaimed. She had been leaning back in the rocking chair, but at Daisy's announcement, she suddenly snapped to attention. "He wants to buy the inn? But where would we live? And what would happen to my salon?"

"That was my reaction, too," Daisy said.

"How about Aunt Emily's reaction? She must have been stunned at the idea. And appalled!" Beulah's grin resurfaced. "I wish I would have been there. I bet she put him in his place good."

"She might have been stunned, but she definitely wasn't appalled," Daisy corrected her. "For a few minutes, she seemed to be considering the idea pretty seriously."

The grin vanished. "I—I can't believe it."

"I can," Lucy countered, taking the teacup from the nightstand.

Both Daisy and Beulah looked at her in surprise.

"Of course Emily would never sell this place," Lucy told them with a gentle confidence. "It's her home. And she considers it our home, too. But she likes to dream just the same as the rest of us. What it would be like not to have to worry about the taxes and the constant upkeep and the guests and all the bills."

"Kenneth did promise that she would be well compensated," Daisy remarked.

Her mama nodded. "I've heard him discussing it with his wife."

Beulah's hazel eyes widened. "You have?"

Lucy smiled. "Old Southern houses and their ridiculously thin walls, my dear. And the fact that Mr. Lunt booms like a bull elephant when he talks. They're in the Pickett room right next door."

"But he was discussing it with Sarah?" Daisy was thoughtful for a moment. "That's interesting, because when he made the offer to Aunt Emily, Sarah acted as though it was a new idea to her."

"It most certainly wasn't," her mama replied. "I distinctly heard them talking about the size of the property."

"Odd. Maybe I misunderstood."

"Or maybe the wife isn't the shrinking violet that she makes herself out to be," Beulah retorted.

Daisy turned to her. "You think she's pretending?"

Beulah shrugged.

"Whenever I've seen her, she's always been mousy and sort of hesitant about everything," Daisy said.

"Too mousy and hesitant to be even half believable," Beulah responded. "Last night when we were having supper she couldn't make up her mind whether she wanted bread or not. We were passing the basket around the table like we always do, and she stopped and just held it in her hands, staring at it for what must have been five minutes. They were dinner rolls, for criminy sake. No one was asking her to decide if she should eat the family pet hen."

Lucy smiled again. "Oh, Beulah. You forget that not all women are quite as independent as you."

"They should be! You can't spend your life sitting around and waiting for a man to tell you whether or not you should eat a dinner roll."

Daisy laughed. "If I had done that with Matt, I would have starved and been drunk all the time. He would have just kept handing me more beer."

"Ain't that the truth." Beulah gave a little snort. "Well, Sarah didn't finally make up her mind until Kenneth made it up for her and reminded her to keep the basket moving—"

"Was Georgia there?" Daisy interjected suddenly.

"Huh?"

"Was Georgia with you yesterday at supper?"

Beulah scrunched up her nose. "No. She wasn't. Why?"

"She walked into the dining room this afternoon while everybody was there and dropped a tray of glasses."

"A whole tray?" Lucy shook her head. "Poor Emily."

"Poor Georgia," Beulah chimed in. "That girl has a bad clumsy streak."

"Except I'm not sure that it was clumsiness," Daisy said. "At least not this time. I think that she might have recognized one of the guests and dropped the tray in surprise. I'm trying to figure out who it was. She's seen the Lunts before, hasn't she?"

Lucy took a sip of her tea. "I'm afraid I'm the wrong one to ask, considering that I've barely been out of this room since they arrived, which was three days ago."

"Have they been here only three days? It seems a lot longer."

"That's because Kenneth talks so much," Beulah commented dryly.

"But in three days Georgia must have seen them, right?" Daisy said.

Scrunching up her nose some more, Beulah considered it. "Not necessarily. She always eats breakfast alone. Then she spends most of the day either in the kitchen or cleaning the rooms with the door closed. And lots of evenings she eats alone, too. I'm trying to remember if she was at the dining table the night before last."

"The Lunts went out to eat the night before last," Lucy replied. "I know because they came back late, and I couldn't help overhearing. It was some place down in Danville, although I didn't catch the name."

Daisy nodded. "I heard part of their conversation when they were coming down the hall. Sarah liked it, but Kenneth didn't."

Beulah gave another snort. "No great secrets of national security could ever be kept here."

"But our little secrets are so much more fun," Lucy rejoined, reaching for a piece of shortbread.

"So it's possible," Daisy returned to the more pertinent point, "that Georgia hadn't seen the Lunts before this afternoon."

"It's possible," Beulah agreed.

"Although it's probably more likely that she was surprised to see someone else," Daisy went on.

"Maybe Henry Brent," Beulah suggested. "And maybe instead of being surprised, she was shocked. That burgundy-striped seersucker of his is enough to blind you."

Lucy stopped chewing. "He's wearing the burgundy seersucker?"

"It matches the burgundy velvet draperies in the parlor perfectly," Daisy answered, deadpan.

Her mama chuckled. "Henry always was a snappy dresser. But somehow I doubt that was what made Georgia drop a tray of glasses."

"She was staring hard at the person afterward," Daisy told her. "And then she was staring at Aunt Emily's Remington in the kitchen."

"Hmm." Lucy took a contemplative bite of shortbread. "I always thought there could be more to Georgia than met the eye. She's very secretive."

"That's what Drew said, too."

Stretching out in the rocking chair, Beulah put her feet back up on the bed. "I'm not sure that I trust her."

"Why not?" Daisy asked.

"For starters, we know nothing about her."

Daisy couldn't argue with that. She had thought the exact same thing only a short while earlier.

"She also doesn't give me my phone messages," Beulah added somewhat peevishly.

"That was only one time," Daisy reminded her. "It was on the inn's phone line, so she got confused about it being a guest."

Beulah responded with a dubious grunt.

"Well, we can find out more about Georgia tonight," Daisy proposed. "You can help me watch her at dinner. See who she reacts to, or doesn't react to."

"Tomorrow. Tomorrow I'll have the eyes of a hawk. But not tonight. No can do."

Daisy looked at Beulah questioningly.

She squinted back at her with impatience. "I have my date!"

"You have a date? Since when?"

"Since Wade's schedule changed. He's driving through the area this evening, so I agreed to meet him."

Lucy set down her teacup. "Beulah, dear, are you sure that's safe? You don't really know this man, do you?"

"That's why I picked somewhere public to get together. Friday night at the General is always busy, so there will be plenty of people around in case things turn sour."

The General—a tribute to Robert E. Lee, a recurring theme in southern Virginia—was the local roadhouse. The place was old, damp, and crumbling, but it had a pleasant, comfortable atmosphere and was viewed fondly throughout the county.

"Good choice," Daisy said. "But I can tell you that Aunt Emily won't be overjoyed with you skipping out this evening. I know that she was counting on you to be charming and entertaining with the guests."

"She doesn't need me. She has you." Beulah batted her eyelashes. "You can be plenty charming and entertaining for both of us."

"Golly, thanks."

"Sorry, Daisy, but I've already cancelled on Wade three times. I can't cancel again. And he doesn't know when he'll be back this way."

Wade Watson Howard III was a long-haul trucker based in Tennessee. He was the cousin of a neighbor of a customer of Beulah's. She had several antediluvian customers who insisted that she was much too pretty to still be single—they also insisted that no woman could be truly happy unless she was married—and they were continually trying to set her up with their friends of friends and extended relations. As a result, Beulah went on quite a few blind dates, but so far, none of them had stuck.

Daisy shrugged. "Good luck with it. I hope he's better than the last."

"You mean the one who refused to wear shoes?"

Lucy blinked at Beulah in amazement. "He didn't wear shoes?"

She nodded. "Wouldn't put 'em on. Ever. No matter what."

"Why on earth not?"

"He said that he was training his feet."

"Training them for what?"

"That, he wouldn't say."

Lucy could only shake her head and take another bite of shortbread. "You poor girls. It all seemed so much easier back in my day. What strange frogs you have to kiss to find your prince."

Daisy and Beulah looked at each other. "There's a prince?"

CHAPTER
8

Henry Brent let out a low whistle as Beulah—dressed and ready for her date with her potential prince—came down the stairs and entered the parlor. "Lookin' mighty fine there, Beulah."

Parker agreed with an affable little woof.

Lillian gazed at Beulah appraisingly, and from the way her string-bean body sat rigid and erect on the gold-brocaded settee, it was clear that she didn't share the gentlemen's admiration. "Not appropriate," she declared, like a cranky old judge banging a gavel and pronouncing a verdict.

Daisy ignored her. "Gorgeous," she said to Beulah from the scuffed leather smoking chair. "As you always are."

Beulah's antediluvian customers were right about one thing—she was very pretty. She had thick, naturally auburn hair, fiery hazel eyes, and flawless porcelain skin. Beulah also had a good figure and knew how to accentuate it by picking the right clothes to match her curves.

"So who is—" May began with enthusiasm.

"—the lucky fellow?" Edna concluded.

Raising her chin in exaggerated pride, Beulah responded affectedly, "Wade Watson Howard III."

Daisy laughed. "You do an excellent job of making him sound like royalty."

Beulah grinned. "What's that old saying—we are who we choose to be? Well, I'm taking a cue from your brilliant mama and choosing who Wade is going to be, at least for this one evening."

"Poor chap," Drew chuckled. He was leaning against the side of the smoking chair, sipping a beverage. "He won't know what hit him."

"Is he related—" May started to ask.

"—to the Bristol Howards?" Edna finished for her.

"I don't know," Beulah said. "He could be. He is from Tennessee. But I never met him before, so I have no clue about his family."

"Not appropriate," Lillian repeated, clucking her tongue. "Not appropriate at all."

Beulah rolled her eyes to Daisy, then she turned toward the sour lemon. "What isn't appropriate, Lillian?"

"A first date—or any date, for that matter—dressed the way you are."

"I'm wearing a skirt and a sweater, with tights and boots."

"A sweater that's far too snug," Lillian informed her. "And a skirt that's considerably too short."

Ordinarily Beulah had a short redheaded fuse, one that usually resulted in her taking a shark-size bite of retribution out of her victims, but in this instance, her prospective date had her in too good of a mood. So instead of spitting insults or hurling daggers, she answered only with a derisive snort.

That apparently egged Lillian on, because she added with her own bite, "Those boots could belong to—dare I say it—a lady of the night."

"Now, my dear," Parker protested.

Henry Brent gave a contemptuous clack. "Careful, Lillian. Your claws are showing. Fangs, too."

She shot him a dark look.

Undaunted, he continued, "There's no need to be jealous of a beautiful young thing. You had your day. Once. Long ago. Such as it was."

The look turned black.

Drew rattled the ice cubes in his glass. "She's just mad because she doesn't have the legs for those boots."

Although it was true, Daisy frowned at him. It was good of him to support Beulah, and everyone was more than a little tired of Lillian, but there were still some constraints of civility. Lillian was Daisy's in-law, after all, and it was Aunt Emily's party. Drew offered a halfhearted shrug of apology, to which she replied with a grateful smile.

"Oh, heavens," May fretted. Her eyes darted anxiously from Drew to Lillian to Henry Brent, and she pulled out her handkerchief.

Edna uncrossed, then recrossed her legs.

"If you're heading outside, Beulah, you better take a warm coat," Aunt Emily said, coming through the dining room from the kitchen. "I just popped onto the back porch, and it's starting to snow."

"Snow!" Henry Brent exclaimed, and promptly headed over to the nearest window. He pushed aside its drapery.

Daisy and Beulah exchanged a pair of amused winks. Daisy hadn't been exaggerating to her mama. The burgundy seersucker and the burgundy velvet did match perfectly.

"No doubt about it," he reported, pressing his nose against the pane. "I see flurries."

"Dear me." May rubbed the lace border on her handkerchief.

Edna's legs uncrossed and crossed again.

"Are you sure that you should go?" Aunt Emily asked Beulah.

Beulah winked at Daisy once more. It was just as they had predicted. Aunt Emily was not happy to have her leave.

"I'll be here all day tomorrow to help entertain," Beulah promised. "I might even be back sooner than expected this evening, depending on how things turn out."

"We can entertain ourselves just fine," Aunt Emily retorted somewhat tetchily. "I was more concerned about you driving in this weather."

"No worries. I'm an excellent driver."

Aunt Emily limited her response to a raised eyebrow.

"I am," Beulah insisted.

"What's all the fuss?" Kenneth Lunt interjected. "It's only a few flurries."

"Only a few flurries?" Lillian echoed, aghast.

Kenneth looked at his wife, who was sitting in the damask armchair next to his. Daisy watched her with interest. Beulah had sparked her curiosity about Sarah, whether the woman's mousiness was at all exaggerated. But she was disappointed a moment later when Sarah simply shrugged. A shrug proved nothing either way.

Henry Brent turned from the window. "Where exactly did you say you were from?" he asked the Lunts.

"I can tell you that they ain't from around here," Parker remarked.

"Certainly not," Lillian concurred haughtily.

Sarah's chin quivered. "We—"

Her husband's voice rose over hers. His face was flushed. "I didn't say. And I don't see how it's any of your business!"

The entire group grew still, uniformly taken aback by Kenneth's sudden vehemence.

"None of your damn business at all—"

"I would remind you to watch your language," Henry Brent cut him off in a stern tone. "There are ladies present."

Daisy and Beulah glanced at each other, and both restrained a grin. There was something awfully endearing about a ninety-four-year-old who wore a polka dot clip-on bow tie and worried about the delicate ears of the ladies in the room.

Kenneth's face flushed further. "My language? Are you kidding me! I didn't even use a—"

This time Daisy cut him off. "It's the snow," she said lightly.

He turned to her with a hard gaze.

"It's the snow," she repeated, hoping that she was correct in her assumption that Kenneth's enmity was a defense mechanism from everybody ganging up on him rather than actual anger.

Aunt Emily nodded at her and mouthed a word of thanks. Encouraged, Daisy continued.

"In this area," she explained, "even a little snow is enough to shut down the world. We usually get some only once or twice during a winter, and it typically melts within a day, if it sticks at all. The mountains can get more, of course. But there aren't enough plows to cover all the country roads, and there aren't big piles of salt and gravel waiting at the ready like up north and in larger cities. So if there's snow and ice around here, lots of people tend to get nervous and bunker down 'til it's over. That's why when you talked about it being only a few flurries, the natural conclusion was that you weren't from these parts."

"Precisely." Aunt Emily nodded at Daisy again.

"Well said, Ducky!" Commending her with a clack, Henry Brent let the drapery fall back over the window. "I can remember the storm of sixty-two like it was yesterday."

Beulah's nose twitched. "Was that 1862 or 1962?"

He chortled. "If it were 1862, I'd be one heck of a dinosaur, and they'd have me locked up for study and testing."

"They should have you locked up anyway," Lillian muttered under her breath.

Fortunately she said it quietly enough so that only Daisy and Parker heard her. They both gave her a reproving look. She pursed her lips, but didn't mutter anything more.

"That storm of sixty-two was a doozy," Henry Brent reminisced. "A solid inch of ice, followed by more snow than I'd ever seen in my whole life, even in pictures. It was like somebody had busted a snowmaking machine up in the sky. It just kept on coming. Day and night. Heaps of the stuff."

"Every road was blocked," Aunt Emily said. "We couldn't leave the inn for a week. And the electrical was out even longer."

The Fowler sisters chimed in.

"We were only young girls at the time—"

"—but we remember it, too."

"No school—"

"—for days and days."

"We thought it was wonderful—"

"—but our mama complained and complained."

Drew cleared his throat in Daisy's direction. She answered him with a smile. She didn't know if Edna and May had spoken in tandem as children, but if they had, she could well imagine that even the most doting and affectionate parent would eagerly welcome the peaceful respite of schooltime.

Lillian noticed the exchange and evidently found it too intimate for her taste, because she glared at Drew.

Unfazed, he turned to Beulah. "I know that you're not panicked about the snow, but if you want, you can take my truck tonight, just to be extra-cautious."

"What a good idea!" Aunt Emily appeared relieved.

"It's got four-wheel drive," Drew went on, "and it hasn't let me down yet, not even in some really nasty mud and serious inclines."

"My car is kind of a wimp," Beulah said.

Reaching into his pocket, Drew pulled out his keys. As Beulah walked over to collect them, she passed close to Daisy.

"Don't look now," she whispered, "but Georgia's watching."

As surprised as Daisy was, she followed Beulah's advice and didn't immediately snap her head up to look around. Instead she leaned back and pretended to casually stretch in her chair. Out of the corner of her eye, she caught a glimpse of pixie-cut strawberry blond hair. Beulah was right. Georgia was watching. She was hiding in the kitchen, peering into the parlor from the edge of the dining room doorway. How long had she been standing there? And why?

"Thank you, Drew," Beulah purred, as she took the truck keys from him. "I'll try really hard not to break it."

Drew laughed. "I'd appreciate that."

"I told you," Beulah whispered, passing by Daisy again. "You shouldn't be so quick to trust her."

Daisy wondered if Georgia was watching all of them, or just one of them. Was it the same person that she had been staring at earlier?

"Is it the secretary, Ducky?"

Although she heard Henry Brent's words, her mind was focused elsewhere, and she didn't respond.

"That's what you're looking at?" He moved slowly from the window to the nook between the parlor and the dining room.

When she still didn't answer, Drew nudged her with his elbow. "Daisy?"

She blinked at him. "Sorry?"

"The secretary," Henry Brent repeated. "You were looking at the secretary?"

Daisy had been looking at Georgia and not the secretary, but she understood from the way her head had been turned toward the dining room how he could have drawn the wrong conclusion.

"You think it's tippy too, Ducky?" he asked.

"Well . . ." She hesitated a moment, shifting her attention to the piece of furniture. "It does seem to be tilting a bit."

Drew nodded in agreement.

"But maybe it's not a problem," Daisy added after another moment, studying the two parts of the secretary. "Maybe it's just what you were talking about before. It can't sit flush against the wall because the back of the bookcase extends beyond the back of the desk."

In an attempt to better examine the issue, Henry Brent

approached the secretary. He twisted his neck and shoulders and pressed himself as close to the back of it as he could.

"Don't hurt yourself!" May cried.

Edna jumped up in alarm. "You mustn't do that!"

He responded by squeezing his body further behind the secretary.

"They're right, Henry." Aunt Emily hurried over to the nook. "You're not a stretchy rubber band. You could snap."

"I'm okay," he assured them. "I'm just seeing if I can . . . There's some thingamabob here . . ."

Although he might have felt okay, he didn't look okay. He looked half squished and, before long, fully stuck. The secretary wobbled slightly.

"Henry!" Edna and May exclaimed in unison.

The secretary wobbled some more.

"That's not good," Drew mumbled, and a minute later, he was pulling the man out like an obdurate beagle that had gotten itself wedged in a drainpipe chasing after a rabbit.

"Thank you for the assistance," Henry Brent said, when he had been wrenched free. "Much obliged to you."

A chorus of reprimands from Aunt Emily and the Fowler sisters followed. Henry Brent replied by brushing his suit, straightening his bow tie, and clacking his dentures at the chattering hens.

"Well, this has been exciting," Beulah said, heading toward the entrance hall. "But if I don't hurry, I'll be late for my date."

The adventure with the secretary was quickly forgotten as everyone wished Beulah a safe drive and a good time. As usual, Lillian was less generous.

"Better do the best you can with it," she advised Beulah.

"You aren't getting any younger, you know. You won't have many opportunities left."

Beulah stopped and turned on the heel of her boot. Blowing a parting kiss to the rest of the group, she threw Lillian such a taunting look that Daisy knew Lillian would one day pay for that remark, no doubt when she least expected it.

CHAPTER
9

Although Daisy would have enjoyed Beulah's company at dinner, it turned out that she didn't need her hawk eyes to help watch Georgia and see whom she reacted to. That was because Georgia reacted to no one. She assisted in serving the meal and cleaning up afterward, but she didn't sit at the table and eat with the rest of the group. Her head and gaze were kept studiously down each time she appeared from the kitchen with a new bowl of string beans or an extra dish of scalloped potatoes. And she never opened her mouth. Even when she had to get close to someone to replenish their water glass or was thanked for a clean napkin, Georgia didn't utter a syllable or lift her eyes from the floor.

Her limbs did twitch occasionally, and Daisy also noticed that Georgia's hands weren't the steadiest. But as far as she could tell, the twitching didn't get worse next to any specific person, and the shaky fingers were in keeping with Georgia's general clumsiness. The only time Daisy spotted any response from her was when Sarah Lunt lingered over the breadbasket. It was just as Beulah had described from the night before. The basket was moving merrily around the table, until it came to Sarah. Then she stopped and just held it in her hands, staring at it as though its contents required the utmost contemplation. The surrounding conversation slowly died, and everyone in turn began staring at Sarah.

As the seconds ticked by and the group's focus remained on Sarah, Georgia started shifting her weight back and forth from one leg to the other. But Daisy was inclined to think that instead of taking a particular interest in Sarah, Georgia was merely being impatient. The basket was nearly empty, and she wanted Sarah to make up her mind so she could grab it and run back to the security of the kitchen. Based on the long minutes that it took for Georgia to complete each refill and every other mini-errand, she was clearly eager to leave the dining room whenever she could.

Sarah's behavior was more intriguing. Daisy couldn't decide what to make of it. It was odd how paralyzed she became by the breadbasket. Beulah really had said it best. *They were dinner rolls, for criminy sake.* She didn't have the fate of nations resting in her petite palms. There was also something in the way she was gazing at it, like the bread wasn't simply bread. Like it had greater meaning somehow, although Daisy had no clue what that meaning could possibly be. It did seem as though Sarah was waiting, however. If she was waiting for her husband to tell her what to do, then she wasn't held in suspense for too long. After a pause, Kenneth reminded her—firmly but not crossly—to keep the basket moving, which she did, leaving the rolls untouched.

The remainder of dinner passed smoothly and enjoyably. Even Lillian managed to keep her complaints and criticisms to a minimum. The evening ended soon thereafter. The group was tired from all of the earlier excitement, with everyone's arrival and the hullabaloo regarding the secretary. Once the first person announced their intention to retire for the night, the rest soon followed. Daisy was glad for it. She had been up early and worked hard at the bakery that day. She was more than ready to put up her feet and lay down her head.

Ironically enough, the oldest in the party had the most energy. With his stomach pleasantly full, Henry Brent proceeded to settle himself in the parlor and start in on a convivial bottle of Aunt Emily's gooseberry brandy. As the others toddled off to their rooms, he kept looking around for somebody to share a nip and a good story. Daisy would have obliged him, but she couldn't stop yawning like a grizzly in need of a lengthy hibernation. So Drew pulled up an armchair instead. After a quick kiss good night—one that they did their best to conceal from Lillian—Daisy headed upstairs.

Her body hit the bed with all the force of an anvil dropping on concrete. She slept hard, at least in the beginning. Then noises started to creep in. There was a rumble. It sounded like thunder. Maybe it was the storm outside, except she didn't think that snow usually had thunder. The hinge of a door squeaked. There were footsteps in the hall. It was probably Drew. He and Henry Brent had finished their brandy and were finally calling it a day. Drew's room was the Stonewall Jackson, which was only one away from hers.

Another rumble, followed by footsteps on the stairs. Still more asleep than awake, Daisy couldn't tell if they were coming up or going down. It could be Drew again. But it couldn't be Henry Brent. He was in the Jubal Early. That was on the ground floor, on the other side of the dining room from the parlor. A car—or truck—door slammed. Beulah had made it back to the inn at last. The date hadn't ended early, after all, so that meant Wade Watson Howard III must have passed muster, even if only temporarily. Although Daisy thought for a fleeting second about checking the time, the clock on the nightstand was too far away. She didn't want to bother rolling over.

Voices. Were those voices? If they were, they weren't close by. She couldn't hear more than a garble. Or maybe she was dreaming it. Daisy was pretty sure that she had dozed off again. Maybe all the noises were part of her dream, too. A deeper rumble, then the crash of lightning. That seemed strangely out of order to her. There was a thump. It was a dull, heavy sound, like somebody had dropped a big mud-caked boot. A second thump. Then a third. They kept coming, a whole string of them. *Thump, thump, thump.* Pause. *Thump, thump, thump.* Daisy cracked an eye. She was in her room. It was still dark out. And she definitely wasn't dreaming.

As she lay there slowly regaining her senses and listening to the continued thumping, it started to sound more like pounding. Then it occurred to her that somebody wasn't dropping muddy boots, they were pounding on the front door of the inn. Beulah? She must have forgotten or lost her key. Daisy knew with the thin walls of the inn that she couldn't be the only one who heard the pounding. But she very likely would be the only one who was going to respond to it. She certainly couldn't expect the guests to rise and open the front door for who-knows-who in the middle of the night. Her mama was too ill to get out of bed. And Aunt

Emily was either sleeping like the dead or dashing down to the kitchen for her shotgun.

Rising and pulling a robe around herself, Daisy opened her own door and shuffled out. The hall was dimly lit by a small stained glass lamp at the opposite end. As far as she could see, the other room doors were closed. The pounding went on, growing progressively louder and harder. It had probably begun as a normal polite knock, and when nobody had answered it, Beulah had gotten impatient. Daisy couldn't blame her for that. Nobody wanted to be stuck outside on a February night in the cold and wet.

The steps creaked under her as she descended. Daisy remembered Kenneth Lunt's comments about being able to hear her moving around the previous morning, and she shrugged. If he was indeed such a light sleeper, then he was already awake anyway. Somewhere above her a door opened. It sounded like it came from the third floor. Lillian and Parker were in the James Longstreet on the third floor. Maybe Lillian was coming to protest the pounding. Another door opened. There were also footsteps. Daisy couldn't tell the direction of either. The closer she got to the pounding, the more it obscured everything else.

When she reached the bottom of the stairs, she was surprised to find the entrance hall dark. A trio of brass sconces lined the wall. Although they originally held candles, they had been wired for electricity long ago. Their soft light was more decorative than functional, but Aunt Emily always left them on so that no one would accidentally go careening down the steps in the pitch black, especially not guests, who weren't used to the narrow passages and tight corners of the inn like Daisy was.

Even more surprising to her was the parlor. It was dark,

too. To the best of Daisy's recollection, there had been at least four lamps switched on when she had left Drew and Henry Brent earlier in the evening. It seemed peculiar that the two men would have been fastidious enough to turn them all off, particularly after enjoying what had no doubt been a considerable amount of gooseberry brandy. And then they both would have had to make it to their respective rooms in the dark. Granted, it wasn't completely dark. There was no light coming from the kitchen or the dining room, but there was a faint yellow illumination from the porch lights shining through the leaded-glass panel above the front door.

Suddenly, she felt movement behind her. Daisy spun around. No one was there, or at least no one appeared to be there. She squinted down the hall. Was that shadow at the edge of the kitchen a person?

"Hello?" she asked.

She received no answer. The shadow didn't budge an inch. Daisy shook her head at herself. How silly. Of course it wasn't a person. Her eyes and mind were just playing nighttime tricks on her.

By this point, the pounding on the front door had become almost frenzied. Turning back around, Daisy hurried to put a stop to it. She flipped the locks and threw open the door.

"Hey there," she began with a smile. "How was the date? Did you lose your key . . ."

Both Daisy's voice and her smile faded in the same instant. She had been mistaken. It wasn't Beulah on the front porch of the inn. It was a man. A strange man.

"Mercy me, Ducky! What's all the racket?"

There was no mistaking Aunt Emily. She was plodding

down the stairs in her scarlet slippers, fastening her matching chiffon dressing gown. Apparently she had been sleeping like the dead, because there was no shotgun in her hands.

"I—" Daisy stammered, still startled from not finding Beulah at the door.

Aunt Emily rubbed her eyes to wake herself up, after which she carefully ran her fingers over her hair to correct any wayward silver strands. When she had finished her toilette, she looked at Daisy, then at the man standing in the doorway, and finally back at Daisy again. "Who's this?" she said.

"I—" Daisy started once more.

The man cut her off.

"Bud." He took a step forward and stuck out his hand. "Bud Foster."

Bud Foster appeared to be about fifty, and he didn't have a nice hand. The nails were ragged, the skin was thick and callused, and the knuckles had that misshapen quality often noted in those with pugilistic tendencies. After a brief hesitation, Aunt Emily shook the hand, but she did so with obvious reluctance.

"This isn't an appropriate hour, Mr. Foster," she remarked.

Although Aunt Emily's tone wasn't hostile, it also couldn't have been described as welcoming. Apparently good hostess standards were less rigid between the hours of midnight and dawn when strangers on the front porch were involved.

"Bud," the man corrected her with an unnervingly large smile of chipped and yellowed teeth.

Neither Aunt Emily nor Daisy smiled back.

"It's my car," Bud said, after a short pause. "I got lost. Then the storm hit, and I couldn't see a damn thing—"

Aunt Emily cleared her throat to express her displeasure.

He paused again and seemed momentarily confused. "Oh. Okay." He gave a little nod. "I couldn't see *any*thing. The snow was coming down in these huge flakes. They were clumping together on the windshield like a blanket, and the wipers couldn't get 'em off fast enough. I didn't know if I was still on the road or had gone off it. I couldn't tell what was ahead of me or on either side. It all just blurred together in one giant cloud. I think it must have been what they call a whiteout. Take a look for yourself." Bud turned and gestured behind him.

For the first time since she had opened the door, Daisy's eyes moved past the man. She was so astonished by what she saw that she took a step backward. It was as though the world had disappeared. There was nothing beyond the inn. The doorway, the front porch, and then a wall of gray. Common sense told her that it was a sheet of white snow against the black night sky, but it looked like a solid wall of gray.

"Well, I'll be," Aunt Emily exhaled.

Bud nodded vigorously. "I was driving real slow, hoping that I wouldn't hit something, or that nothing would hit me. But then I went down into a ditch and got stuck. After a couple of tries, I knew that I wasn't going to be able to work myself out. Of course my phone couldn't get a signal, not that a tow truck could reach me now anyway."

"Certainly not," Aunt Emily concurred.

"So I sat there for a while," Bud continued, "wondering what to do. After a lot of looking around, I thought that I saw some lights in the distance. I got out and headed toward them. Five minutes into it, I was wondering if I hadn't made a big mistake and should have just stayed put. With the snow piling on and the wind whipping it around like a tornado, half the time I couldn't see my hand in front of my face and kept losing track of the lights. Let me tell you, I was getting pretty worried. You hear those stories about people in blizzards wandering ten feet from their house or barn and not being able to find their way back. They just get covered and freeze. When I finally saw that the lights belonged to this place, I said a prayer of thanks."

"I can well imagine," Aunt Emily concurred again.

Daisy glanced at her. Her tone had warmed, but only slightly. It still couldn't have been considered friendly. Did Aunt Emily not believe the story? There was a somewhat artificial, almost rehearsed quality to it. But that could have been because the man was cold and stressed. Why would he want to fabricate such a tale? Of at least one truthful element there could be no doubt—the heavy snow.

Maybe there was something else about Bud Foster that Aunt Emily didn't trust. He definitely didn't have the most confidence-inspiring appearance. His stubble was a good three days old. His tan trench coat was fraying in spots and had several large inkblot stains from coffee or cola having been dribbled down the front. And he kept cracking his pugilist knuckles while he talked.

"Sorry for banging on the door like I did," Bud apologized, "but I was worried that everybody might be asleep. I couldn't very well stay out here on the porch all night, not in this miserable weather."

"Everybody?" Daisy echoed. The word struck her. It seemed as though he knew that there were a lot of people in the house.

"It is an inn, isn't it?" he replied immediately. "I saw the sign coming up the front walk, or what I assume is the front walk, and the part of the sign that isn't coated with ice. 'The Tosh Inn. Rooms available.' I'm hoping that you'll have a room available for me."

It was a smooth response. A bit too smooth, perhaps. Daisy glanced at Aunt Emily again, wondering if she thought so also. She must have had some reservation, because as with taking Bud Foster's hand, Aunt Emily hesitated with his request.

"Of course we'll find you something," she answered after a moment. "None of God's creatures should be left outside on such a night."

"Thank you, ma'am. I sure do appreciate your kindness."

Stomping his feet and brushing the snow from his coat, Bud stepped into the inn. A hefty black duffle bag was slung over one shoulder. Daisy blinked at it in surprise.

"You trekked through the snow and wind carrying luggage, not knowing in advance that this place was an inn?" she said.

This time the response wasn't so smooth.

"I couldn't tell—" Bud began. "I thought maybe—"

He was interrupted by the onslaught of voices and footsteps on the stairs. His pounding on the door, along with their talking in the entrance hall, had evidently stirred the guests. There was a mixture of sniffling, shuffling, and general drowsy mumbling. Aunt Emily switched on the sconces. Drew was the leader of the pack, followed by Lillian, who was sputtering about the injurious disruption to her sleep regimen.

With the front door still partially open behind Bud Foster, there was a frigid breeze gusting through the hall, so none of the guests lingered. Like sheep pushing into a cozy pen, they all crowded into the parlor, where Drew and Parker started turning on lamps and arranging seats. Daisy was about to shut the door and show Bud where he could hang his wet coat when she heard Drew's voice rise abruptly. A second later, the light clicked on in the dining room. And Lillian screamed.

CHAPTER

10

"Oh, for pity sake," Aunt Emily said, rolling her eyes at Daisy. "What is that woman bellyaching about now?"

Daisy didn't roll her eyes back. She knew that something was truly wrong. For all her grousing, Lillian never shrieked like a panicky schoolgirl about spiders and spooks. Which meant that she wasn't just startled. She was shocked. And so was the rest of the group as they turned one by one almost in slow motion toward the dining room. Gasps. A cry of horror. May Fowler sinking to the carpet in distress.

Leaving Aunt Emily and Bud Foster in the entrance hall, Daisy hurried toward the others. Her feet stopped the moment she reached the French doors that separated the parlor from the dining room. They were wide open, providing an unobstructed view of the nook where a mere twelve hours earlier Henry Brent had proudly revealed his gift to Aunt Emily. The antique secretary was no longer standing grandly, albeit tippy, against the wall, its golden tiger maple and brasses gleaming. It was now lying facedown on the floor, the two pieces—the desk and the bookcase—

separated, no doubt from the impact. Except the impact wasn't with the floor. Between the furniture and the ground lay a body. It was Henry Brent.

There was no need to check for a pulse or seek emergency medical care. Daisy could tell that instantly. Henry Brent's eyes were open and unblinking, staring without seeing up at the ceiling. His mouth was open also, forming a stiff circle. And his limbs were stretched out in every direction like a jumping jack. The exact injury wasn't clear. A heart attack, a shattered spine, internal hemorrhaging. They were all possible based on the great size and weight of the secretary. The end result was the same, regardless. Henry Brent was dead.

He must have seen it coming, considering that he was lying on his back rather than his stomach. Daisy dearly hoped that it had been a quick death. She thought it might have been. There was no visible blood from slowly seeping wounds. Neither his hands nor his arms were scratched and bruised as they would have been had he struggled to get out from underneath or push the secretary off. On the contrary, his right palm was closed and appeared to be holding something.

Daisy felt a warm touch on her shoulder. Glancing up, she found Drew leaning over her. Only then did she realize that she was no longer on her feet but on the ground next to Henry Brent, her fingers mechanically straightening his bow tie.

"Daisy—" Drew began, trying gently to get her to rise.

She stayed put, gazing with some confusion at the bow tie and the accompanying suit—the burgundy seersucker that matched the burgundy draperies.

Drew tried again. "How about if we go sit in the parlor?"

Still not moving, Daisy lifted her head and looked at the group gathered before her. May remained on the carpet where she had sunk at the first glimpse of the body. Edna knelt beside her, patting her hand and crooning in soothing tones. They were dressed in nearly identical long-sleeved, floor-length flannel nightgowns with a ribbon of ivory lace stitched to the collar and hem. Lillian was on her usual settee, wearing a pair of pumpkin-orange pajamas featuring an array of cats chasing mice. In his cartoon wiener-dog pajamas, Parker paced back and forth behind his wife, grimacing and mumbling intermittently to himself.

The neighboring settee was occupied by the Lunts. Sarah perched at the edge of the brocaded fabric with the agitated expression of a caged canary waiting to fly off at the first available opportunity. She was clad in a scanty turquoise silk negligee with an equally flimsy turquoise silk cape. It was a surprising—and rather daring—choice of attire, considering both her personality and that she was at an inn with relative strangers instead of in the privacy of her own home. Kenneth lounged next to her, wearing such crisply starched pajama bottoms that they displayed not even a hint of a wrinkle. They were topped by a sweatshirt from his presumed alma mater.

Finally there was Georgia. Dressed in tie-dye boxer shorts and a faded Dairy Queen T-shirt, she was pressed against the wall in the far corner of the parlor with her gaze studiously averted from everybody else. But it wasn't what each person was doing or individually wearing that struck Daisy. It was the fact that they were all—including her—in their nightclothes, while Henry Brent was in his seersucker. Unlike them, he had never gone to bed.

"Can you get a blanket?" Drew said to Parker.

Parker stopped pacing. "A blanket?"

"A big one, to cover him. Or a bedsheet?" Drew suggested.

"Right. Good idea." Parker took several quick paces toward the hall before pausing with a frown. There were an awful lot of blankets and bedsheets at the inn. He turned to Aunt Emily questioningly.

Up until that point, Aunt Emily had been standing mute and motionless at the edge of the parlor. "I know just the one," she murmured, more to herself than to him, and then disappeared down the hallway toward the linen closet.

Parker's frown deepened as his focus shifted to the person that had been next to her. "Who are you?" he asked Bud Foster.

Glancing intermittently at the body on the floor, Bud started to give the same explanation that he had to Daisy and Aunt Emily about getting lost while driving, and the storm hitting, and his car subsequently ending up in a ditch, but May cut him off halfway through.

"I must see Henry," she said abruptly, paying not the slightest attention to Bud or his story.

"I'm not sure . . . ," Edna's voice trailed away, her brow heavily furrowed.

"I must see him," May repeated emphatically, "before they cover him."

Edna shook her head, as though she thought it far better for her sister not to see the deceased any more or any closer than she already had. It was certainly understandable. May, twisting her handkerchief taut and clutching it to her bosom, clearly did not have the strongest of nerves. But as May looked at her imploringly and reached out feebly for support, Edna didn't have the heart to say no and helped her to rise.

Parker came over to offer his assistance, and together he and the sisters moved slowly, arm in arm, toward Daisy and the nook. The rest of the group seemed to take it as a sign that now was the time when they should collectively pay their respects. Lillian joined her husband. Sarah and Kenneth followed. Even Georgia tiptoed over.

They circled around Henry Brent like a bereaved family of elephants closing ranks around a lost member of the herd. Some stood, others bent down or knelt by his side. It was Daisy who closed his eyes. She wanted to close his mouth, as well. She could see his dentures, and it made her think fondly of his clacking. But his jaw looked as if it was already too rigid, and she decided that it would be best to leave it rather than forcing it.

The wind hollowed outside, and an arctic blast of air whistled through the front door, which was still partly open. There was a communal shiver.

"Shut the door, would you?" Kenneth hollered at Bud, who had yet to move from the entrance hall.

Bud complied without speaking, although not before a second gust carried a shower of snow and ice inside. May swallowed a sob.

"Henry would have been so excited," she said mournfully. "He would have wanted to see if this storm could have topped the one in sixty-two."

Edna gurgled.

Parker heaved a sigh. "I sure will miss the old dog." He gave a farewell woof.

Lillian's lemon lips puckered, and she harrumphed under her breath. Daisy shot her a reproachful look. It was no secret how much Henry Brent's banter—especially with Parker—had annoyed Lillian, but that didn't excuse her being disrespectful to the dead.

"He seemed like such a lovely man," Sarah remarked quietly.

"He was so kind," May told her.

"And smart," Edna added.

"He asked after my mama every chance he got," Daisy said.

May nodded. "That was Henry. Always thinking of others."

"Always able to make you laugh," Parker chimed in.

Lillian harrumphed again.

Daisy's reproachful look repeated itself, and this time, it was joined by a pointed glare from Drew. Sniffing indignantly, Lillian turned her back on them, although she remained next to her husband as the eulogizing continued. Soon thereafter, Aunt Emily appeared with a large wool blanket cradled in her arms. It was a dogwood-colored tartan, the official state tartan of the Commonwealth of Virginia. Daisy knew it to be Aunt Emily's favorite, and she thought it very appropriate under the circumstances.

The circle parted to make room for her, and Aunt Emily approached them with wobbly steps. Rising to her feet, Daisy nodded at her encouragingly. The steps steadied the closer she came.

"Oh, Henry," Aunt Emily said, gazing at the man lying before her.

She didn't weep, but that didn't surprise Daisy. Although Aunt Emily would occasionally shed a happy or sentimental tear, she never cried out of sadness. Daisy had asked her about it once many years earlier. Aunt Emily had gotten a faraway look in her blue eyes and didn't respond. Ever since then, when the subject came close to being broached, she always deflected it by calling herself a tough old biddy.

"I shall miss you, my friend," she went on.

Edna gurgled as she had before. May swallowed another sob.

"I should have paid more attention," Aunt Emily chastised herself. "Everyone was talking about it being tippy. I should have listened better. It's my fault."

"No, no!" May exclaimed. "It's my fault! The secretary wouldn't have been here at all if I hadn't sold it to him."

"It never should have left the shop," Edna said plaintively.

"But it didn't look tippy at the shop!" May wailed.

"Indeed it didn't," Edna agreed. "And that's why it's not your fault. You couldn't have known what would happen."

"I should have known," Aunt Emily interjected severely. "When Henry was squeezing himself behind it last night before dinner, and it wobbled. I should have insisted right then and there that we move it, or at the very least, that we set something up against it, so it couldn't tumble over. I should have . . ."

As Aunt Emily continued her dour self-reproaches, Daisy remembered the noises—the rumbles and the crash—that she had heard in her bed before Bud Foster's pounding on the front door. She had originally thought that she might have dreamed them, but now it occurred to her that maybe they had been real, after all. Maybe they had been Henry Brent twisting himself behind the secretary again, trying to make it less tippy, or to see whatever thingamabob he said he had been looking at the first time. The rumbles could have been him pushing or shifting the secretary for a better fit or view, and the crash could have been it falling over. That would explain why it had seemed like the thunder came before the lightning.

Daisy also remembered that in between the rumbles—

but before the crash—there had been footsteps in the hall on the second floor and also on the stairs. Door hinges had squeaked. There had been voices, too. Garbled voices, some distance away. Were those part of a dream? Drew and Henry Brent had been together in the parlor when she retired to her room, and she had assumed that some of the sounds were from Drew going to bed. But were they all from Drew? Or maybe none was from Drew. The footsteps on the stairs could have been going up or down from the third floor, just as easily as from the second. And the voices had come after the hinge squeaks and footsteps, or at least so she thought.

She looked at Drew, who was standing close by her side with his arm wrapped supportively around her waist. His hair was rumpled, and he was wearing an old hockey jersey. He had definitely gone to bed. But Henry Brent in his seersucker hadn't gone to bed. Which meant that he must have remained in the parlor—or returned to the parlor—to tinker with the secretary after he and Drew had called it a night. So was one of the voices his? Had Henry Brent been talking to somebody? Or maybe she was confused, and she had just imagined the voices.

"Ducky?"

Drew gave her waist a prodding squeeze.

"Ducky?" Aunt Emily repeated. "Would you take that end?"

Waking from her musing, Daisy found Aunt Emily holding a corner of the dogwood-colored tartan in her direction. Apparently she was supposed to take it and help cover Henry Brent.

She grasped the proffered corner. Parker held the opposite corner across from her. Removing his arm from her waist, Drew took the third corner, and Aunt Emily retained possession of the fourth. Together they stretched the blanket wide.

"Under or over?" Parker asked.

For a moment, Daisy didn't understand him, then she realized what he meant. Did Aunt Emily want the blanket to go over the whole secretary, or under the secretary and only over the body?

"Just Henry, I think," Aunt Emily said.

"We'll have to lift the secretary for that," Drew told her. "At least partway."

"Oh, no," she responded quickly. "We don't want to lift it. We might see how he—Oh, no."

"I'm afraid the blanket isn't big enough to cover everything," Parker said.

"We can do the top of the secretary and wrap the blanket under him," Daisy suggested.

And that was precisely what they did. The entire bookcase was covered, while the desk was left open. The edges of the blanket were tucked under Henry Brent, so that none of him remained visible. In a flurry of activity, everybody in the group lent a hand, and then they all stepped back.

"Gracious, Parker!" Lillian cried. "Can't you even cover a body properly?"

She gestured toward Henry Brent's right arm, to which Parker was the closest. The arm was sticking out of the tartan like a stray caterpillar leg protruding from a cocoon.

"How did that . . ." Parker gazed at the arm quizzically. "I thought I—"

"Well, obviously you didn't!" Lillian snapped.

"Dear me." May looked back and forth between them, then at the arm—which in its present state had a rather disturbing disembodied appearance—and she started to swoon.

"Come sit down," Edna said to her sister, although not before chiding Lillian with a stern shake of her head.

Drew helped Edna guide May to the nearest settee, and as he passed Lillian, he muttered, "Instead of griping, fix it."

Lillian glowered at him.

"I'll fix it," Daisy said, not wanting to turn the sad arm into a circus. And before anyone could respond, she came around and pulled the blanket over the offending appendage.

"Thank you, Ducky," Aunt Emily said gratefully.

But Daisy didn't hear her. She was too busy thinking about the arm that she had just covered. It was Henry Brent's right arm. The palm of the hand was open and empty. And that was what troubled her. Because the last time she had looked at Henry Brent's right palm—before the blanket and before the eulogizing—it had been closed and holding something.

CHAPTER
11

It had looked like a piece of paper. Not a scrap torn from something else, but bigger and with straight edges. Daisy thought it had been folded in the shape of a letter, although she couldn't remember the color. White or cream, maybe a light yellow. She had only noticed it for a second. It had been a consoling sign to her that Henry Brent hadn't struggled under the secretary, because if he had, he presumably wouldn't have kept his palm closed, holding whatever it was that he had been holding. Except he wasn't holding it anymore.

She could be mistaken, of course. Daisy had enough experience with death to know that the shock and grief of it could easily play with one's senses. But she was pretty sure that the paper had been there. So why wasn't it there now? The most obvious answer was that it had fallen out of Henry Brent's hand. Her eyes took a quick survey of the surrounding floor. No paper—or anything else. It could be under the blanket.

Leaning down, Daisy slid her fingers along the edge of

the tartan. She had to be subtle about it. She couldn't just lift up the blanket for all to see. May, who was being bolstered on the settee by Edna and Drew, couldn't handle another view of the body. Daisy felt around carefully, pretending to tuck in the corners of the blanket with great diligence. Henry Brent's right shoulder, then his elbow, and finally his hand. She flinched slightly when she touched his skin. It was like waxy plastic. With some reluctance, she checked his palm. It was definitely open, and there was definitely nothing in it. There was also nothing around it, at least not that she could find.

The stiffness of his skin made her glad that she hadn't tried to close his mouth earlier. It also made her realize that it was unlikely for Henry Brent's palm to have opened up all by itself and whatever had been in it to just drop out. That left only one other option—somebody had taken the paper from his hand. But why? And for that matter, why had Henry Brent been holding it in the middle of the night, in the nook between the dining room and the parlor, while looking at an antique secretary?

It could have been anything. A bill from the electric company, a note confirming a doctor's visit, even a grocery list. And it could have been anyone who had taken it. That was obvious enough. They had all crowded around the body to pay their respects. They had all helped with the blanket. Straightening back up, Daisy looked about expectantly. One of them should be holding it. One of them should have it in their hand. But none of them did.

"I don't like to interrupt—" Bud Foster said.

Every head turned toward him. He had at long last moved from the entrance hall to the parlor, although he remained distinctly separate from the rest of the group. It was the first time he had spoken since May interrupted the story of his arrival.

"—but shouldn't someone call the police?" he went on.

"Call the police?" Parker echoed.

Bud nodded.

"Why would we do that?" Lillian asked with considerable disdain.

The question seemed to surprise Bud, and he answered by gesturing at the shrouded figure.

"What's the use of calling?" Kenneth said. "The man's stone cold dead."

"No one—" May began tearfully.

"—can do anything for him now," Edna concluded, adding a weary exhalation.

"All the same," Bud responded, "there needs to be an investigation."

"An investigation?" Parker echoed as he had before.

"What on earth needs to be investigated?" Lillian snapped.

"He was plainly crushed," Sarah squeaked, her thin frame quivering.

Kenneth's nostrils flared at Bud. "You're upsetting my wife."

In Daisy's opinion, Sarah looked more chilled from her lack of clothing than upset by Bud Foster.

"I don't mean to upset anyone . . ." Bud hesitated, as though he couldn't quite decide how to continue.

"Just so you know," Daisy said to him after a moment, "we don't have the police around here. We have a sheriff."

She deliberately kept her tone light, as though it wasn't really an important distinction, merely one of law enforcement nomenclature. But in truth, there was something important about it. By mentioning the police, Bud had shown that he wasn't from the area. In Pittsylvania County, Virginia—like many counties in the country—there was no police. There was a sheriff. Except Daisy wasn't sure whether Bud's error helped to prove or disprove his lost-and-stranded-motorist story.

Aunt Emily gave her a shrewd sideways glance. Evidently she had noticed Bud's faulty word choice, as well.

"Police or sheriff," Bud retorted with some impatience, "they have to be contacted, regardless."

"He's right," Drew said.

Out of the corner of her eye, Daisy saw Georgia shrink back against the wall.

Parker turned to Drew. "You think so?"

"I do."

Lillian wrinkled her nose. "I don't see why."

"I don't, either," May whispered, blinking from one person to the next. She seemed confused by the entire discussion.

"But is it right to bother the sheriff?" Edna's cleft chin jutted out as she spoke. "Especially in this frightful weather. There must be so many accidents and other problems that need his attention."

"Well, this was no acc—" Bud began brusquely.

Drew cut him off before he could finish. "It doesn't matter how many other problems there are," he said, addressing the group as a whole. "The sheriff needs to be notified. It wouldn't be bothering him. It's his job. There's been a death, after all."

"Yes," Parker remarked thoughtfully. "I can see your point. It should be reported."

May went on blinking. Edna gurgled and nodded, apparently seeing the point also. Lillian harrumphed.

Daisy looked at Drew. He looked back at her with

meaning and shook his head ever so slightly. He realized what Bud was going to say, the same as she did. Only, he didn't want everybody else to realize it, too. Unlike the rest of them, Bud didn't think what had happened to Henry Brent was an accident.

Bud was wrong. Of course it was an accident. It was obviously an accident. The secretary had been tippy. They had all noticed it and talked about it. They had even seen the piece wobble. Henry Brent had pushed it, or tried to adjust it, or was just standing in the wrong place at the wrong time, and the behemoth secretary had fallen on him and killed him. Terribly sad, but simple enough. Everyone thought so. Everyone had been shocked and horrified at the accident. No one supposed it to be anything but an accident. Except Bud Foster.

Except Bud didn't know that the secretary had been tippy. He also didn't know Henry Brent. The man had been ninety-four years old. He had been witty, generous, and extremely amiable. No one wanted to kill him. And that was what it boiled down to—killing him. Because if it wasn't an accident, then it was murder. The idea was so startling to Daisy that she had difficulty wrapping her mind around it. *Murder* Henry Brent?

"I'll make the call," Kenneth volunteered.

"I think that would be wise," Sarah concurred.

"Why you?" Lillian countered. "You don't even know the sheriff."

"No, but I—" Kenneth started to say.

"Parker could do it better than you," Lillian informed him crisply.

"Now, my dear," Parker protested. "This is Emily's house. She's the one who—"

"Daisy should do it," Drew interjected.

They all turned toward him.

"Daisy," he repeated with such decisiveness that nobody argued, "should call the sheriff's office."

The group looked at her. Daisy, in turn, looked at Aunt Emily. She was squinting at the tartan blanket.

"Yes, yes. By all means," Aunt Emily responded absently, her thoughts clearly not on the conversation at hand. "You talk to the sheriff, Ducky."

Daisy didn't mind talking to Sheriff Lowell. He was smart and efficient, and her dealings with him in the past had been amicable. But she was curious why Drew insisted on her being the one to make the call. Her eyes went to him, and he once more looked back at her with meaning. He definitely had some reason. Maybe it was because he knew that she would handle the matter without making a great fuss, unlike Lillian and some of the others. A quick call and a quick appearance by Sheriff Lowell would be good all around. Drew and Edna were still propping up May on the settee, and by this point, everybody had an equally gray and worn appearance. Depressing as it was, May and Edna were right. No one could do anything for Henry Brent now. There was no purpose in dragging out the necessary formalities.

The clock on the marble mantel chimed six. It was early, but at least it was morning. Even though Sheriff Lowell wouldn't in all likelihood be in his office yet, she could leave a message for him. As Daisy headed toward the phone in the entrance hall, she glanced at the glass panel above the front door. There was no sign of dawn, and the yellow glow from the porch lights had disappeared in the swirling snow. Wind rattled the door.

She shivered, although she wasn't cold. This wasn't how

the weekend was supposed to go. It was meant to have been a party. She had planned on peacefully sleeping in that morning, not calling the sheriff's office to report a dead body—dear Henry Brent's body—lying squashed on the floor.

With a cheerless sigh, Daisy picked up the inn's phone from the hall table and dialed. While it rang, she tried to figure out what she should say and how much to explain. Better to make it short and fast, she decided, like ripping off a bandage. She could go into all the unpleasant details when Sheriff Lowell arrived.

To her surprise, the phone kept on ringing and ringing, which was odd. Somebody was always at the office, all hours of the day and night. They had to be. It was the sheriff's department. Daisy wondered if maybe she had misdialed. She checked the screen. The number was correct. Finally, there was a click and a friendly—albeit drowsy—female greeting.

"Pittsylvania County. George Lowell, Sheriff. Janice, here."

"Hey, Janice. This is Daisy McGovern. Over at the Tosh Inn. I know it's a bit early, but I wanted to leave a message for the sheriff."

Janice yawned. "Sure can, luv. Only, he won't get it today."

"Oh." Daisy was disappointed. "I thought he usually came in on Saturday mornings."

"Sure does, luv." Another yawn. "Only not today."

She hesitated. Should she ask which deputy was on duty that day, or would it be better to wait and call Sheriff Lowell later at his home? He knew her and Aunt Emily well enough, so it wouldn't be too great of an imposition.

"It isn't an emergency, is it?" Janice inquired.

"No. Not exactly. But—"

"Good, because you won't get nobody."

Daisy frowned. "I won't?"

"Nobody," Janice repeated. "Can't get here. Can't get there."

"What? Why not?"

"The storm, luv. Haven't you looked outside? We've got a monstrous blizzard going on. It's been going on all night. Trees toppled. Roads covered. Bridges blocked. Sheriff Lowell can't make it down the mountain from his house. I talked to him just a little while ago. And Deputy Johnson's truck slid off into a ravine. Nobody can get anywhere. It's a real mess."

"I didn't know it was that bad," Daisy said frankly.

"It is," Janice confirmed, clucking her tongue. "I can't get out, neither. Been here since yesterday afternoon. I was supposed to go off my shift at two this morning, but the car wouldn't start. It's buried now anyways, and no one can make it in to replace me. So I'm stuck camping on the sofa in the coffee room until things clear up. I was having a nap when you rang. That's why it took me an age to answer. Who knows how long I'll end up having to stay here! At least the power hasn't gone yet, thank heavens."

Although Janice couldn't see it, Daisy nodded earnestly in agreement. She hadn't thought of it before, because she didn't realize how severe the weather was, but under such nasty conditions, they were very lucky to still have power at the inn. The wiring was old and unstable, and the electricity often went out from nothing more than an ordinary summer thunderstorm. Having no power wasn't much of a problem when there was only Aunt Emily, Beulah, and her mama to consider. But having the inn jammed full of hungry, anxious, trapped guests was another thing entirely.

It suddenly occurred to Daisy that Beulah hadn't made it back to the inn. Either her date with Wade Watson Howard

III had gone really well, or she was having trouble with the storm, too. Daisy made a mental note that she needed to call Beulah to make sure everything was all right. She also had to check on her mama and tell her about Henry Brent.

"Do you still want to leave a message, luv?" Janice asked her.

Did she still want to leave a message? There didn't seem to be much sense in it. Not if no one could get to the inn. It truly wasn't an emergency, and Edna had made a good point earlier: there probably were some serious accidents and other problems out there that should take priority. Awful as it sounded, Henry Brent wasn't going anywhere.

"Thanks," Daisy responded, "but I think I'll just call back later."

"Better make it tomorrow," Janice advised. "Or better yet, Monday. It doesn't look to me like this snow is going to let up any time soon, and nobody can do anything until it stops. Even then, we're going to have to be plowed out first. Lordy, it could take forever. I hope the vending machine isn't running low."

Daisy said that she hoped so too, thanked Janice again, and set down the phone. Then she walked to the front door and pulled it open. She was greeted by a squall of snow. The gray wall of pale flurries against the dark sky that she had seen when Bud Foster first arrived was gone. Now there was only snow. Layers upon layers of it, moving up and down, left and right. It looked like a flock of white ibis in flight, continually shifting direction.

Aunt Emily turned toward the hall and open door in surprise. "Is Sheriff Lowell coming already, Ducky? That sure was quick!"

She didn't answer. She simply stared—at nothing. There was nothing visible through the blowing snow. No objects.

No shadows. No horizon. Without the clock on the mantel, Daisy wouldn't have been able to even guess the hour. It was neither the black of night nor the light of day. They had been replaced by a curtain of opaque nothingness. And there was nothing to be heard. Only the wind as it howled, lonely like a wolf, but with the deep roar of a freight train and the merciless ferocity of an angry god.

"I assume he was in the neighborhood?" Aunt Emily went on. "I hope it won't be too difficult for him to get up the driveway."

"No," Daisy replied without thought. She didn't move from the entry. The icy sharpness of the air brought the blood to her cheeks. It felt good, clearing her head and refreshing her body.

"I hope not," Aunt Emily said again, "because the sooner he gets here, the sooner—"

Daisy drew a deep glacial breath, then she closed the front door and proceeded to recite the relevant portions of her conversation with Janice to the group in the parlor. She received a mixed reaction. Kenneth was doubtful that the storm could really be causing so much trouble. Lillian announced her intention of returning to bed. Edna advocated for an early breakfast with a strong pot of tea. May seconded the proposal. Parker's gaze drifted wistfully toward the liquor cart. And Sarah mumbled something in relation to a hot bath.

Drew and Bud were the only ones to focus on Henry Brent.

"If it's going to be a day or two before anyone official can get here," Drew said, rising from the settee and looking from Daisy to Aunt Emily, "then we should come up with a way to cover him better."

"My thoughts exactly." Bud drew a square in the air

with his calloused hands like he was cordoning off a crime scene. "Restrict access."

"I was referring more to blocking the view." Drew motioned surreptitiously toward May, who was leaning against Edna and still quite pallid.

"Indeed," Aunt Emily murmured, squinting once more at the tartan blanket. "Seeing him there . . . The constant reminder . . ."

Daisy watched Georgia slip silently from the parlor to the dining room and then disappear into the kitchen. It gave her an idea. With swift steps, she headed toward the nook. Aunt Emily followed her.

"I wish it wouldn't have happened, Ducky," Aunt Emily said in a low tone.

"Of course not. None of us do."

She shook her head. "Not just Henry. The party. The party started it all."

"Of course it didn't," Daisy rejoined, only half listening. She was looking at the French doors that separated the parlor from the dining room. Although the upper panels were made of glass, the bottom portion was solid wood. With the lights turned off in the dining room and the doors closed, Henry Brent and the secretary would no longer be visible from the parlor. The guests couldn't go into the dining room anymore, but that was all right. They could eat in the kitchen, or their bedrooms, or picnic-style in the parlor.

Not waiting for confirmation, Daisy flipped the switch in the dining room. She began to shut the door on the left. Aunt Emily, quick to understand the plan, took the door on the right.

"I told you yesterday that it was a bad omen for the weekend," Aunt Emily reminded her.

"Oh, Aunt Emily . . ."

Together they latched the French doors, concealing the nook and the body.

"And bad things always happen in threes," Aunt Emily said.

CHAPTER

12

Aunt Emily may have been a wise old owl, but she also tended to be a superstitious one. Daisy shrugged off her ominous remark as a fatigued and strained rambling. It was a sign that Aunt Emily needed a hot bath and a strong pot of tea just the same as Sarah Lunt and the Fowler sisters. Daisy encouraged her to go upstairs, promising to talk to Georgia about the eating arrangements and to find some accommodation for Bud Foster. Aunt Emily complied, and the rest of the group slowly followed. They were all still in their nightclothes, and they were gradually realizing that it was no longer the night.

If things did happen in threes—good or bad—in Daisy's case, it was two more telephone calls. She had just finished getting dressed herself when Brenda rang. She was at home and worried about getting to the bakery. Daisy told her not to try. Given the conditions, there would be no customers that day. And she certainly shouldn't come to the inn. She would never make it through. Being a nervous driver to begin with, Brenda sounded greatly relieved at not having to brave the storm. She said that she would settle in with Blot—her beloved portly cat—and try out some new recipes. Daisy hung up the phone with a smile. By the end of the weekend, Blot would be even more portly.

That settled one issue, at least. Bud could take Brenda's room. Talking to Brenda reminded Daisy that she hadn't yet checked on Beulah. She figured that now was as good of a time as any. Her mama was still sleeping, Georgia was in the process of organizing breakfast, and it was no longer too early for a wake-up call if Beulah had settled somewhere comfortable with Wade Watson Howard III.

Daisy dialed and waited.

"Hello, darlin'."

For the second time that morning, Daisy glanced down at the screen, thinking that she had pressed the wrong buttons. She hadn't.

"Darlin'?"

"Rick?"

He laughed. "Now admit it. You missed me yesterday at the party, didn't you?"

"What are you doing with Beulah's phone, Rick?" Daisy said, surprise temporarily trumping annoyance.

"She left it on the table."

"On the table?" Daisy frowned. "Where is she?"

"Where are you?" Rick countered.

"At the inn. You?"

"The General."

"Oh." Daisy understood now. The General was where Beulah had arranged to meet Wade. Apparently Rick had been a Friday-night customer as well. "Did Beulah get stuck there?"

"We all did," he told her. "Can't get out of the parking

lot. Aside from being buried, it's got that incline up to the road. The snow's turned it into a mini-mountain of ice."

"It must be really bad," Daisy said, and she meant it. Rick and his trusty rusty pickup were not timid when it came to traversing tough terrain. He—together with his brother, Bobby—lived further in the backwoods than Sasquatch.

"How is it at the inn?" he asked. "Your mama okay? And Aunt Emily?"

Her frown faded. For all Rick's faults, he was always sweet toward her family. "We're snowed in, too. Mama's got a nasty cold and cough, but I think—or at least, hope—she's on the mend. As to Aunt Emily, well, she's . . ."

Daisy hesitated. Should she tell Rick that Aunt Emily, along with everybody else at the inn, was shaken up by what had happened to Henry Brent? He'd want details, and she didn't feel like recounting the whole awful scene, especially when she was also going to have to do it with Beulah.

"Did you meet Wade?" she said instead. Rick was usually a pretty savvy judge of character, and she was curious to know what his impression of Beulah's date had been.

"You eventually meet everybody when you're trapped in a bar overnight with them, darlin'."

"And what do you think of him?"

"He's all right."

Daisy rolled her eyes. Rick was never very chatty on the phone, but that was laconic even for him.

"You're so helpful," she remarked dryly.

Rick chuckled. "Wade seems like a decent enough chap. Is that better?"

She gave a little grunt.

"But I am sorry," he drawled, "that you didn't come along with them. Then *we* could have spent the night together."

Even through the phone, Rick's serpent tongue had an

undeniable magnetic quality. Over the years, Daisy had seen countless women's knees grow weak at his hypnotic hiss. But she knew how to break the spell.

"It would have been just like old times," she drawled back at him. "When I used to have to pick you and Matt up at the General after the two of you had gotten so drunk that you couldn't even walk out the door."

Rick growled at her in warning.

"Why do you have my phone? Give it to me!" An instant later, Beulah's voice replaced Rick's. "Daisy?"

"Yup."

Beulah snorted. "I knew he was talking to you. I could see it on his face. He's got that predator expression, like he's stalking you in the jungle—" She interrupted herself. "Are you going to sit right next to me and listen to our entire conversation, Rick?"

"I was thinking about it," he said, loudly enough for Daisy to hear.

"Well, don't! It's none of your business what we talk about. And you can stop grinning at me like that. Daisy isn't interested in you. She's got Drew, and he's—"

This time Daisy interrupted her. She had to. Rick had a talent for getting under Beulah's skin. Their spats could go on for ages if not promptly nipped in the bud. "Beulah, I've got news. It's important."

"News?" Her voice rose excitedly. "Is it about you and Drew?"

She could tell that Beulah was dropping Drew's name just to pique Rick, and ordinarily Daisy would have been amused, but her mind was on Henry Brent.

"Have you finally decided to get serious with Drew—" Beulah cooed.

"Henry died," Daisy said.

Beulah went mute. Daisy could picture her sitting at one of the rickety, beer-stained tables, her hazel eyes bulging in disbelief.

"I hate telling you this way," she apologized, "but I thought you should know."

"He died?" Beulah echoed in a whisper. "But he seemed so—so healthy and in such good spirits yesterday."

"Who seemed healthy and in good spirits? Who died?" Rick demanded. When Beulah didn't immediately answer, he reclaimed the phone. "Who died, Daisy?"

"Henry Brent."

"His ol' ticker finally gave out, eh?"

"No. It was—Put the phone on speaker, Rick, so Beulah can hear, too." She waited for the telltale click, then continued, "It was an accident. One of the new pieces of furniture, a secretary, fell on him in the dining room when we were asleep."

There was a momentary pause.

"Are you sure?" Rick said.

"Of course I'm sure," Daisy responded with irritation. "I saw him lying on the floor. I touched him. The man was no longer alive."

"That's not what I meant. Are you sure it was an accident?"

The question startled her. Why would Rick ask that? Why would he even think it? It reminded her of Bud Foster's similar remark and how adamant he had been about them contacting the police.

"I called the sheriff's office," she told Rick.

"What did they say?"

"Nothing. I talked to Janice. Sheriff Lowell is stuck at his house. And nobody else can get anywhere with the storm."

There was another pause.

"You said that it happened when you were asleep. Was everyone asleep?" Rick inquired.

"I don't know. I assume so. It was the middle of the night, dark and quiet, with everyone in their rooms . . ."

It was Daisy's turn to pause, as it occurred to her that it hadn't actually been quiet. On the contrary, there had been quite a few noises. The rumbles and the crash, presumably from Henry Brent fussing with the secretary, and it tumbling over. The door hinges squeaking, followed by the footsteps in the hall and on the stairs. Then the garbled voices, which Daisy was still uncertain about. And finally the pounding on the front door, courtesy of Bud.

"I don't know," she repeated slowly, this time with a furrowed brow. "I really have no idea who was asleep or in their rooms."

"Where was Lillian?" Beulah remarked tartly.

"Lillian!" Daisy exclaimed in surprise.

"She's the first person that I'd suspect of anything bad," Beulah said. "She couldn't stand Henry, especially when he and Parker would team up against her."

"That's true, except Lillian was the first person to find him in the dining room. She screamed like a banshee."

"It could have been a fake scream."

"Well, yes, theoretically, but be serious now, Beulah. I know you're mad at what she said yesterday. Lillian can be a royal pain in the—"

"She's worse than an army of fire ants crawling into your bikini!"

Beulah must have made a face to match, because Rick gave a hoot of laughter.

Daisy smiled, too—it was such an apt description of

Lillian—then she said again, more earnestly, "Be serious now, Beulah. You can't honestly think Henry's death was anything other than an accident. You saw how the secretary wobbled."

"It was tippy," Beulah acknowledged, "but not so tippy for it to fall over all by itself, especially in the middle of the night when no one was around to witness it. It's awfully coincidental—and convenient. My money is still on Lillian's helping hand. Or maybe Georgia's!"

"Georgia is the new maid?" Rick said.

Before Daisy could respond, Beulah answered, "Exactly. She came out of nowhere a couple of weeks ago, and she's very secretive."

"She's just young and nervous," Daisy explained.

"You're too trusting," Beulah rejoined.

"You're right about that, Beulah," Rick concurred. "Daisy is far too trusting."

"Heaven help us when you two start agreeing on things," Daisy muttered.

"And there's Sarah Lunt," Beulah added with enthusiasm. "It could have been her also."

"Sarah Lunt?" Rick asked.

"She and her husband, Kenneth, have been staying at the inn while house-hunting in the area—or so they claim," Beulah informed him. "Would you believe that they offered to buy the inn from Aunt Emily? Something isn't right with them. I can tell."

Daisy sighed. Apparently Beulah had decided to become suspicious of everybody, and she sounded like she was greatly enjoying it.

"Where are you in the inn, Daisy?" Rick said suddenly.

"My room. Why?"

"Good. You have to be careful when talking about this. You don't want folks to overhear and think that you're suspecting them."

"But I'm not suspecting them. See what you've started, Beulah? Now Rick's suspicious of everybody."

"Not suspicious," he corrected her. "Cautious. And you should be cautious too, particularly when you've got odd sorts roaming around who you don't really know."

"If you think that now," Daisy replied drolly, "just wait until I tell you about Bud."

"Who?" Rick and Beulah chorused.

"Bud Foster. He showed up on the porch shortly before we discovered Henry. He said that he got lost and his car went into a ditch near the inn because of the storm. But his story seemed slightly off. He looks . . ." Daisy searched for the right word. "Rough. Almost like he's been living in his car. Only, I don't think that he has. He definitely isn't a fool. He was the first one to suggest calling the sheriff."

"If he did that," Rick mused, more to himself than to them, "then he can't be running from the law."

"What does Drew think about everything?" Beulah asked Daisy.

"Drew?" Rick's voice stiffened. "Is he at the inn?"

Beulah tittered. "Of course he's at the inn. Thank him again for letting me use his truck last night, Daisy. It really helped in getting here. The roads were already pretty bad. But I'm afraid I probably won't be able to get it back to him today."

"He won't care," Daisy said. "It's not like he's going anywhere."

"No, he's not. Drew's at the inn for the *entire* weekend."

From her tone, it was clear that Beulah was directing

the statement at Rick, no doubt to needle him. Evidently their brief moment of harmony had passed.

There was a tense silence, then Rick snickered. "He must be having a miserable time with Lillian. We all know how devoted and protective she is when it comes to dear Matt."

Rick was spot on, unfortunately, but Daisy wasn't about to give him the satisfaction of telling him that. She changed the subject.

"I've got to go. My mama needs her cough medicine, and I still haven't given Bud his room."

"I'll call you as soon as it looks like I'll be able to get out of here," Beulah said.

"Sounds good—"

"You have to be careful, Daisy," Rick interjected.

"She'll be fine," Beulah responded. "She's got Drew."

"What good is he going to do?" Rick scoffed. "He obviously couldn't help Henry."

That launched a spirited rebuttal from Beulah on Drew's many manly virtues, followed by an even snappier retort from Rick on how those supposed virtues hadn't done a lick to stop a secretary from crushing Henry Brent. The exchange had the hallmarks of becoming a long argument.

As she hung up the phone, Daisy drew an unsteady breath. Rick's words lingered in her mind. Twice he had told her that she needed to be careful, and she was beginning to have a worrisome feeling that he might be right.

CHAPTER

13

"*That's* the room key?" Bud said, frowning at the large, tarnished brass key in Daisy's hand.

She nodded. "Aunt Emily is a bit old-fashioned when it comes to locks. She doesn't like those coded cards they use at hotels."

"I assume since I didn't see one in the entry downstairs that she also doesn't like security systems?"

"Not if they're electronic." Daisy suppressed a smile as she thought of Aunt Emily's shotgun on the pegs in the kitchen. At the same time, she noted to herself that in addition to not being a fool, Bud Foster was evidently quite observant.

"The thing is humongous," he muttered, watching her push the clunky key into the matching brass lock on the door.

"And heavy," she added, for no reason other than it was true.

"Then how does anyone carry it in their pocket?"

"They don't, usually. Either they drop the key off with

Aunt Emily when they go out, or they just leave the door unlocked."

Bud stared at her with his red-ringed, bloodshot eyes.

"If it's any comfort," Daisy said, "there hasn't been a theft at the inn for years. We don't get many complete strangers to begin with. Most of the guests have some connection to the neighborhood. And because of all the creaking and squeaking when it comes to the porches and doors, no one can go in or out without everybody noticing. So folks don't generally walk off with other folks' hats and trousers."

He raised a bushy, skeptical eyebrow.

She could only shrug as she turned the knob and swung open the door. "Welcome to the Joseph E. Johnston."

The room was snug and pleasant, one end tucked up into the attic. It was a favorite with Brenda when she occasionally spent a night or weekend, because it had an excellent view of the fuchsia rhododendrons surrounding the gazebo. They weren't blooming in February, of course. Now they were being pummeled with wind and snow.

Bud walked through the doorway, glanced once around, and immediately said, "Isn't there anything else?"

It was Daisy's turn to raise an eyebrow. "Is there a problem with the room?" she asked, her voice frosty.

If there was, she certainly couldn't see it. The Joseph E. Johnston was warm, clean, and, even with the unfriendly conditions outside, cheery. Daisy couldn't help thinking the man should be a little more grateful that he wasn't stuck in his car, freezing into an ice cube.

"No. Not a problem." He spoke slowly, as though choosing his words with care. "But it's the third floor. Don't you have something lower?"

Lillian had objected to being on the third floor, too, although that was because she enjoyed being indignant and complaining about whatever she could—in this case, an extra set of stairs. Bud Foster didn't seem like a habitual complainer, and he didn't have any apparent difficulty climbing the stairs, so Daisy knew there had to be more to the request.

"I'm sorry," she responded lightly, "but there isn't another room available on any floor. This one is only empty because the woman who was going to stay here couldn't make it through the storm."

Bud appeared thoughtful. "Who else is on the third?"

That was a mighty interesting question, considering that he was supposedly a lost and stranded motorist and therefore not acquainted with anybody at the inn. Daisy's doubts about his story were starting to grow.

"Georgia's room is up here," she said. "Lillian and Parker's also."

She watched him curiously, wondering how much that would mean to him, particularly since she didn't use surnames or offer any additional elucidation. But Bud's expression remained flat, telling her nothing.

"There are four doors in the hall," he observed.

"Three bedrooms and one storage room, with steps up to the attic."

"And who's on the second floor?"

There were eight bedrooms on the second floor. Four were permanently—more or less—occupied by Daisy, her mama, Beulah, and Aunt Emily. The other four were allocated for the weekend to Drew, Edna and May Fowler, and the Lunts. It wasn't any sort of a secret who was where. The rooms were all plainly marked, and every door was visible along the hall. But Daisy didn't feel like giving Bud a comprehensive list, let alone drawing him a map. If he was that interested, he could simply pay attention and figure it out for himself.

"Everyone else is on the second floor," she told him.

Bud's gaze flickered, and Daisy could see that it was not the answer he wanted, or expected.

"What about that man?" he inquired brusquely. "The old fellow who died. Where was his room?"

She blinked at him in surprise. "Downstairs, on the other side of the dining room."

"Why can't I have that one?"

Daisy bristled. It was no longer a request for a different room. Now it had become a demand for Henry Brent's room. Beyond being rude and aggressive, it also struck her as odd. Very odd. What was wrong with the Joseph E. Johnston on the third floor? Was it too close to someone else? Too far from someone else? Or maybe there was something specifically about Henry Brent's room that drew Bud to it. But why on earth would anyone want a dead man's room?

They were questions that she couldn't answer. But Daisy was sure of one thing. She was not giving Henry Brent's room to Bud Foster. Except she had to give him a reason, a solid excuse that he couldn't argue with. She remembered how Bud had said that there needed to be an investigation. An investigation surely included looking at the deceased's room, and that meant no one else could be allowed in before Sheriff Lowell had been there.

She shook her head. "The room is off limits until the sheriff has given his okay. So it's either this room," Daisy concluded firmly, "or the rocking chairs outside on the porch."

For a moment, she had the impression that Bud might

suggest an alternative, like sleeping on one of the settees in the parlor, but then he seemed to change his mind and decided to accept the Joseph E. Johnston, after all. It was a wise choice. Wartime aside, Aunt Emily would never allow anyone to camp in the parlor, and the rocking chairs on the porch didn't offer hot coffee or after-dinner cordials.

Sliding the black duffle bag that he was carrying off his shoulder, Bud tossed it next to the bed. It landed on the wooden floor with a heavy thump. Daisy's first reaction was annoyance, because the noise had probably woken up her mama, whose room was directly below. Then she thought of how the bag had been one of the things that made her mistrustful of Bud and his story to begin with, and she used it as an opportunity to go digging.

"It was awfully smart of you to bring that bag along from your car," she remarked, her tone sweet in an effort to sound more complimentary than suspicious. "Especially since you didn't know this place was an inn."

Bud turned to her.

"Now it would be nearly impossible to get anything out of your car with all the snow," Daisy continued. "What road did you say you were on when you went into the ditch?"

"I'm not sure," he answered. "I got lost."

"Yes, of course. And where were you headed?"

"I had an appointment."

"Oh, dear." She widened her eyes like a guileless lamb. "Well, at least they can't be too upset with you for not making it. It's not your fault, after all. You can't control the weather. Have you been able to reach them? Would you like to use the inn's phone?"

"I have a phone," Bud informed her.

"Yes, of course," Daisy said again. "But didn't you mention something about not being able to get a signal in your car? I thought you might still be having trouble, considering the terrible conditions outside. We could also look up a number for you, if you needed. Who was your appointment with?"

Bud flinched. It was so slight that ordinarily it would have gone unnoticed. But while intentionally chattering like a perky hen, Daisy was also scrutinizing the man closely. Tiny as it was, the balk was enough to confirm to her that something about his story was most definitely fishy.

"I do hate missing appointments," she chirped on. "My friend Beulah almost missed one herself yesterday evening because of the storm. I hope yours wasn't too important. Will you be able to reschedule?"

"It's no big deal," Bud replied, giving an inconsequential shrug. "Door-to-door life insurance. That's my line. I schedule and reschedule all the time. In the end, I get there when I get there."

"How interesting," Daisy drawled. "I didn't realize that anyone still did door-to-door life insurance sales."

"Indeed they do. An excellent business. Booming."

An excellent and booming business, door to door on a Friday night, in a rural area during a winter blizzard? That didn't just smell fishy. That stunk like a passel of skunks.

"Everybody you know needs life insurance," Bud told her with gusto. "Everybody wants a good send-off."

Daisy was tempted to respond that on the contrary, she did know someone who no longer needed life insurance, and she was quite confident that Henry Brent was past caring about his send-off. But she shrewdly stayed silent.

Bud's chapped lips curled into a crooked grin. "Never

too young or too old, too healthy or too ill for life insurance. That's my motto."

He sounded like he was playing a part, reading aloud from a script or advertising brochure, and it gave Daisy an idea.

"Do you have a business card?" she said.

The grin vanished.

"And an informational pamphlet? I think my mama and I might be interested in getting some of that insurance."

"I . . ." Bud started patting his pants' pockets. "Well, I . . ."

Daisy's nose twitched. It was exactly as she had supposed. The man's story was a bunch of hooey. It might have been reasonably well rehearsed and constructed with sufficient detail to be passable to someone who wasn't paying too much attention, but it was still hooey.

He continued patting. "I can't seem to find any at the moment . . ."

She swallowed a chuckle, waiting to see how long the faux search would last.

"Maybe in here . . ." Bud fumbled with his trench coat.

A folded newspaper, accompanied by a mass of crumpled tissues, fell from the coat onto the floor. The tissues looked used and wet, and Daisy—ever the waitress—promptly reached for the little wicker wastebasket in the corner by the bath.

Bud mumbled a halfhearted apology while she collected the unappetizingly soggy wad. Daisy gingerly lifted the damp newspaper with two fingers to avoid staining her entire hand with ink. It was a small local paper. The sports section was turned up, with an article about the new baseball coach at the community college in Rocky Mount.

"Do you want to keep it?" she asked Bud.

"No." His back was turned toward her. He had given up searching for the elusive business card and informational pamphlet, and had moved on to brushing off his coat and hanging it in the armoire.

Setting the paper in the wastebasket, Daisy noticed that a photograph accompanied the baseball article. Although not in color, it was large enough for her to see the age, build, and general appearance of the new coach. He was about thirty years old, tall and fit, trim and tidy. According to the caption, his name was Bud Foster.

Startled, she looked up at the man standing in front of the armoire. He was twenty years older, thirty pounds heavier, unkempt and unshaven—clearly not the same Bud Foster. What a strange coincidence. And then it occurred to Daisy that maybe it wasn't a coincidence. Maybe it wasn't only his story that stunk. It was Bud himself, because he wasn't actually Bud Foster. That was just a name he had seen in the newspaper. A name that he had assumed somewhere between the door of his car and the door of the inn.

Daisy's mouth opened, ready to accuse the man of being a liar and demand an immediate explanation for his deception. But a second later, she shut it again as Rick's warning echoed in her head. She needed to be careful. She had already pressed Bud—or whatever his real name was—hard enough for one day, or at least for that morning. She didn't know how he might react if she confronted him with the truth.

Reluctantly, Daisy returned the wastebasket—with the newspaper—to its corner. She wanted to take the paper along as evidence to show Aunt Emily and the others, but she worried that it would be too obvious and put Bud on guard. It would be better if he believed that his secret remained safe, even if only temporarily.

"I'll leave you to get settled," Daisy said, forcing herself to be polite and composed.

Still busy at the armoire, he grunted a word of thanks.

"The key is in the lock," she added, before slipping as quickly as she could out of the room and away from Bud Foster.

CHAPTER
14

"He said he had appointments and his business was door-to-door sales?" Aunt Emily asked Daisy.

"That's right," she answered. They were sitting in her mama's room as Lucy finished a late breakfast, Daisy on the foot of the bed and Aunt Emily in the yellow painted rocker across from her.

"What utter rot!" Aunt Emily exclaimed. "It's either door to door *or* appointments. It can't be both."

"I think the more important point," Daisy's mama interjected, gazing contemplatively at a last bite of toast, "is his name. Could it be a coincidence?"

"No, it could not, Lucy. Absolutely not!"

That was as agitated as Daisy had seen Aunt Emily in some time, but she wasn't surprised, and she didn't blame her in the least. Aunt Emily had been circumspect toward Bud Foster from the moment she saw him standing in the doorway of the inn. She had been reluctant to shake his hand and invite him into her home in the middle of the night, and her misgivings had been proven correct. Now she had someone that she didn't know, didn't trust, and who was in all likelihood a fraud occupying one of her rooms.

"I agree. It's too . . ." Lucy wiped the crumbs from her fingers, then set the napkin on the tray at her side. ". . . too improbable. If everything else were going for him, I might be more inclined to believe it. But there's his peculiar arrival, and him having the newspaper in his coat as though he had just read it and picked up the name, and you both said that he didn't seem quite right from the outset."

Aunt Emily sniffed defensively. "I only let him in because of the weather."

"Of course." Lucy nodded. "It would have been uncharitable not to."

Her approbation seemed to soothe Aunt Emily, who nodded back at her.

"So what do we do with him now?" Daisy asked.

"I'll tell you what I'd like to do," Aunt Emily responded, more cheerfully. "I'd like to give the man a good punt in the rear. It would teach him a lesson."

Lucy chuckled. "That it might, but it still wouldn't solve the problem."

"Well, something has to be done," Aunt Emily went on. "We can't allow a potentially crazed criminal to run willy-nilly around the place."

"Rick doesn't think that he's a criminal," Daisy said.

"Rick?" her mama and Aunt Emily echoed in astonishment. They exchanged a glance.

"Yes, Rick," Daisy returned dryly. "And there's no need for that look. We haven't been whispering sweet nothings. I called Beulah earlier to check on her and tell her about Henry—"

"Beulah's with Rick?" Aunt Emily's blue eyes bulged like a trout's.

"She's not *with* Rick. She's with Wade, her date. They got stuck at the General last night, and Rick happened to be there, too."

"Oh, I'm very glad to hear it." Lucy sighed in relief. "I always worry when Beulah goes on those blind dates all alone. And now with the storm, she can't leave if there's a problem. It's a comfort to know that Rick is watching out for her."

"Watching out for her?" Daisy gave a dubious snort. "It's more likely that Rick and Beulah will throttle each other if they're trapped together too long."

"Nevertheless," her mama said, "I feel better with Rick there. We don't know Wade. We know Rick."

"That's true. We know Rick is a philandering, carousing—"

"What did Rick say about Bud?" Aunt Emily cut her off impatiently.

"I told Rick that Bud was the first one to suggest calling the sheriff," Daisy explained. "He said if Bud did that, then he can't be running from the law." She added with a wry smile, "And if anybody knows about running from the law, it's Rick."

"But Rick doesn't know Bud?" Aunt Emily asked.

"No. Not from his name, at least."

"Except it's not his real name," Aunt Emily reminded her.

"I doubt there's much chance of us finding out his real name," Lucy remarked.

Aunt Emily clucked her tongue. "It's too bad Rick isn't here."

Daisy's gaze narrowed at her.

"Now, Ducky, don't get cross with me. You know I'm fond of Drew. I didn't mean that I wish Rick were here instead of him. It would just be helpful to have Rick's opinion on Bud. He has a knack for seeing through people."

Although Daisy didn't admit it aloud, she knew that Aunt Emily was correct. It was precisely why she had asked Rick about his impression of Wade.

"You shouldn't sell yourself short, Emily," Lucy said kindly. "You're a mighty good judge of folks yourself."

She blushed at the praise. "That's what comes from being a tough old biddy. But Rick is much better at gauging the more," Aunt Emily clucked her tongue again, "unsavory types."

"That's what comes from being an unsavory type," Daisy muttered.

Her mama and Aunt Emily exchanged another glance, which further ruffled her feathers.

"Well, Rick isn't here, and he can't get here," she snapped, "so we'll have to figure out Bud by ourselves."

There was a loud thump overhead, and all three of them looked up. The noise had come from Bud's room. Perhaps he had thrown down his duffle bag again.

"I think," Lucy mused, her eyes still raised toward the ceiling, "that you were right before, honey. The question isn't his name, but what do we do with him now?"

"Chuck him out," Aunt Emily promptly proposed, and she made a motion of drop-kicking the man.

Daisy had to laugh, because she could well imagine her booting him straight through the front door just like a football. "When he wanted a different room, I told him that it was either the Joseph E. Johnston or one of the rocking chairs on the porch."

Rocking in her own chair, Aunt Emily nodded approvingly, but Lucy shook her head.

"We can't put him out on the porch," she scolded them. "Not in the freezing temperatures and with all the snow."

As if to prove her point, the wind howled fiercely against the side of the inn and rattled the bedroom windows. With a shiver and a cough, Lucy pulled up the patchwork quilt, which had been folded back while she ate.

"I suppose it would be uncharitable," Aunt Emily agreed after a moment, although she looked disappointed by the lack of drop-kicking. She turned to Daisy. "Why did he want a different room?"

"I don't know, but he's definitely got some reason beyond the usual nonsense of objecting to the color of the wallpaper or not fancying the view that nitpicking guests like to use, especially when it comes time to pay the bill. I'm sure there's more to it. He wanted to know who was on what floor, and he even asked for Henry's room."

"Henry's room?" Her mama frowned.

"I said he couldn't have it because Sheriff Lowell hadn't been in it yet."

"That was quick thinking, Ducky," Aunt Emily complimented her.

Lucy frowned harder. "But Henry's room? It seems suspicious, doesn't it?"

"It does," Aunt Emily stopped rocking, "except Bud—or whatever his name actually is—couldn't have done dear Henry in. He wasn't in the inn when it happened."

"Done him in!" Daisy exclaimed.

It was Aunt Emily's turn to frown. "I'm afraid there's a good chance of it, Ducky. Don't tell me you haven't considered it yourself."

Daisy looked hastily at her mama, worried what effect the shock of Aunt Emily's words could have on her fragile health, but she didn't appear at all startled by the idea that Henry Brent's death might not have been an accident. On the contrary, Daisy had the distinct impression that she and Aunt Emily had discussed the possibility previously. It was Aunt Emily—and not herself—who had first told her mama about the tragic event downstairs.

"Could there be something in Henry's room?" her mama remarked thoughtfully.

"But if there is," Aunt Emily started rocking again, "how would Bud know about it? From the way he looked at the body and talked about the need for an investigation, he didn't seem to know Henry at all. Unless . . ." She hesitated.

"Unless he knows someone else here," Lucy continued for her. "And that was why he asked Daisy who was on what floor—"

"So he could slip into their room and speak to them privately," Aunt Emily concluded, "unnoticed by the rest of us."

There was a short pause. Daisy couldn't help being a little amused. Listening to her mama and Aunt Emily finish each other's sentences was a bit like following along with one of the Fowler sisters' conversations. But she was also more than a little concerned, because what they were saying had a strong ring of truth to it. Bud could indeed know a person at the inn. In his questions to her, it had felt as though he was trying to locate the room of someone—surreptitiously.

"I wonder who he could know." Lucy turned to her daughter. "Didn't you mention something last night about Georgia recognizing or being surprised to see someone?"

Daisy nodded. "She was surprised enough to drop that

tray of glasses. And afterward, she was staring hard at somebody. But it couldn't have been Bud. He wasn't here yet."

Suddenly Aunt Emily burst out with a cackle. "Maybe Bud knows Lillian! Maybe he's come to the inn for a tryst with her!"

"Oh, Emily, please," Lucy groaned. "Lillian and a romantic rendezvous? I've only just finished my breakfast."

She went right on cackling. "Can you imagine how delicious the scandal would be? Lillian's always getting on her high horse and complaining about the supposed improprieties of others."

Half suppressing a smile, Lucy replied, "What about poor Parker?"

"Pish, pish." Aunt Emily waved a nonchalant hand. "After the initial shock wore off, Parker would be as happy as a raccoon with a jar of peanut butter. Getting untethered from his sourpuss wife would be the best thing that ever happened to him."

"I wouldn't mind it either," Daisy added, more earnestly than the others. "If Lillian and Parker were officially on the rocks, then she would have to stop trying to make me feel guilty about Matt."

"You don't have a speck to feel guilty about, Ducky!"

"Nothing at all, honey," her mama concurred.

Daisy shrugged. "It doesn't matter, regardless, because I think we can be pretty confident that Bud is not having a dalliance with Lillian."

"He's here for something, though," Aunt Emily countered. "And it darn well isn't selling insurance. If that man is in the business of life insurance, then I'm a monkey's uncle."

Lucy laughed. "You would be an excellent organ grinder, Emily—"

She was interrupted by another loud thump from above.
"What on earth is he doing up there?" Aunt Emily cried.

Remembering Rick's caution about people overhearing,
Daisy hushed her. "We should be careful what we say. The
walls—and the ceiling—are thin."

"Too thin for comfort, on occasion." Her mama spoke
in a low tone. "Last night I heard the Lunts talking about
buying the inn again."

Aunt Emily's brow furrowed. "But I told them it wasn't
for sale."

"They seem to be under the impression that you might
change your mind."

"Change my mind?" She was taken aback. "Why would
I do that?"

"You said the timing didn't work," Daisy reminded her.
"Maybe they believe the timing's better now."

"Because Henry is dead?" Aunt Emily's astonishment
switched to indignation. "They have some bloody nerve—"

"I doubt it's that," Daisy broke in hurriedly, motioning
for her to keep her voice down. The Lunts' room was the
George Pickett right next door. She didn't know if they were
presently in it, but she did know that if her mama could
overhear them, then they might also be able to overhear
Aunt Emily. "Timing can include a lot of things. Honestly,
it was sort of an odd answer you gave them."

Aunt Emily pressed her raspberry lips together hard, but
she didn't respond.

Lucy changed the subject. "I keep thinking about Bud
wanting Henry's room. What could Henry have that would
interest Bud?"

Daisy's mind went immediately to the mysterious disappearing piece of paper. But that had been in Henry Brent's

hand, not his room. And Bud couldn't have taken it, because unlike all the others, he didn't get near the body. He wasn't close enough to have even seen the paper.

"We could check the room," Aunt Emily proposed.

"It couldn't hurt," Lucy said. "One never knows what one might stumble across."

Aunt Emily nodded. "Pop in, take a peep around, pop back out."

In unison, the pair turned toward Daisy. Understanding the inference, she arched an eyebrow at them.

"So you want me to do it? I'm the one who's supposed to go snooping?"

"Your mama's cough is just beginning to mend, Ducky," Aunt Emily pointed out. "She can't go downstairs without potentially catching her death."

Although Daisy would never have suggested that her mama climb up and down the steps with her lungs in such a weakened state, let alone take the chance of her being caught in an icy draft, she still found it rather ironic that the two women were so quick to volunteer her for the task of poking about in Henry Brent's room.

The eyebrow remained raised. "And I presume that you're far too busy with the guests, Aunt Emily?"

"Well, as a matter of fact, yes." She fussed with the sleeves of her blouse. "It's nearly time for lunch, and then there are afternoon cocktails to think about . . ."

"You could take Drew with you, honey," Lucy suggested.

"Oh, what an excellent idea!" Aunt Emily commended her. "An extra set of eyes is always beneficial."

"And it would let you and Drew have a moment's privacy," her mama added.

Daisy smiled at her in gratitude. She didn't consider

rooting through a dead man's room to be a particularly am-
orous activity, but it would get her and Drew away from
Lillian's ever-watchful gaze, even just for a little while.

Her mama started to smile back when a severe coughing fit suddenly overtook her. Daisy swiftly got up and
handed her a dose of medicine. It helped, but only slightly.
The coughing continued.

"Enough talking," Daisy said, throwing Aunt Emily a
stern glance, because she had the tendency to chat with her
mama indefinitely. "Now you need to rest." She plumped
up the pillows behind her head and tucked the quilt snugly
around her.

Lucy patted her daughter's hand and coughed some
more.

Picking up the breakfast tray, Daisy headed toward the
door. "Come on, Aunt Emily."

As she rose from the rocker, she gave Lucy an encour-
aging nod. "We'll report back as soon as Ducky and Drew
find something."

"*If* we find something," Daisy corrected her.

"I have every confidence," Aunt Emily returned opti-
mistically.

But Daisy couldn't share in such a rosy view, because it
occurred to her that in all their discussion of Bud Foster's
fake identity, and what Henry Brent might have in his room,
and someone doing the dear man in, there was one thing
they didn't mention. If someone had indeed done Henry
Brent in, then that person was certainly still at the inn.

CHAPTER
15

Daisy's foremost challenge wasn't finding something of importance in Henry Brent's room. It was finding Drew. She checked his room, the kitchen, and the parlor, but he wasn't in any of them. The stairway leading down to the cellar was dark, and the French doors that concealed the nook and the body were still closed. He couldn't be wandering around outside in the storm, and he also would have no reason to climb up to the attic. Drew seemed to have evaporated into thin air.

Puzzled, she was about to go back up the steps to see if he had returned to his room in the interim when she noticed Lillian sitting on the Windsor bench in the hallway across from the linen closet.

"Have you lost something?" Lillian said, with a not-quite-friendly twang.

Daisy stopped and looked at her. She was wearing a yellow-and-brown-spotted sweater, topped by a large cowl that made her neck stretch up like a giraffe's. Her mouth was puckered even tighter than usual, and she was holding a goblet that contained a liquid more closely resembling whiskey than water.

Not wanting to broach the subject of Drew, Daisy motioned toward the glass. "A bit early in the day, isn't it?"

"Just a drop of sherry. Takes the edge off."

She swallowed a laugh. No goblet was big enough to take the edge off Lillian. A bathtub full of sherry might have done it.

"Not much of a party," Lillian grumbled.

"It certainly hasn't gone like Aunt Emily planned."

As she said it, Daisy couldn't help thinking that all of the unpleasantness had begun with Lillian's arrival. But if Aunt Emily was right that bad things did always happen in threes, then maybe they were done now. First there had been Lillian's unexpected and unwelcome appearance. Then came Bud Foster. And finally—with the worst occurring last—Henry Brent's death. The bad omen for the weekend had been fulfilled, and a sunny sky would soon follow. Hopefully.

Lillian sipped her sherry. "I told Parker I wanted to leave."

Although Daisy would have been delighted to see her go, she knew it wasn't possible. "I don't think you can get to your car. The parking lot is buried."

"That's what Parker said. I told him then I wanted to walk."

"Walk home in this weather! Oh, Lillian, I know it's only a mile or so to your house, but you wouldn't make even half of that. You can't see your own arms and legs out there. You and Parker would get lost and covered before you reached the end of the inn's driveway."

"That's what he said," she repeated.

"He's right. But it's okay that you have to stay." Daisy tried to buck up her spirits, well aware that an unhappy Lillian was liable to make everybody else unhappy, too. "Lunch should be ready shortly, with cherry pie for dessert. If I remember correctly, isn't cherry pie one of your favorites?"

Lillian answered with a half nod, then she took another drink.

"Where is Parker?" Daisy asked, hoping that after another minute of polite conversation, she could excuse herself and return to her search for Drew.

"With those Fowler sisters." She rolled her eyes. "Apparently they're still all shook up, and Edna was worried that May would be too unsteady on her feet to make it down the stairs by herself. So she asked Parker to come and help. I don't know what's keeping them. They're only on the *second* floor."

It took Daisy some effort not to roll her eyes back at Lillian. Even with all that had happened, the woman was still holding a grudge and grinding an ax over the location of her room. She replied lightly, "It's nice of Parker to help. May did look pretty shaky earlier."

"Too indulgent." Lillian sucked on her teeth. "Far too indulgent."

Daisy wasn't sure if she was referring to her husband, Edna, or everybody at the inn generally—aside from her unsympathetic sour lemon self—but she didn't seek any further explanation or dispute the point. She could see that Lillian's mood was not improving, and she was eager to distance herself as soon as possible.

"Well, lunch should be ready shortly," she said once more, unable to think of any other innocuous topic. She turned to walk away.

Lillian sucked on her teeth again. It was a grating sound. "You've lost him, haven't you?"

Daisy stiffened.

"I don't mean Matt." Her voice was harsh and bitter. "I mean the one you replaced him with."

To her surprise, Daisy found herself more fatigued than angry. With a weary sigh, she turned back around. "Really, Lillian? Do we have to have the same argument over and over?"

"I'm simply looking out for you, Daisy. Matt would want that."

She was tempted to respond that if Matt had any interest whatsoever in her well-being, he wouldn't have left her in the first place, but there was no sense in egging the woman on.

"I can't shirk my responsibilities to my family," Lillian continued, haughty and grave.

The sigh repeated itself.

"And I don't trust him."

At that remark, Daisy's brow furrowed. Since when did Lillian not trust her darling nephew?

"It's very suspicious," Lillian said.

"What is?" Daisy asked her hesitantly.

"That boy, of course."

She was confused. "Matt?"

Lillian's nostrils flared. "No, not Matt! How would Matt be suspicious? I'm talking about Drew!"

Daisy closed her eyes and took a deep breath. "Lillian, I am *not* going to keep doing this—"

"Listen to me, Daisy." Her words tumbled out fast. "He was ahead of me on the stairs. He was the first one down. But I think he was down already."

"I don't have the slightest clue what you're—"

"Last night," Lillian said. "Although technically, it was already this morning. When we were all woken up by that banging on the door."

"You mean from Bud?"

She nodded. "I was behind Drew on the steps. He was the first in line. Except he wasn't really."

"Yes, he was," Daisy responded curtly.

"No, he wasn't."

"I was in the entrance hall, Lillian. I saw it. Aunt Emily and I were talking to Bud when everybody came down the stairs. There was Drew, then you—"

"But I think he was just pretending."

Daisy shot her an irritated, impatient look. "That's absurd. How could Drew be pretending to be on the stairs when we both saw him there?"

"You don't understand." Lillian shook her head in a state of agitation. "I was in bed when I heard the pounding on the front door, and I complained to Parker about it."

"Naturally you did," Daisy muttered under her breath.

"Being lazy like he is, Parker wouldn't get up. He said I should mind my own business and go back to sleep."

"Which naturally you didn't," she added, also under her breath.

"Well, I couldn't just lie there without knowing what was going on." Lillian drained the remainder of her sherry. "So I opened our door. There was no one in the hall. Of course there wouldn't be on the *third* floor."

Daisy felt an overwhelming desire to gulp down a glass—or bottle—of something considerably stronger than sherry.

"I stepped out on the landing and was just about to start

down the stairs," Lillian went on, "when suddenly there was this movement."

"A movement?"

"It was like when an animal scurries in the night. You can feel it better than you can see it, but you know something is there. And then came the shadow."

That grabbed Daisy's full attention. She remembered a movement, followed by a shadow, too. It was right before she had answered the door and spoken to Bud Foster. She had come down the stairs and felt something behind her in the hallway. When she turned around to look, there had been a shadow at the edge of the kitchen. Or at least she had thought there was a shadow at the edge of the kitchen.

"It was only in front of me for an instant." Lillian held the empty goblet before her as though pointing at the shadow. "On the second-floor landing."

"Did it move?" Daisy asked. Her shadow didn't budge an inch, which was why she had dismissed it as her imagination.

Lillian hesitated. "I'm not sure. It was awfully dark."

"So it just disappeared?"

"Of course it didn't just disappear," she retorted, more adamant than indignant. "It must have gone somewhere."

Daisy was thoughtful. Had her shadow gone somewhere, as well? At the time—for a brief moment—it had seemed to her like a person. She had even spoken to it. When it didn't respond, she had assumed that it was her eyes and mind playing a nighttime trick. But maybe it wasn't a trick, after all.

"It couldn't have gone up, because I was there," Lillian declared, waving the goblet in the relevant direction. "And it couldn't have gone down, because you were there. Which

means that it must have gone into the second-floor hall. It's
the only option left."

"And then?" Daisy questioned.

"And then it came back out again! It was Drew acting
like he was coming from his room when he had actually
just come up the steps."

Daisy blinked at her. It was Drew? Drew was the
shadow?

"So you see he wasn't really first on the stairs," Lillian
concluded in triumph. "He was only pretending."

"Why?" Daisy said slowly.

"I don't know that," Lillian replied with a careless air,
as though it were an unimportant detail. "But I do know
it's suspicious. Very suspicious."

There was a pause as Daisy considered whether she
could be right. Not about Drew being the shadow, but about
the shadow generally. The timing fit. If Daisy saw her shadow
before she opened the door, and Lillian saw her shadow after
she started speaking to Bud, then the shadows could be one
and the same. The same person that was ghosting about the
inn in the middle of the night. And the same person that
might have been talking to Henry Brent before he died.
There had been those voices.

"Did you hear anyone talking?" she asked Lillian.

It was Lillian's turn to blink at her. "I heard you—and
Emily—at the door with that man Bud."

"No, before that. Before the pounding on the door."

"Well, Henry and Drew were talking to each other in
the parlor when the rest of us were going to bed." Suddenly
Lillian's eyes stretched wide. "That could be why Drew was
pretending! He already knew what had happened to Henry
with the secretary, and he didn't want us to know that he

knew. So he snuck back upstairs, making it seem like we were all discovering Henry together."

Daisy frowned. If Drew had known about Henry Brent, he would have immediately called an ambulance, not snuck upstairs.

"I told you I don't trust the boy," Lillian said disdainfully. "And you shouldn't either. How well do you know him anyway?"

The frown deepened as her resentment began to rise.

"With all of this shady behavior," Lillian continued, "it makes me wonder if maybe that secretary tipping over like it did was no accident."

"Are you accusing Drew of—"

"I'm not accusing anyone of anything. But if the shoe should happen to fit . . ." Lillian gave her a smug look. "Now Matt, on the other hand . . ."

Oddly enough, the mention of her estranged husband calmed Daisy down. It reminded her that Lillian was intentionally goading her in support of Matt. As she proceeded to rattle off his innumerable merits—nearly all of which were imaginary—Daisy reflected on what she had said a moment earlier. Lillian certainly wasn't the first person to suppose that the accident might not actually have been an accident. She also wasn't the first one to point the finger at somebody. Beulah had accused her, Georgia, and Sarah Lunt all in the span of five minutes. But Lillian was the first to base the idea on something that could be considered tangible, or at least semi-tangible. The shadow.

Someone could have gone downstairs after Drew had retired for the evening, leaving Henry Brent alone in the parlor. That would explain the footsteps that she had heard in the hall and on the steps and the door hinges squeaking.

It would also explain why Drew had been in his night-clothes, while Henry Brent had never gone to bed. Henry and the person could have argued. That would account for the garbled voices. And the person could have pushed the secretary over on top of him. But why? Why would he—or she—want to kill Henry Brent?

Daisy felt a growing sense of urgency. She shouldn't be wasting time squabbling with Lillian over Matt. She should be looking in Henry Brent's room. And she needed to find Drew. She had to ask him if he had seen the shadow, or anything else.

Mumbling a vague apology to Lillian about having to check on something, she started to hurry away. Lillian's sharp voice called after her.

"If you're checking on Drew, you better find him soon, Daisy. You don't know what he could be getting up to."

And to Daisy's considerable chagrin, Lillian was proven correct not long thereafter when she discovered Drew standing on the third-floor landing, with Georgia whispering in his ear.

CHAPTER
16

It didn't look romantic. It did, however, look clandestine. Georgia was leaning into Drew, her voice low and her gaze shifting about apprehensively, like some undercover agent about to pass along crucial state secrets. Drew was paying close attention to her, nodding and responding with short questions or one-word answers. They hadn't noticed Daisy in return, so she retreated silently into the second-floor hall. She stood just far enough back that they couldn't easily see her, but she could still watch them.

Straining her ears, she caught a few snippets from Georgia. *He shouldn't . . . I had . . . You can't . . .* Without more, they weren't very useful. Her tone was anxious and also somewhat belligerent, although Daisy had the impression that the belligerence was directed more toward the subject matter of the conversation than Drew. It also reminded her why eavesdropping wasn't good. You heard bits and pieces of things, and you weren't sure exactly what they were, but you tended to jump to conclusions anyway.

The chief conclusion Daisy drew was that her mama

was right. There was definitely more to Georgia than met the eye, and she was clearly secretive. It made her wonder if Beulah was right, as well. Had she been too quick to trust Georgia? After all, they knew so little about her. And she had been exhibiting some strange behavior. There was a lot of furtive peering around corners, and staring hard at people, and shrinking against walls at the mention of the sheriff being called. Except Daisy couldn't fault her too much for watching folks while hiding, because that was precisely what she was doing herself at the moment.

Georgia's voice rose slightly from the landing. "In the kitchen—"

At that remark, Daisy recalled another odd incident, when Georgia had been gazing so intently at Aunt Emily's shotgun on the chimney. She had tried to ask her about it, but Georgia had talked instead of tea bags and sticky fingers, after which she had gone skipping into the cellar in search of potatoes.

A door opened on the third floor. Immediately quieting, Georgia and Drew turned toward it. Lillian was still downstairs, probably refilling her goblet with a second installment of sherry. According to her, Parker was with Edna and May in one of their rooms. So it had to be Bud coming from his room. Daisy wasted no time in taking advantage of the opportunity. With Georgia and Drew focused on him, she had a chance of slipping away unnoticed. She wasn't eager to see Bud again so soon, and she really didn't want Drew and Georgia to find her skulking in the hall.

With fleet feet and averted eyes, Daisy hurried down the steps. Almost unconsciously, she succeeded in avoiding the creaky spots. It wasn't until a floorboard in the entryway groaned beneath her that she stopped. That was when it occurred to her that if the shadow she had seen in the night at the edge of the kitchen had gone up the stairs when her back was turned, then it had done so in true phantom fashion without making any noise.

Who could have managed that? It had to be someone familiar enough with the inn to know where—and where not—to step. That included herself, Aunt Emily, her mama, and Beulah. There was also Georgia. Georgia had been up and down those stairs hundreds of times over the past few weeks. By now, she must have learned which spots creaked and which didn't. Which meant that she could be the shadow.

Daisy tried to remember in what order Georgia had appeared in relation to Drew, Lillian, and the rest of the group when they had trooped down the steps, but she couldn't. Then there was the all-important question of why. Why would Georgia be creeping about in the dark, and why on earth would she kill Henry Brent by pushing a secretary on top of him? She hadn't even known the man. Unless, of course, she had. He could have been the person that startled her and at whom she had been staring.

Taken as a whole, it seemed rather far-fetched to Daisy. Beulah, no doubt, would have told her that she was being too trusting again. There was another possibility, however. The shadow could have simply gotten lucky. The steps didn't always creak, and even if they did, Daisy might not have heard them over Bud's pounding on the door, especially if the creaks happened to be soft. A smaller person usually made smaller creaks, and the smallest person at the inn was Sarah Lunt.

The problem with Sarah being the shadow—aside from her not knowing or having a reason to kill Henry Brent, either—was that her husband was a light sleeper. He would have noticed her getting out of bed and wandering around the inn for an extended period of time. Unless, of course, he had been aware that she was going to commit murder, and he didn't mind or was supportive of it. But that seemed pretty far-fetched, as well.

The most troubling part for Daisy was that she couldn't come up with a motive as to why anybody would want to harm Henry. Lillian was the only one who had disliked him, and she had seen the shadow, too. Unless, of course, she hadn't actually. She could have made it up. Someone who didn't scruple to kill a man could certainly also lie about it in an attempt to frame someone else for the deed. Lillian had been awfully fast in pointing the finger at Drew, although Daisy didn't know if that was just because he wasn't Matt, or if she was seriously trying to blame him.

As Daisy walked slowly down the hall, her lips curled into a morbid smile. She was shifting the guilt among Lillian, Georgia, and Sarah Lunt, exactly the same three people that she had chastised Beulah for accusing earlier that morning. She felt somewhat comforted by the fact that she didn't really think it had been any of them. Except it had to have been somebody. Unless, of course, it was an accident, after all. But the chance of that decreased significantly in her mind the moment she entered the kitchen.

Lunch was nearly ready. Pots were steaming on the stove; serving dishes were lined up, waiting to be filled; and the lovely smell of fresh, warm bread was wafting from the oven. It was all set for the finishing touches, only there was no one in the kitchen to make them. Georgia was upstairs. Aunt Emily was somewhere else, apparently. And the guests were probably getting hungry. But Daisy wasn't concerned with them. She wasn't thinking about the people that weren't there. She was thinking about what else wasn't there. The mottled throw rug lay as usual at the edge of the hearth. Next to it stood the wrought-iron log holder stacked half full. Then came the old stone fireplace with its worn wooden pegs. The pegs, however, were empty. Aunt Emily's Remington was gone.

Daisy's eyes went immediately to the wall behind the log holder. Unlike the gun, the needlepoint bag was still hanging from its hook. It looked full, and she hastily checked it to be sure. Although she had no way of knowing if every last shell was there, the raggedy bag seemed to contain as many shell boxes as it had the day before. That was some relief, at least. The Remington was never kept loaded, so whoever had it didn't have any shells. Theoretically, they could have brought their own, but that didn't seem too likely. Most people didn't carry around shotgun shells without the accompanying shotgun.

Her gaze returned to the chimney. Who would take the gun? The one person that she could rule out with complete certainty was Aunt Emily. She would never move the Remington without also moving its shells. Georgia, on the other hand, ranked high on the list. Except her staring at the shotgun didn't necessarily equal her taking the shotgun. And from an opportunity standpoint, it could have been anyone at the inn. With proper timing, anyone could have walked into the kitchen, picked up the gun from the pegs, and walked right back out again, entirely unnoticed. It was only by chance that Daisy had even noticed the gun was gone now.

Under ordinary circumstances, she would have merely

shrugged at the missing Remington. But these were far from ordinary circumstances, considering that Henry Brent was lying dead in the adjacent room, a man using a false name was presently on the third floor, and half the inn was acting peculiar. The disappearance of the shotgun confirmed the worst to her. For Daisy, it could have only one of two interpretations: the person who took the gun wanted to use it, or the person wanted to keep someone else from using it. Either way, it meant that there was little chance of anything having been an accident, and there was a great chance that more trouble was coming.

"There you are!" a voice suddenly exclaimed.

Whirling around in surprise, Daisy found Drew standing behind her.

"I've been searching all over for you. Sometimes this place can seem too darn big, especially when I can't find you." With a warm smile, Drew took hold of her hand and pulled her toward him.

She resisted, and he immediately loosened his grip.

"What is it?" he said, the smile fading. "What's wrong?"

For a moment, Daisy hesitated. Lillian's allegations lingered in her brain, along with the clandestine meeting that she had witnessed on the landing.

"Nothing's wrong." Shaking off her doubts, she took a step forward. "You spooked me. That's all."

Wrapping his arms around her, he drew her close.

"You had me worried there for a minute," Drew murmured in her ear. "I thought something might really be the matter."

Daisy hesitated again, this time debating which subject to broach first. The sound of footsteps on the stairs made the decision for her.

"Quick!" she exclaimed in a low tone. "We have to leave before they come!"

Although he appeared somewhat startled, Drew didn't argue with her. He followed Daisy as she moved swiftly out of the kitchen and into the dining room. With the French doors closed and the chandelier turned off, the room was dusky, but there was enough gray light from the windows to see the bulky combination of the secretary, blanket, and body on the floor at the far end. Daisy paused and gazed at it somberly. In all likelihood, somebody had killed Henry Brent, and now that someone might be in possession of a shotgun.

"What are we doing?" Drew asked her. "I thought lunch was supposed to be buffet-style in the sunroom. Parker and I set up a couple of folding tables and carried some chairs in there earlier. It's a bit chilly, but Emily thought it would be better than making a mess on the furniture in the parlor."

Daisy only half heard him. She was still focused on the missing gun.

"I should have taken the shells," she mused aloud. "They could go back for them."

"Go back for them? What shells?"

"You remember the Remington that Aunt Emily keeps on the chimney in the kitchen?" Daisy didn't wait for his answer. "Well, it's gone. Somebody took it. But the shells are kept in a separate bag, and the bag is still there."

Drew took a long, slow breath as he considered what she had said. "When?"

She shook her head. "I don't know. Sometime between yesterday afternoon and a few minutes ago when I came into the kitchen."

"Do you have any idea who it was?"

Although she shook her head again, she replied, "Georgia is a possibility."

He frowned doubtfully.

Daisy frowned back at him. "What exactly is going on with you and her anyway? I saw you two talking together earlier, on the third-floor landing. You looked pretty cozy."

"That wasn't cozy," Drew corrected her. "This is cozy."

Putting his hand firmly under her chin, he lifted her mouth to his. It was a hard, strong kiss, and Daisy kissed him back.

Drew grinned when they came up for air. "It's a good thing Lillian didn't see that one. She would have passed out from the shock."

"Maybe she could still sense it," Daisy returned, with a laugh. "And she spontaneously combusted in the sunroom."

"It wouldn't be quite so chilly then!"

They were about to kiss again, but Daisy heard pots and bowls clanging in the kitchen. Lunch was being served.

"I hope you're not hungry," she whispered to Drew.

Taking his hand, she led him through the archway on the other side of the dining room into a short, narrow hall. At the end of the hall stood a closed door. It was the Jubal Early—Henry Brent's room.

Drew looked at the door, then at her. "Why do I have the feeling that we haven't come here for more smooching?"

Daisy sighed. "Aunt Emily thinks we should take a look around Henry's room."

He grunted. "Poor man. Going along merrily until he comes to this place and stumbles into something that he shouldn't have."

"So you believe it was murder, too!"

Drew glanced quickly behind them. "Not here," he told her.

Nodding, Daisy reached for the doorknob. Although the hall and dining room were both empty, and everybody was probably in the sunroom eating, it was best not to take the chance that someone would hear them. "Let's go in," she said.

As expected, the Jubal Early was unlocked. Like the dining room, it was dark except for the gray light filtering in through the windows. The tall, thick draperies cast murky shadows onto the walls. They reminded Daisy of what she had wanted to ask Drew.

"Last night," she began, closing the door softly behind them, "did you see anything after you left the parlor?"

"See anything? Like what?"

"Like a shadow. A shadow that could have been a person."

Daisy switched on the little lamp that stood on the nightstand. Drew was squinting at her, his brow furrowed.

"When I came downstairs because of that pounding on the front door," she explained to him, "there was a shadow at the edge of the kitchen. I didn't think much of it at the time, until Lillian told me that she saw a shadow, too—on the steps, shortly afterward—and she thinks it was a person. She thinks it might have been the person that tipped over the secretary."

Drew let out a low whistle.

"She also thinks," Daisy added, a tad sheepishly, "that it might have been you."

He responded with an aggrieved snort. "She would."

"That part is rubbish, of course. Lillian's just being Lillian. But if she did see a shadow, and I saw the same shadow, then there could be something in it. So I was wondering if you noticed anything. You were the last one—excluding whoever pushed the secretary—to see Henry alive."

With his brow still furrowed, Drew walked over to the pecan desk in the corner, pulled out the accompanying straight-backed chair, and sat down on it. He was thoughtful.

"There was one thing," he remarked slowly, "but it wasn't a shadow. After I left Henry and came up to my room, I thought I heard a door open. It was only about a minute later, maybe less, even. Somebody went into the hall."

"It was a door and the hall on the second floor?" Daisy asked him.

Drew looked at her questioningly.

"There were a lot of footsteps and door hinges squeaking last night," she said. "And with half of 'em, I couldn't tell if they were going up or down, second floor or third. But it might be significant, even if we don't know why right now."

He nodded. "It was the second floor. I'm sure of that. Although I'm not sure where they went afterward."

"So it could mean nothing. They could have just turned around and gone back into their room."

"It's possible. Except . . ." Drew paused. "There was something else. I was getting into bed when I heard these two voices."

Daisy's eyes focused on him with keen interest. The garbled voices. They were definitely significant. "Downstairs? Were they arguing?"

"As a matter of fact, I think they were. I remember thinking how strange it was, partially because it was the middle of the night, and also because one of the voices belonged to Henry. He wasn't really a quarrelsome sort."

"No, he wasn't," she agreed. "He was too jolly. But more importantly, who did the other voice belong to?"

"That's where it gets muddled." Drew shook his head at himself. "I was falling asleep, so it became less and less clear, like it was slipping into a dream. I know I heard it, and I know at the time I thought I could identify it, but I can't remember who it was now."

"Well, you need to try," Daisy replied grimly. "Because unless I'm very much mistaken, that voice was the murderer's."

CHAPTER
17

The lamp on the nightstand in Henry Brent's room flickered. Daisy went to the window and drew back the draperies as far as they would go. Ordinarily the Jubal Early had a nice view of the side lawn. In one corner, the parking lot and a portion of Beulah's salon were also usually visible. But not today. The lawn was lost in a swirling mass of snow, lashed and scoured by the raging wind. The salon and parking lot had vanished behind a frozen veil. It looked like a bleak and desolate landscape, one where nothing could exist, but Daisy knew that somewhere beneath the towering, shifting drifts there were camellia borders, the old potting shed, and the Fowler sisters' hatchback.

"At least we still have power," she said.

"As long as it lasts," Drew returned, doubt in his tone.

The words were barely out of his mouth when a violent gust battered the panes of glass, causing the whole room to shudder. The lamp flickered again.

"Before the lights do go out," he continued, "what exactly did Emily want us to look for in here?"

"I don't know. I don't think she knows. Something that would make Bud interested in the room."

The doubt moved to Drew's eyes. "If Bud believed there was something of real value or importance here, I don't think he would have asked you for the room. He would have simply come in and taken whatever it was at the first available opportunity. Granted, I've only just met the man, but he seems plenty smart to me."

He was right. Daisy herself had told Rick and Beulah that Bud wasn't a fool. If he was sly enough to use a false name, then he was also sly enough to sneak into Henry Brent's room. Except that left the question of why he had wanted to switch rooms. If it wasn't for some*thing*, then it had to be for some*one*.

"Have you noticed anything," she asked Drew, "that would make you think Bud might know somebody at the inn?"

"Now that you mention it," he replied after a moment's reflection, "he was looking at all of us very carefully in the parlor when he first arrived, like he was trying to identify someone, although it's hard to say for certain."

"But if he knows someone, why the fake name and story?"

Drew shrugged. "I have no idea. It could be that we're reading too much into it. Maybe he just enjoys playing make-believe, like some people do at hotels and on cruise ships. They pretend that they're a completely different person for no reason at all."

"Then what about him asking to change rooms?"

He shrugged again. "Maybe the man hates heights and was hoping to be on the ground floor."

That still didn't explain to Daisy why Bud had wanted

to know precisely who was on which floor, but it was useless to belabor the matter further when Drew had no better
answers than she did.

Stepping back from the window, her eyes circled around
the room, searching for a clue of any sort. There was the
pecan desk where Drew was sitting. On it stood a pair of
bronze elephant bookends, an accompanying row of tomes
for perusal by the guests, and a large, old-fashioned leather
blotter. It reminded her of the piece of paper in Henry
Brent's hand. Had he written it on the blotter? There was
no other paper on the desk, nor any writing instruments.
Perhaps the paper belonged to someone else. That could be
why it had so mysteriously disappeared from his palm. Its
owner had reclaimed it.

One door of the armoire was open. Henry Brent's overnight bag sat on the bottom shelf, neat and buckled closed.
The bed was similarly tidy and untouched. Its pillows were
fluffed. The blanket was straight and smooth, except the
bottom edge had come untucked.

Daisy looked at Drew. "When you left Henry in the
parlor last night, do you know if he was planning on going
to bed?"

"I assume he was, although he didn't actually say it."

"I've been wondering about that," she mused, "almost
from the very beginning when I noticed that he wasn't in
his nightclothes. If the shadow that I saw and the voice
that you heard belonged to the person that killed him,
was Henry sitting there waiting for them—knowing they
were coming, but not knowing what they were going to
do? Or was the person waiting for you to leave and then
surprised Henry as he was heading from the parlor to his
room?"

"He wasn't heading to his room," Drew told her. "At least not right away. He was going to the kitchen. He said he needed to get something."

"Probably a glass of water after all that gooseberry brandy. The stuff is potent." Daisy gave a sad little chuckle. "Too bad he didn't get the Remington instead, *with* the shells. That would have changed things."

"That's not the only way things could have been changed. I should have paid more attention," Drew reproached himself.

She shook her head sympathetically. "I don't think paying more attention would have helped much, under the circumstances."

"It might have," he countered. "Something was bothering Henry."

"Bothering him? What do you mean?"

"He was worried. There was something weighing on his mind last evening. Looking back on it, that's probably why he decided to stay up when everybody else headed off to bed. He wanted to think—and talk—things over."

"He did seem interested in sharing a drink and a story," Daisy agreed.

Drew nodded. "And I should have listened better."

"What did he say?"

"Nothing. That's the problem. It was all just the usual sort of trivial late-night chitchat. Except something was troubling him. I'm convinced of it. At the time, I didn't want to pry, and frankly, my mind was on you. But I should have asked him about it." Drew's face was grave and regretful. "It's my fault."

"No, it's not," she responded gently. "It's not your fault any more than it is Aunt Emily's or May Fowler's. There's only one person to blame in all of this—the person that pushed the secretary on top of him."

For a long minute, they were both quiet. Daisy watched the lamp on the nightstand as it flickered repeatedly, like it was sending out Morse code. Finally she sunk down on the bed with a sigh.

"I guess there's not much point in continuing to look around—Ouch!" Feeling something hard and jagged beneath her, she immediately stood back up.

Drew rose from his chair. "What is it?"

"I don't know." Daisy frowned at the bed. "I don't see anything, but . . ."

She put her hands on the spot where she had been sitting and pressed down. Her behind hadn't deceived her. Although it wasn't outwardly visible, there was definitely something more than sheets and a mattress beneath the blanket. It was bulky and rigid.

Daisy stepped to the end of the bed where she had noticed earlier that the bottom edge of the blanket had come untucked. Reaching beneath it, she felt around for a moment and promptly discovered that it wasn't loose by accident. Someone had lifted the blanket—and the mattress—intentionally for use as a hiding place.

An instant later, with minimal effort, she pulled out a double-barreled 20-gauge. It was Aunt Emily's missing Remington.

"Well, hell," Drew muttered.

Her thoughts exactly. Daisy turned over the gun in her hands. Its signs of age aside, it looked fully functional. No one appeared to have tampered with it. She popped open the breech. There were no shells. The shotgun wasn't loaded. It was in the same condition as it had been on the pegs on the chimney.

"It must have been Henry, don't you think?" Drew said.

Daisy nodded, having not the least doubt. "Of course it was him. He's the only one who would put a shotgun under his mattress. It's a terrible hiding place, considering that anybody could find it just by sitting on the bed, like I did. And nobody but Henry would have used his room. It's too risky to keep slipping in and out of here, because each time you have to go through the dining room and kitchen, where everyone can see you."

Drew nodded back at her. "I guess that explains what he was talking about when he said he needed to get something from there. Apparently it wasn't a glass of water, after all." Suddenly his eyes widened and his voice rose at a disturbing realization. "But why did he leave the shells? For God's sake, they could have saved his life!"

Slowly, Daisy sat back down on the bed. She stared at the gun in her lap, trying to make sense of it.

"Henry was as sharp as a tack," she said, talking almost as much to the Remington as she was to Drew. "He may have had a good funny bone, but his actions—when it really mattered—were always logical. So if he didn't take the shells, then he wasn't planning on using the gun. Which means that he took the gun to keep someone else from using it. And he must have done it quickly, hence the poor hiding place."

"Then he obviously realized that someone was coming after him," Drew replied. "Why not try to defend himself?"

"I can only assume," Daisy chewed on her lip, "that he didn't think it would get that far. He knew that someone was upset or angry. He knew that they might act rashly with a gun in their hands. But he must have figured that once he took the gun, he could talk to them rationally, calm them down, and it would be all right."

"Except it wasn't all right. They just found a different way to kill him."

"Yes, but *why*? That's what I don't understand. What would make someone want to kill him? Henry must not have fully understood the reason, either, or he underestimated it somehow, because otherwise, I believe you're absolutely right. If he had thought that he was about to be killed, he would have tried like the dickens to defend himself—with the shotgun and everything else in sight. The man may have been ninety-four years old, but he certainly hadn't yet lost his zest for life."

"And if we can't figure out why," Drew said, "then we also don't know whether that same someone wants to kill anybody else."

Daisy sucked in a ragged breath. "I hadn't thought of that."

"Which leaves us with an unidentified—and potentially unfinished—murderer roaming about the inn."

She tightened her grip on the Remington. "At least they don't have the gun."

"That's one thing in our favor," he agreed. "What do you want to do with it?"

"Well, it definitely can't go back in the kitchen. Even without the shells, it makes a nice weapon. It's heavy enough to be used as a club."

"Good point."

"To be really safe, we need to put it somewhere no one will go, like the attic or—" Daisy cut herself off. "I know the perfect place! My mama's room."

Drew was hesitant. "Are you sure that's wise?"

"Oh, yes. It's the ideal spot. With her cold, my mama can't leave the room, so no one can possibly find the gun or even look for it in there. It's almost better than hiding it in the barn under three tons of muck and hay."

"Considering the weather, I don't think the barn is an option at the moment," he responded with a slight smile.

"If it were, the sheriff would be able to get here, and we wouldn't be in this situation."

The clock on the mantel in the parlor could be heard softly chiming the hour.

Daisy hastily stood up and began straightening the bed. She didn't want to leave behind any sign of their visit. "They could all still be in the sunroom, finishing up dessert. If we hurry, we might be able to sneak out and get upstairs without any of them seeing us."

Drew returned the chair to the desk, then he helped her adjust the draperies. When they were done, they took a step back and looked around. Everything was orderly and just the same as when they had arrived. Aside from the Remington tucked under Daisy's arm, it was like they had never been there at all. They moved toward the door, but Daisy stopped with her hand on the knob.

"There could be one problem," she said. "Georgia. She loves to lurk in the kitchen, especially during mealtimes when nobody else is there."

"I can distract her," Drew replied.

She laughed. "I bet you can."

"You shouldn't joke. The girl is scared, Daisy."

"We should all be scared with a murderer on the loose."

"That's not what I mean. She's scared of you."

"*Me!*" Daisy exclaimed. "Why in heaven's name would Georgia be scared of me? Nobody's ever scared of me. I'm as harmless as a flea."

"She says while holding a double-barreled shotgun,"

Drew retorted wryly. "And fleas aren't harmless, as you well know."

Daisy responded with an arch smile.

"Georgia's scared of talking to you," he explained. "She's worried that if she tells you something important, you'll tell Emily."

"Well, she's right. If it's something that Aunt Emily should be made aware of, then of course I'll tell her about it. She's my family, blood or not. And she's given me and my mama a home when we needed it the most. My loyalty will always lie with her, particularly over someone I've known for barely a month."

"I told Georgia that. I also told her that you were fair and wouldn't jump to conclusions. You'd probably tell Emily, but you wouldn't automatically hold it against her."

"This doesn't sound good," Daisy grumbled. "What is it? What did she do?"

"It's not so much what *she* did—"

"It's what somebody else did?" She was suddenly apprehensive. "Does Georgia know something in connection to what happened to Henry?"

"I'm not sure about that." Drew frowned. "I did ask her, but she wouldn't give me a straight answer, which makes me think that maybe she does."

"So ask her harder!"

He shook his head. "It won't work. She's too jumpy, and she'll just clam up. Then she'll go hide in some cranny where no one can find her until a week after the storm has cleared and everybody has gone home."

Daisy gave a little grunt. "That's not really such a bad idea. Maybe we should all do it."

Drew grinned. "Only if you and I can hide in the same cranny."

"Then it'd better be far away from Lillian's."

He chuckled for a moment, then returned to the matter at hand. "But Georgia did see something. It doesn't have anything to do with Henry. Or at least, it doesn't seem to me to have anything to do with him. And she's afraid that if she tells you or Emily, she might lose her job. She's very concerned about that. She doesn't want to leave the inn."

"Why don't *you* just tell me?" Daisy prodded him.

"I can't. I promised her I wouldn't."

Her gaze narrowed.

"It's nothing that would harm you," Drew said quickly. "Or your mama or Emily. Of course I'd never keep anything like that from you. Georgia simply saw something yesterday afternoon that she wishes she hadn't."

"Yesterday afternoon?" Daisy echoed thoughtfully. "Wait a second. Does this have any relation to her dropping that tray of glasses in the dining room when everybody was first admiring the secretary?"

Drew nodded.

"I thought Georgia might have recognized someone and was staring at them in surprise," she went on.

"Surprise, yes. Recognize, no."

"I don't follow."

"If I say any more," he answered apologetically, "I'll have told you. And I really shouldn't, Daisy. In a way, Georgia's just a kid. She needs to learn to have more confidence in herself. I hate breaking her trust over something like this, because then she might not trust anyone again for a long time."

Although she certainly wasn't keen on Drew keeping secrets from her, Daisy couldn't argue with his reasoning. She knew firsthand—courtesy of Matt—how hard it was to trust after having your faith shattered.

"Okay," she said. "Maybe if Georgia believes that she can trust you on this, then she'll also trust you with anything that she might know in connection to Henry."

"Maybe," Drew agreed, his brow furrowed. "It's hard to figure her out exactly. Even for a kid, she's a bit peculiar. When I was talking to her on the stairs earlier, she kept mentioning your mama's tea."

Daisy blinked at him. "My mama's tea?"

He could only shrug.

"She does seem to like my mama," Daisy remarked, remembering how Georgia had decided to hide Lucy's favorite tea bags in the Rhett Butler cookie jar to protect them from so-called sticky fingers. "And she worries a lot about her tea."

As Drew shrugged once more, Daisy turned the knob and swung open the door. A minute later, she was down the hall, up the steps, and in her mama's room, depositing the Remington and the needlepoint bag full of shells, which she had snatched from the hook in the kitchen along the way.

CHAPTER

18

"We missed you at lunch," Parker said to Daisy, as she walked into the parlor where the guests were gathered. "But of course you needed to take care of your mama. How's she feeling?"

"A little better, I think. Thanks for asking. Her cough isn't quite so—"

Lillian cut her off mid-sentence. "You weren't at lunch, either," she observed sharply in Drew's direction.

He turned toward her from the scuffed leather smoking chair. Lillian was in her usual spot on the gold-brocaded settee, with Parker next to her. Edna and May sat across from them on the emerald-brocaded settee. The Lunts occupied the damask armchairs. Bud Foster had chosen a straight-backed chair from one of the tea tables. Georgia, to no one's surprise, was absent. And Aunt Emily was busy at the liquor cart, taking stock of the decanters and murmuring occasionally to herself.

"I don't suppose you were taking care of Lucy, as well," Lillian continued to Drew in a derisive tone.

"Now, my dear—" Parker began.

She didn't pay the least heed. "So what were you getting up to? Where have you been poking around?"

When Drew didn't immediately answer, Lillian pursed her lips at Daisy and tittered. Daisy understood her perfectly. She was trying to prove that she had been right earlier—Drew wasn't trustworthy, and he was engaging in some sort of shady behavior. What Lillian didn't know, of course, was that Daisy hadn't been taking care of her mama during lunch, either. She and Drew had been poking around together.

Under different circumstances, Daisy would have simply let the matter slide and brushed aside Lillian's snickering spitefulness as another fruitless attack on Drew in support of Matt, but she saw that the entire group was now looking at Drew. And they were looking at him with considerable interest. Lillian had sparked a general curiosity with her comments, and it couldn't just be ignored. Presumably somebody in that parlor was a killer, and Daisy couldn't let them think that Drew might be poking around their secret. It was too dangerous.

The lamps in the parlor chose that moment to flicker, and it gave her an idea.

"What was he getting up to, Lillian?" she replied. "While you were lounging in the sunroom and tucking into that cherry pie, Drew was working. For your benefit, I might add. As I'm sure you're aware, the inn's wiring is old and not the most reliable during storms. With the lights sputtering like they have been, Drew was afraid that the power might go out, so he was organizing wood for the fireplaces."

It wasn't actually a lie. When they had passed through the kitchen from Henry Brent's room, and Daisy had grabbed the needlepoint bag from the wall behind the wrought-iron log holder, Drew had noted that the holder was only half full. He had then remarked that he should talk to Aunt Emily to find out if she wanted him to bring in some more wood from the larger stack on the porch.

"How very thoughtful," Edna said.

"Yes, indeed," May agreed. Her fingers fiddled with the lace on her handkerchief, which had moved permanently from her skirt pocket to her hands. "But—oh, my—do you think that we could really lose power?"

"It's nothing to be concerned about," Drew told her in a comforting tone.

"Nothing at all," Aunt Emily chimed in, glancing up from the stack of cocktail napkins that she was meticulously straightening. "There are already candles in every room. We have an army of oil lanterns waiting in the cellar. And there's a big enough pile of firewood out back to keep us warm and fed from the Dutch oven for a month."

"Stay here for a month?" Lillian echoed sullenly. "Not on your life, thank you."

Daisy concealed a grin. Her little ploy had worked. Everyone's attention had been diverted from Drew poking around where somebody might not want him to, and as an added bonus, she had also managed to dampen Lillian's mood. Maybe that would silence her lemon lips for a bit.

"I don't like the cold," Sarah Lunt squeaked, as she huddled in her chair.

"No worries there," Drew responded in the same comforting manner that he had with May. "We can build you a roaring blaze."

"I'm fully capable of looking after my wife," Kenneth snapped at him.

Drew frowned. "I wasn't suggesting that you weren't."

"It seems to me that you were."

"I'm glad your mama's cough isn't getting any worse, Daisy," Parker interjected, trying to change the subject.

"Me, too—" she started to answer.

"That blasted cough kept me up half the night," Kenneth complained. "I could hear it through the wall like it was in my own room."

Daisy was tempted to reply that her mama could hear him, as well, especially when he and his wife talked about wanting to buy the inn, but she restrained herself.

Aunt Emily must have been thinking something similar, because she said, "Thin walls make for careful neighbors."

Not catching the hint, Kenneth retorted, "Neighbors should mind their own business."

Sarah responded with a shiver and a sigh. "It would be nice to have neighbors like this. Everybody is so friendly around here."

Her husband gave a snort.

"There are lots of wonderful groups in this area to join," May told Sarah. "Something—"

"—for everyone," Edna concluded.

"I was just saying to Edna," May went on, "that at our next Daughters of the Confederacy meeting as president-elect she should nominate Henry for a memorial award."

"What a lovely idea!" Aunt Emily exclaimed.

Daisy smiled. She had no doubt that Henry Brent would have been tickled pink at the prospect of a memorial award. That was partly because he was a great enthusiast of history and heritage, having been a dedicated supporter of the Pittsylvania Historical Society for most of his life. And also because he had always enjoyed teasing the Fowler sisters about the humongous floppy dress hats and white gloves that they so frequently wore to Daughters of the Confederacy events, particularly when those events involved awards.

"With a cape and a horse added to his striped suit and polka dot bow tie," Georgia remarked, "Mr. Brent would have been just as dandy in the cavalry as Jeb Stuart."

Every neck in the room swiveled toward her in surprise. Without any notice, Georgia had crept into the parlor as stealthy as a panther and was now standing next to Daisy, holding a platter of well-organized cheese and crackers.

There was a brief silence, then May said, "Are you a member of the Daughters, dear?"

"Naw." Georgia shook her head. "But my best friend's meemaw is. She used to show us old pictures of Mr. Stuart. He seemed awfully fond of having a flashy uniform and being in parades."

Aunt Emily chuckled. "I've seen those pictures, too. I've also read that he liked wearing a big yellow sash and having an ostrich plume in his hat. They say he cut such a dashing figure leading the cavalcade at reviews that the ladies would swoon by the dozens."

"He was a decorated hero," Edna admonished her sternly. "And a *general*," she corrected Georgia.

"No question about that," Aunt Emily concurred, immediately growing serious, although she cast a quick wink at Daisy as if to say—*When it comes to Confederate generals, don't mess with the president-elect.*

At the moment, Daisy was far more interested in Georgia than in Edna's affinity for Confederate military men. Georgia apparently had a best friend, and that best friend had a meemaw. It was the most that Daisy had learned about her kith and kin over the entire past month.

"Where does your friend's meemaw live?" Edna asked Georgia.

While Edna naturally wanted to find out if the aforementioned meemaw's chapter of the Daughters of the Confederacy was near her own chapter, Daisy was also curious to hear the response, albeit for a different reason. She still didn't know where exactly Georgia had been raised.

Georgia, however, didn't oblige them with an answer. She squinted at the floor for several seconds, then gave an abrupt start, as though suddenly remembering that she had left the kettle boiling on the stove. Depositing the cheese and cracker platter unceremoniously in Daisy's arms, she whirled around and scurried out of the room, not uttering another syllable.

"Goodness!" May said.

"Skittish little thing," Parker observed sympathetically.

Edna's brow furrowed. "Too many people, perhaps."

"Maybe she's cold," Sarah Lunt suggested, shivering once more.

Daisy and Drew exchanged a glance. Drew promptly rose from his seat and left the parlor, as well.

Kenneth watched him go with evident distaste. "He sure does spend a lot of time worrying about other women."

Lillian sniffed and mumbled something under her breath about Matt. Daisy ignored both of them. She understood what Drew was doing, and she was in full accord. It was an excellent opportunity to get Georgia alone and press her on whether she knew anything in connection to what had happened to Henry Brent.

As individual conversations replaced the collective discussion, Daisy adjusted the platter in her hands and walked over to the liquor cart under the pretense of procuring some serving napkins.

"Drew told me about the Remington," Aunt Emily said, barely above a whisper. "That was smart of you to leave it with your mama, Ducky."

"It's the safest place I could come up with on short notice."

Aunt Emily nodded. "Henry must have known something was wrong. He never would have taken the gun otherwise."

Daisy nodded back at her. "Drew and I think Georgia might know something also. He's gone to talk to her, or at least try to talk to her."

"I can't figure it out. Poor Henry. Why would somebody want to . . ." Aunt Emily didn't finish the sentence. "It doesn't make any sense."

"Not a lick," she agreed. "But don't forget that whoever did it is here with us right now. So we have to be careful."

Following her own counsel, Daisy feigned a hearty laugh in relation to nothing and pecked Aunt Emily on the cheek, not wanting to raise suspicion by speaking with her too earnestly for too long. Then she began a circle around the parlor, offering the cheese and crackers with her usual waitress gusto.

Bud Foster was her first stop. Up until that point, he hadn't spoken one word. From the way his arms were folded tightly across his chest and his knees just as stiffly crossed, he gave the impression of not being at all interested in socializing with or getting to know any of the other guests. But Daisy wasn't fooled by his detached demeanor. She could see that Bud was paying close attention to everything that transpired. His gaze was quick and watchful. If it hadn't been for the fake name and fishy story, she might have supposed that he was the law. Except he was too rough, even for being undercover. Daisy didn't know who or why, but she was certain that Bud was focused on someone in the room.

Lillian and Parker came next. Lillian was not a happy camper. She kept glowering at Parker, who was leaning toward the other settee, conversing with Edna and May. The trio was smiling and chattering merrily, obviously trying to make the best out of a less than ideal situation. When Daisy offered the platter to Lillian, she glared at it like she wanted to hurl it—along with her husband—into the entrance hall. Parker and the Fowler sisters, on the other hand, thanked Daisy profusely and stocked up on the cheese as though they were expecting an imminent shortage of all comestibles.

Kenneth Lunt took a polite serving of the snacks. His wife, however, seemed stumped. Sarah gaped at the platter Daisy held before her as if it contained a live octopus waving at her, and she couldn't decide whether she should shake the creature's tentacle in greeting or run away screaming. It reminded Daisy of the similar breadbasket episodes at dinner.

"She doesn't want any," Kenneth said after a moment.

Daisy started to move away, but she turned back when she saw Sarah blink longingly at the retreating crackers. "They're tasty," she encouraged her, pushing the platter a little closer.

Sarah's hand lifted toward it.

"No." Kenneth's voice was low and firm.

The hand retreated.

"If you're hungry, then you should eat," Drew advised, reappearing in the parlor.

"Keep out of it!" Kenneth snarled in fury.

The room instantly grew quiet. Everyone looked startled, including Daisy. Did Sarah want the dinner rolls and crackers, but her husband for some inexplicable reason didn't approve? Daisy remembered that Beulah had thought Sarah's mousiness and hesitancy were exaggerated, so maybe there was more to it. Either way, Sarah's hand remained down, which Daisy could only interpret as her having made a final decision against the snacks.

"Well, I'll leave them here," Daisy said, setting the platter and remaining napkins on the nearest tea table, "if anybody changes their mind or wants a second helping."

After an awkward minute, the group resumed chatting. When they did, Drew cleared his throat softly. Daisy took it as a hint that he had information for her, but she needed a way for them to exit the parlor. She turned to Aunt Emily.

"I'm going to start bringing up those lanterns from the cellar, just in case."

Aunt Emily's shrewd blue eyes understood. "Good plan, Ducky."

"I'll help," Drew volunteered, loud enough for everyone to hear.

Parker rose to offer his assistance, but Aunt Emily swiftly intercepted him with an urgent question about the selection of cocktails before dinner. Meanwhile, Daisy and Drew hastened into the hallway.

"Any luck with Georgia?" she asked him, the instant they were out of earshot.

Drew shook his head in disappointment. "I tried, but

she wouldn't say a thing about Henry. All she wanted to talk about was your mama's tea."

"*Again?*"

He sighed. "I can't explain it."

Daisy was thoughtful. "Maybe it's a nervous tick, like May and that handkerchief of hers. Georgia isn't really focused on my mama or her tea. It's just something that comes out of her mouth when she gets anxious."

"You could be right. Although it did seem awfully important to her. She was looking at me so intently, and she kept going on about it."

It was Daisy's turn to shake her head. "Then I can't explain it, either. But I'm pretty sure that my mama's had more than enough tea today. I suppose I can always check again after we get some of those lanterns."

No sooner had she said it then the lights gave one final flicker, and the inn went dark.

CHAPTER

19

There was a collective cry of surprise from the parlor. Although everyone had been aware that the inn could lose power, it was still startling when it happened. It seemed as though the afternoon had vanished in a flash and the night suddenly collapsed on top of them. The heavy storm clouds with their cascades of snow had sunk low in the sky, almost touching the earth, leaving only a few weak streaks of daylight to sneak through the windows.

"Ducky?" Aunt Emily called.

"I'm in the hall with Drew," she answered. "We're on our way to the cellar. We'll bring everybody a lantern as soon as we can."

"We'll stay here," Aunt Emily told her, "and light some candles in the meantime."

Parker could be heard soothing May. Lillian was complaining that she would no doubt get stuck with the smallest, most ineffectual candle. And Kenneth let out a string of profanities as he banged his knee against some table or other while retrieving the box of matches that Aunt Emily told him were on the mantel.

"Follow me," Daisy said, taking Drew's hand to guide him. "And watch out for the Windsor bench on the left side. It's sturdy enough to break a toe."

She had walked that way so many times with the lights off before dawn for her early morning shifts at the diner and the bakery that Daisy didn't have any trouble maneuvering through the hall or the tight double turn into the kitchen. Because of its big bay windows, the kitchen was slightly brighter. She almost expected to find Georgia there—either making the all-important tea for her mama or huddled on the throw rug next to the hearth—but the room was empty.

The door to the cellar was on the far side of the chimney. Daisy went over to it and gave the glass knob a firm tug. The wood stuck in the frame for a moment, then the door creaked open. A blast of cold air shot up through the opening.

"Chilly." Drew peered into the cellar. "And dark."

Dark was an understatement. There was not even a hint of illumination below. The first few steps were decreasingly visible, then only blackness followed.

"You should take this," Georgia said suddenly.

Both Daisy and Drew jumped at her abrupt appearance. Somehow Georgia had sidled soundlessly into the kitchen— or perhaps she had been sitting in the corner undetected— and was now standing beside them, holding out a large flashlight.

"So you don't fall and snap your neck," she explained. "Those stairs are wicked."

Although *wicked* might have been a bit of an exaggeration, there was no question that the old cellar steps were steep and narrow. It certainly would have been much easier to retrieve the lanterns before the power had gone out.

"Thank you, Georgia." Drew took the proffered light and immediately handed it to Daisy. "I spend most of my days climbing up mountains and crawling around damp caves looking for bats to study, so hopefully I can make it down a few rickety stairs without doing any permanent damage to myself."

Having seen him in action, Daisy could vouch for the truth of his words. When it came to traversing rocky peaks and inky caverns, Drew was as surefooted as a Himalayan goat. Granted, that was with the aid of professional equipment, but all things considered, she didn't mind being the one with the flashlight.

"I'll go first," she said. "To hold the light, and also because I know where the lanterns are kept."

"I'll catch you if you start to tumble," Drew promised.

It was a sweet thought, even if unlikely in practice. Daisy started off slow and cautious, but after the first few steps, she got her bearings and the remainder of the dark stairway proved to be less challenging than anticipated. Maybe that was because after so many years of transporting Aunt Emily's countless jars, crocks, and pots between the kitchen and the cellar during jam, jelly, canning, and pickling seasons, the dimensions of the stairs had become ingrained in her memory.

Drew didn't have any more trouble than she did, and they were soon at the bottom. The floor was packed bare dirt—as hard and unyielding as concrete—having been tamped and compressed for many decades.

"Good golly," Drew's teeth chattered, "it's cold down here."

"Welcome to the country cellar," Daisy replied. "In weather like this, it's a giant refrigerator." She frowned.

"You don't think the low temperature will hurt the lamp oil?"

He shook his head. "No, it just might thicken it up a bit."

"So long as it doesn't damage the likker." Daisy laughed, thinking of Aunt Emily's precious gooseberry brandy.

She directed the flashlight to the vast network of shelves on their left. Long rows of jars lined the wall, perfectly ordered like battalions marching into battle. Pickled products, canned products, and plenty of moonshine.

"Good golly," Drew said again, this time laughing also. "That is a heck of a lot of hooch. Come the next war, this is the place to be. You've got enough provisions and barter goods to last five years."

"Medicine, drink, and entertainment combined in one pretty package!"

He walked over and took a closer look. "Is it all brandy?"

"Mostly," she responded. "There's also some corn whiskey."

"Does Emily make that, too? Because the stuff I had last night with Henry sure was tasty."

"These days Aunt Emily tends to stick to her gooseberries. But the whiskey is from the neighborhood." Daisy didn't add that it was the best corn whiskey he would ever come across, anywhere. It was Rick's moonshine, and the likker was very much like the man—fiery, with an unpredictable finish, and always dancing on the edge of the law.

"Can I try some?" Drew asked. "After we're done with the lanterns."

Daisy joined him at the shelves and scanned the rows with the flashlight. When she came to Rick's jars, she paused. Some were gifts to Aunt Emily, some were gifts to her mama, and some were gifts to the inn in general. None had been purchased. Rick would never accept any money from them for his 'shine. And that was also why none were gifts to Daisy. She, in turn, wouldn't accept them. She preferred not to owe Rick favors. He liked to collect.

"This one." She selected a jar filled with shimmering, copper-colored liquid. "It's aged and really nice."

"Too bad we don't have a happier occasion for it," Drew remarked.

"We'll drink it in Henry's honor."

He smiled. "Based on how he was enjoying that brandy yesterday evening, I think toasting him with a nip would be rather appropriate."

"Um—hello?" Georgia called tentatively. "Are you okay? Did you make it to the bottom?"

"We're fine," Drew called back. "We're getting the first batch of lanterns now."

"Over there." Daisy moved the flashlight to the right. "Along that other wall."

Unlike the jars lined up with methodical neatness on the shelves, the lanterns were clustered in a mass on the ground. They were made of brass and reflected the light with a metallic glint.

Drew started to lift the nearest lantern by its thin wire handle. "Can I assume they all work?"

"I think so. If the globe breaks or something inside goes wonky, Aunt Emily usually sets that one away from the others. But be careful to hold them upright and not tip them too much, or the oil will leak out. It can make a real mess."

Two in each hand was all Drew could carry without banging the glass and spilling oil. Together with the flashlight and the jar of Rick's 'shine, Daisy managed one lantern in each hand. She would have tried adding another, but she didn't want to take the chance of dropping the likker.

Going up the cellar stairs was comparatively easy, because of the daylight—limited as it was—coming into the kitchen. Georgia appeared relieved to see them.

"It's creepy down there when it's so dark," she said, almost in a whisper.

Daisy looked at her. Georgia's usually sunny freckles seemed pale, and her gray eyes were sunken and unsettled. The girl was definitely troubled by something, and Daisy was inclined to believe that it went beyond her mama's tea or the lack of electricity. Hoping that more light would make her feel at least a little better—even if only for the moment— Daisy offered Georgia the first lantern.

"Do you know how to use it?" she asked her.

Georgia nodded.

"Great. Then I can start on these."

With deft movements, Daisy turned the small wheel to raise the wick, lifted the glass mantel, and struck a match. She touched it to the braid cotton wick, and a lovely luminous flame appeared. She lowered the mantel and adjusted the wick once more, then she felt the weight of the lantern. It seemed relatively heavy, which was good. That meant the base was full, and she wouldn't need to refill it with more oil for some time.

"That was quick," Drew complimented her, setting his lanterns next to hers. "Since you're obviously the expert at lighting, I'll get a second load."

"Do you want the lantern or the flashlight?" she said, holding out both.

The lantern illuminated a much wider area, while the flashlight allowed him to carry more.

Drew took the flashlight. "The faster we get this finished, the sooner we can move on to the fun stuff." He inclined his head toward the jar of whiskey that Daisy had put on the kitchen table.

She smiled in complete agreement. Rick's 'shine was exactly what she needed.

"Be careful," Georgia mumbled, as Drew headed back into the dark cellar.

"When you have a free hand, will you grab a bottle of oil, too?" Daisy called after him. "These lanterns all feel pretty full, but it wouldn't hurt to have an extra supply at the ready."

A sardonic snort echoed up the steps. "We'll never hear the end of it if Lillian's should happen to run out."

He was right, and with that thought in mind, when Daisy brought the first set of shining lanterns into the parlor, she made sure that Lillian received hers immediately after Aunt Emily. She didn't want any protests or aggrieved moans from her about being the last in line. In truth, it didn't really matter in what order the lanterns were distributed. One was enough to fill the parlor with a warm golden glow, and the more Daisy carried in, the more pleasant and cheerful the room became. Although she couldn't have said that the group was actually jolly, they did seem to relax somewhat as their surroundings grew brighter. May stopped twisting her handkerchief into a lace pretzel. Sarah temporarily ceased shivering in her chair. Even Lillian didn't voice a complaint.

Drew completed his trips to the cellar before Daisy had finished hers to the parlor. She would have kept pace with him, but it turned out that Georgia needed assistance lighting her lantern, after all. And when it was finally burning after several failed attempts, Georgia promptly disappeared with it and another lantern, murmuring an excuse about bringing it to Daisy's mama. Daisy wanted her mama to have a lantern, of course, and she would never have forced Georgia to help hand out the other lanterns, but her desire to avoid returning to the parlor was so marked that it raised Daisy's curiosity.

Was it simply shyness? Too many people, perhaps, as Edna had said. Except Daisy didn't believe that Georgia was really so shy. On the contrary, she thought her reticence had more to do with a specific person in the room. Maybe it was the same person that had surprised her the day before, causing her to drop the tray of glasses. Or maybe it was somehow connected to what she knew about Henry Brent, and that was why she had raced out of the parlor so abruptly earlier. Either way, Daisy had the distinct impression that Georgia was deliberately staying away from someone, although she had no clue who.

When everybody was in possession of a lantern, Aunt Emily once again resumed the topic of cocktails and began discussing the options for supper, now modified by the lack of power. She suggested a round of bourbon, followed by a light meal of assorted cold cuts. The general response was more enthusiastic toward the drinks than the dinner. It was understandable enough. The buffet luncheon had been ample, and the entire group was weary and on edge.

At the first opportunity, Daisy imitated Georgia and used her mama as an excuse to slip upstairs. To her great joy, she found her sleeping soundly, with only an occasional mild cough. The cold was definitely not becoming bronchitis. It was the first bit of good news that she'd had all weekend. Georgia wasn't in the room, but there was both a lantern and a cup of tea on the nightstand, so she had been there recently. Daisy wondered where she had gone. Certainly not back to the parlor.

Daisy didn't return to the parlor, either. Instead she went to her own room with the jar of corn whiskey. She felt slightly guilty about it, knowing that Aunt Emily could use her help entertaining the group. But she was too tired and worn to have the requisite patience to organize a game of bridge for the Fowler sisters or to listen to Lillian endlessly correct Parker. The only thing that she had the energy or desire for at the moment was Rick's likker.

As the storm howled outside and the inn quaked and shuddered, Daisy waited for Drew to join her. Except he was too late. By the time he came to her room, she had already toasted Henry Brent and fallen asleep.

CHAPTER
20

When Daisy awoke many hours later, it was still. She had become so used to the roaring wind and rattling panes of glass that at first she was confused about where she was. Then she felt the soft bed beneath her and heard the gentle ticking of the clock on the nightstand by her side. She was in her room at the inn. For some minutes she lay without moving, gathering her senses. It was quiet outside. The storm had ended. It was quiet inside, too. Apparently everyone was asleep. The room was dark, so she knew that it wasn't yet morning. She reached for the lamp on the nightstand and turned the switch. Nothing happened. The power remained out.

With a yawn, Daisy sat up. She had slept well and felt refreshed. Her mind was calm. Her body was rested. The inn had cooled considerably overnight. After a bit of blind searching, she pulled on a pair of thick woolen socks and a chunky sweater. Then she shuffled to the window and drew back the sheers. Moonlight flooded into the room. The sky was clear, dotted with what seemed to be a million glittering points of silver. It was bright outside, but not from the approaching daybreak. The dawn was just a mere violet fleck on the horizon. The light came from the stars reflecting against the snow. Together they bathed the world in white, creating a pale, glimmering blanket that stretched over the earth as far as the eye could see.

Daisy thought of Drew. She vaguely recalled him coming into her room during the night and talking to her, although she had been sleeping too soundly to pay much attention. He had said something about their lanterns. Turning from the window, she glanced around the room. With the aid of the moon, she found two lanterns sitting on the mirrored dressing table. She had put hers there the evening before. The second lantern was presumably his.

Neither lantern was burning. Daisy checked the bases and found them empty. The flashlight from Georgia had been next to her lantern on the table, but it was no longer there. Drew must have taken it and perhaps gone to get more oil. Daisy wished that he had woken her. As agile as he was on mountains and in caves while tracking bats, the inn was nevertheless a tricky place to wander about alone at night, especially when you weren't all that familiar with it. It was awfully easy to twist an ankle on the uneven stairs or bang your head against one of the oddly protruding walls. Then you wound up on the floor with a bum leg and a bloody nose, waiting for somebody to stumble over you the next morning.

Without a working lantern, Daisy realized that she was going to have to look for Drew in the dark. Grumbling to herself that she should be smarter about keeping an extra flashlight handy for situations just like this, she opened the door to her room as wide as it would go, hoping that the moonbeam would extend into the hall to help her. It didn't, but somebody—most likely Aunt Emily—had left a chubby candle burning in a dish at the far end next to the stained glass lamp that usually acted as the hall night-light.

She went to the dish and picked it up. The hall was still. All the doors were closed. If someone came out of their room, they were going to have a hard time seeing anything without the candle, but Daisy figured that she needed it more than the rest of them at the moment. She checked Drew's room first, wanting to make sure that she wasn't wrong about the oil and he hadn't gone there instead, but his room was empty. As she proceeded toward the stairs, the little flame on the candle sputtered and started to die. Daisy stopped and hastily circled her palm around the wick, coaxing the dwindling orange spark back to life. The nearest matches that she could think of were in the parlor, and that was a long way to go in the blackness.

Breathing a sigh of relief as the flame regained its strength, Daisy continued to the landing and then down the steps. She was forced to move slowly to keep the candle from snuffing out. When she reached the front entry, she sighed once more, relieved not to see a shadow lurking at the edge of the hall like she had the previous night. She paused briefly, listening. She heard whispering, or at least she thought it was whispering. Daisy strained her ears. It almost sounded like crying, although she couldn't be sure.

There was a dim yellow glow up ahead. It appeared to be coming from the kitchen. Drew with the flashlight, she assumed. He was probably talking to someone. They were speaking in such hushed tones that from a distance it resembled tearful murmurings. Daisy turned the corner with a smile to greet him, but her face promptly fell when she found the kitchen empty. No Drew. Or anybody else, for that matter.

She had been correct about the flashlight, however. Except instead of being in Drew's hand, it was lying in front of the open cellar door. There were also two gallon bottles of oil nearby. She had evidently been right about that, as well. Drew had wanted to refill the lanterns. But where was he? And why was the flashlight on the ground?

"Drew?" she called in a low tone.

There was a muffled noise from the cellar.

Daisy approached the stairs. Unlike the afternoon before, the first few steps were now the darkest. There was more light farther down, because a lantern was burning at the bottom. Kneeling next to it was Georgia. She was leaning over something.

"Georgia!" Daisy exclaimed in surprise. "What are you—"

She never finished the sentence. Georgia raised her head, and the instant she did, Daisy's heart stopped. Georgia was leaning over Drew. He was sprawled on his back on the cellar floor, his body twisted and broken. Although in that moment Daisy couldn't have uttered a syllable, she didn't need to. She knew without asking that Drew was dead.

Her eyes met Georgia's, and for some minutes, the two stared at each other, neither one moving or even blinking. Finally Georgia spoke.

"No," she croaked.

Daisy didn't respond.

"No," Georgia said again, with increasing volume. "No, no, *no!*"

Suddenly she jumped to her feet. Grabbing the lantern, Georgia sprinted up the cellar stairs. When she reached the top, she halted for a second and gazed at Daisy with the most pitiful expression, like a wounded animal trapped in a snare.

"No," Georgia whispered once more.

Then she ran sobbing from the kitchen.

Under other circumstances, Daisy would have followed her, or at least made some effort to listen to where she went. But she didn't. All she could think about was Drew.

Holding the candle in front of her, she descended toward him. When she reached the bottom, Daisy sank down at his side. The ground was icy cold beneath her, but she barely felt it. She was already numb, and she simply let it numb her further.

She didn't know how long she remained there. Her mind was empty. Her eyes didn't see. She just held Drew's stiffening hand. At last, she bent down and kissed his lips. Then she rose, and forcing herself not to look back, returned up the steps.

Without stopping, Daisy left the kitchen and went upstairs. Her mama answered when she knocked. She was in her bed, propped up with pillows, reading a paperback by the light of a lantern.

"Drew—" was all Daisy could get out, but somehow her mama understood.

Her feet made it across the room to the edge of the bed, then her legs crumpled under her. Daisy sat on the floor, her head resting against the side of the mattress. Her mama reached down and stroked her hair in silence. There was nothing to be said. No kind words—no matter how sweet or sympathetic—could change what had happened. No pat expressions could make the truth any less real.

And the truth was that it had been murder. Daisy held

not the slightest doubt. Drew was too steady, too dexterous. He wouldn't have slipped or tripped. Even if he had stumbled and wasn't able to catch himself, then he would have landed on his stomach, not his back. The way he lay left no room for uncertainty. Drew had been pushed down the steps, and he had been looking at his killer when he had been dealt the fatal blow.

Unlike with Henry Brent, Daisy didn't wonder why. She knew that it was because Drew had gotten too close, or at least his killer—Henry Brent's killer—believed that he was getting too close. Drew had said the wrong thing or asked the wrong question, and the murderer had gotten nervous about being exposed. Lillian was probably partially to blame. All her talk of Drew poking around and suspiciously disappearing during lunch. It hadn't just sparked a general curiosity. It had proven lethal.

So who had done it? And what was Georgia doing roaming about at that hour? Could she be responsible for two murders? Daisy's instinct told her no. It wasn't because she didn't believe Georgia to be capable. As horrifying as it was, Daisy realized that she had to assume everybody was capable. But in Georgia's case, it wasn't logical. She had been weeping over Drew's body. She had repeatedly proclaimed her innocence, albeit with one word. Most important, however, Georgia had trusted Drew with a secret—a secret about something that she had seen the day before. She wouldn't have done that if she had killed Henry Brent. On the contrary, she would have kept her lips firmly zipped and not drawn any extra attention to herself.

Logic was the only thing Daisy had. Unfortunately, there was so little of it. But she needed every bit, desperately. That way she had something to focus on, something to keep her from breaking down completely at the thought of Drew lying dead on the cellar floor. The world outside the inn may have been quiet and at peace, but inside Daisy, a new storm raged—one of grief.

Time passed without notice. The room grew light. Brilliant bands of sunshine streamed through the windows. There were voices in the hall and downstairs. Pounding footsteps and loud exclamations. The inn's occupants were up, and Drew's body had been discovered. But neither Daisy nor her mama moved.

At some point, there was a tap on the door.

"Come in," Lucy responded softly.

The door opened, and clicking heels entered the room. Daisy still didn't move.

"Oh, Ducky . . ."

Aunt Emily said no more. The accompanying sigh contained everything else. Her sorrow, her regret, her compassion, and her consolation.

Eventually Lucy began the conversation.

"We need to call the sheriff."

"I already have," Aunt Emily told her. "I talked to Janice at the office, same as Daisy did yesterday. I explained the situation in full. She understands that we can't wait any longer, that we need someone to come as soon as possible. She's working on contacting everybody—including Sheriff Lowell—as quickly as she can. Now that the snow has ended, it shouldn't be too long before they can reach us. The main problem is the lack of plows in the area. Janice says that more are on their way from Richmond, along with trucks filled with salt and gravel. We're at the top of the list. We just have to sit tight until they make it through."

Lucy nodded. "How is everyone downstairs?"

"Pretty much like we are. Dazed and distressed. I'm most concerned about May. She's as pale as the ice on the porch, and she can't stop shaking. Edna and Parker have been trying their best with her, but I'm not sure how much good it's doing."

"Perhaps a small glass of brandy?" Lucy suggested. "It does soothe the nerves." Then she added, to her daughter, "Maybe you'd like a few sips, too, honey?"

Daisy didn't want to drink, whether it was a few sips or half a bottle. She wanted to turn back the hours of the clock and have it be two days earlier. Friday morning instead of Sunday. Then she could cancel the party, and none of this would ever happen.

After a long pause, Aunt Emily said, "I should get the woodstove started to heat the water for the coffee and fig-ure out something for breakfast. I do wish Georgia would help, but she seems to have vanished."

The remark reminded Daisy of what Drew had said when they were in Henry Brent's room. Georgia was so jumpy that if she was pressed too hard, she would likely clam up and disappear into some cranny, not to be spotted again until a week later. Seeing Drew dead and realizing that he had been murdered certainly could be traumatizing enough to make her go into hiding.

"I've looked in all the usual places," Aunt Emily con-tinued.

"You won't find her," Daisy interjected. "Not until she's ready to come out, or you're willing to tear apart the walls in a full-scale search."

Still sitting on the floor next to her mama's bed, she turned to meet Aunt Emily's gaze. The benevolent blue eyes were brimming with commiseration, ready to offer all the support that was needed. Daisy was grateful, but she shook her head. She didn't want to talk about what she felt. It was guaranteed to unleash a wellspring of emotion, and she wasn't so sure that she would be able to plug it again.

Aunt Emily seemed to comprehend and didn't press her. Instead she remained on the subject of Georgia. "But why wouldn't she come out? She doesn't have any more reason to be upset than the rest of us."

"She found—" Daisy's voice quivered. She took a breath to steady herself. "Georgia found him before I did. I think she's pretty shaken up."

"Well, she is young," Lucy pointed out. "And we know very little about her upbringing or her past. This could be her first experience with . . ."

Although she let the sentence trail away, they all understood how it ended. *Death*. Sadly, death was no stranger to the three of them, but it might have been—at least prior to that weekend—to Georgia.

"She found him before you?" Aunt Emily echoed with a deep frown. "You don't think . . . I mean . . . She couldn't have—"

"No," Daisy answered, quietly but firmly. "I don't think Georgia is the one who killed Drew."

"Oh, honey," her mama exhaled.

"There doesn't seem to be much reason for Georgia to have done it," Aunt Emily remarked.

Her tone was matter-of-fact, and Daisy greatly appreciated it. Analyzing the situation rationally somehow made it hurt less.

"There's no reason for her to have killed Henry, either," Daisy added.

"And we have to assume it's the same person, don't we?" Aunt Emily said.

"I don't see how it couldn't be." Daisy rose and sat on the corner of the bed. "It's the only thing that makes sense. Why else Drew? It must have been because the killer got scared."

Aunt Emily nodded. "So we have to go back to the beginning. We have to figure out why Henry—"

"But there could have been two," Lucy mused.

They turned to her.

"Not two people acting separately," she explained. "Two people working together."

Daisy was thoughtful. There had been only one shadow at the edge of the kitchen on the night Henry Brent died. But it was possible that the shadow Lillian had seen on the landing shortly afterward wasn't the same. That could mean two people. Except two people managing not to make a sound while marching around the inn in the dark seemed unlikely, especially going up and down the creaking staircase. And Drew had heard only one voice arguing with Henry in the parlor.

"Who do you have in mind, Lucy?" Aunt Emily asked her. "You look as though you're referring to someone—or rather, two people—in particular."

She hesitated. "I hate to accuse folks."

"I really don't think this is the time to stand on scruples, Mama."

"I know, honey. But I don't have any actual proof. And I can't be entirely sure of what I heard, because I only caught part of the conversation through the wall."

Aunt Emily gasped. "It was the Lunts!"

"Now hold on, Emily." Lucy sat up straighter in her bed. "I just told you I don't have any proof. All I know for certain is that Kenneth Lunt is awfully intent on buying the inn."

"He and Sarah were talking about it again?" Daisy exclaimed.

Her mama nodded. "At length. But not so loudly as before. I had the impression that they were trying to be more careful."

Daisy nodded back at her. "So what exactly did they say?"

"Well, Sarah started off by talking about how pretty the inn was and that everybody was so kind. I missed a part, then her tone changed and she said that she wanted to leave. She didn't like what happened to Henry."

"None of us like what happened to Henry," Aunt Emily responded briskly.

"But that doesn't sound as though she had a hand in his death," Daisy said.

"Not at first," her mama agreed. "Kenneth replied that she should stop being so squeamish. This is what they had decided on. They couldn't turn back now. They had to follow through."

"Follow through?" Aunt Emily's brow furrowed. "Follow through on what?"

"Buying the inn from you. Kenneth said—" Lucy bit her lip, hesitating once more. Finally, with evident reluctance, the words came out. "He said that murder always lowers the asking price."

CHAPTER
21

Murder always lowers the asking price.

Although Lucy had spoken them only once—quietly—
the words seemed to echo around the room. Aunt Emily,
who was rarely so staggered as to be speechless, stared at
her with a jutting neck and a gaping mouth. For the first
time in Daisy's recent memory, Aunt Emily looked old. Her
immaculate silver hair had become a rumpled mass of
washed-out gray. Her laugh lines had deepened into heavy
creases. And her lips were thin and colorless.

The callousness of Kenneth's remark startled Daisy, too,
but instead of being shocked into a stupor, her mind went
immediately to Drew.

"When did the Lunts have this conversation?" she asked
her mama, careful to keep her voice low in case they—or
anybody else—were attempting to listen in.

"Early evening sometime. I didn't think to check the
clock. It was after we lost power, but before everybody went
to bed."

"So Drew was still alive then."

Lucy shuddered, grasping the implication. "I'm sorry, honey. So terribly sorry. It didn't occur to me that Kenneth could mean—that they might—"

Daisy shook her head. "You couldn't have known."

"I never imagined . . . ," her mama continued mournfully.

Looking from one to the other with an expression of horrified disbelief, Aunt Emily stammered, "You think the Lunts wanted the inn so badly that they . . ."

"It's possible," Daisy replied. "We said before that the same person, or two connected people, were in all probability responsible for both deaths. Why not husband and wife, who also happen to be house-hunting in the area? Sarah really likes this place, and Kenneth *really* likes getting his way. He has the necessary physical strength, and she's small enough to sneak around without making a sound."

Aunt Emily stammered some more. "But to kill Henry . . . and then Drew . . ."

"If one murder doesn't get the desired result, try again." Daisy's grief had begun to harden. "The more deaths, the better the price, from the Lunts' perspective."

"That's what they think!" Lucy exclaimed with force. "They're never getting their grubby hands on the inn, are they, Emily?"

There was a pause as Aunt Emily's mouth closed, the color returned to her face, and she carefully smoothed her hair. The tough biddy was back, and she hissed with the ferocity of a snapping turtle.

"They ain't gettin' this house. I can assure you of that. Not even if it involves my own corpse."

As morbid as the topic was, Daisy almost smiled. When

Aunt Emily slipped into her heartiest Southern twang, she meant business.

"Of course, we can't be sure it was them," Lucy said, taking a more pragmatic tack. "They could just be very interested in the inn and are hoping to get a good deal. They're simply capitalizing on the situation, so to speak."

Aunt Emily's blue eyes blazed with anger. "What sort of loathsome people would capitalize on two dead bodies!"

Daisy was quick to motion that she should drop her voice.

"I don't care what they hear," Aunt Emily went on at the same volume, not heeding her caution.

"You should," Daisy responded, "because Mama is right. We don't have any proof, and we don't know anything for certain, other than that the Lunts seriously want to buy this place." She remembered her phone conversation with Beulah from the previous morning and sighed. "I should have listened when Beulah said something was off with them. But I thought she was just having fun being suspicious, and she accused Lillian and Georgia, too."

Aunt Emily was thoughtful. "She may have a point there. Georgia has gone into hiding, which isn't usually a sign of innocence. And Lillian was never fond of Henry or Drew."

"Beulah only accused them in regard to Henry," Daisy said. "She doesn't know about Drew—yet." The sigh repeated itself. "I guess I had better call and tell her."

"Sooner rather than later," her mama urged. "With the storm over and the roads starting to open, Beulah could dig her way out and get here before Sheriff Lowell does. We don't want to risk that."

Daisy nodded in full agreement. One death had become

two, which could far too easily become three if they weren't vigilant, especially considering that there was still some doubt as to who precisely they should be vigilant of. Beulah was much safer where she was. Returning to the inn was dangerous.

"Beulah's at the roadhouse?" Aunt Emily asked her.

She nodded again.

"And Rick is there, too?"

The question surprised Daisy. With all that was going on, it seemed odd for Aunt Emily to be concerned with Rick Balsam's whereabouts. "Yes," she said. "Or at least he was there yesterday, so I assume that he still is. He couldn't have left the General any more than we could have left the inn."

Aunt Emily nodded back at her. "When you talk to Beulah, you should ask Rick what he thinks."

"What he thinks?" Daisy frowned. "But how could Rick have any clue who's responsible for the deaths? He hasn't even met some of the people, including the Lunts."

"Not who he thinks the killer is," Aunt Emily corrected her, "but what we should do with them. At some point, we have to go back downstairs, Ducky. We can't stay up here forever, and Sheriff Lowell may not arrive until this evening, or—heaven forbid—tomorrow."

"Heaven forbid," Lucy echoed. "That would mean another night, and so far, it's always happened during the night."

"You're the safest of all of us, Lucy," Aunt Emily said. "Since you've been forced to keep to your bed, no one would suspect that you know anything."

"Actually, I don't think that's true," Daisy replied. "It may have been before, but not now that I've been in the room for so long. And you, too, Aunt Emily. If anybody's paying attention, they'll know that the three of us have been together in here for quite some time. Unless they're a complete fool—which they clearly aren't, based on how clever they've been up to this point—they've got to realize that we're talking it all through."

"She's still the safest, Ducky. Your mama is the only one who can stay put and lock the door."

"Don't fuss about me," Lucy protested. "I'll be fine."

"Of course you will." Aunt Emily's lips curled into a slight smile. "You've got the Remington."

"If you want to take it and put it back in the kitchen—"

"We are not taking it," Daisy cut her mama off. "And we're certainly not putting it back in the kitchen. I can't think of a worse possible place for a gun at the moment. Anybody can get to it there. Henry hid the Remington for a reason. Unfortunately, it didn't do him much good in the end. But he obviously knew that someone might use it."

"I wonder," Lucy's brow furrowed, "is everybody at the inn familiar with how to use a shotgun? Would Henry know who was and who wasn't?"

Aunt Emily could only shrug. "He might have simply assumed that anyone could figure it out. It isn't very complicated, after all."

Lucy turned to her daughter. "Didn't you say something about Georgia staring at the Remington when it was still in the kitchen?"

"I did," Daisy confirmed. "It was after she dropped that tray of glasses and stared at somebody in the dining room, hard. Drew talked to her about it, and he said that it didn't have anything to do with what happened to Henry."

"So what did it have to do with?" Aunt Emily asked.

"He didn't tell me. He didn't want to break her confidence."

Aunt Emily raised a disapproving eyebrow. "It's all well

and good to hold a secret, Ducky, but Drew shouldn't have kept one from you. Particularly under these circumstances, when he's no longer able to spill the beans."

"He didn't know that he was going to die," she argued in Drew's defense.

"Even so—"

"That isn't helpful, Emily," Lucy interjected in a stern tone. Then she added, returning to the previous subject, "Dropping glasses and staring aside, I'll say one thing about Georgia. She's been extremely conscientious about my tea."

"Drew said the same thing," Daisy told her. "Apparently she kept mentioning it to him."

"Georgia kept mentioning my tea to Drew? How odd."

"We thought so, too. I just assumed it was some sort of nervous tick, but Drew had the feeling there was more to it. He said that it seemed awfully important to her. She wouldn't stop talking about it."

"How odd," Lucy repeated, squinting at the empty cup and saucer that were sitting on the adjacent nightstand.

"And to think I was trying to be nice and do my duty by giving the girl a job and a place to live." Aunt Emily clucked her tongue in self-reproach. "Clearly my ability to judge character has become as rotten as an egg."

"Don't be silly, Emily," Lucy retorted. "It was very kind of you to take Georgia in, and there's nothing rotten about your judgment. I have no doubt that in due course everything will be explained to our full satisfaction."

Aunt Emily responded with a dubious grunt, then she looked at Daisy. "Speaking of judging character, that brings me back to Rick."

It was Daisy's turn to raise an eyebrow.

"Do you remember when I said that it would be helpful

to have Rick's opinion on Bud?" Aunt Emily didn't wait for her to answer. "Well, that's what I want now. Only not in relation to Bud. Although that would be helpful, too. Of all the folks here, we still know the least about him."

She couldn't argue with that. Bud Foster was disturbingly good at disappearing. He didn't run off and hide like Georgia. On the contrary, he was almost always together with the group. Except somehow he managed to fade into the background, unnoticed. He would sit quietly in one corner or another, watching everybody and listening to everything, but never revealing a stitch about himself. The only information they had was the false name that he had adopted from the newspaper and the fishy story regarding his arrival at the inn.

"I want you to ask Rick," Aunt Emily continued, "what he thinks we should do with everyone."

"What do you mean?"

"It's as I said before, Ducky, we can't stay in this room much longer. Eventually we have to go back downstairs. But there's a killer down there, and we have to do something with them. We can't simply pretend that they don't exist and hope for the best. So do we send everybody to their room, or would it be safer to keep everybody together?"

That was an excellent question. Daisy considered it for a moment. "Well, if everyone was in their own room, then that would obviously separate the murderer, or murderers, from the rest of the group. But the problem with that is how do we stop somebody—namely the killer—from sneaking out and going into another room?"

"We can all lock our doors," Lucy reminded them.

"In theory, yes," Daisy agreed. "But I'm afraid that it would be far too easy to convince some of the guests to open their door again. Both Edna and May, for example. And also Parker probably, depending on Lillian's mood."

Aunt Emily nodded. "I would suggest locking everybody in. I have a duplicate key to all the rooms. Except everybody still has their own key. They could just let themselves out whenever they wanted."

"So then maybe it would be better to keep the group together," Daisy said. "There is protection in numbers, after all. No one can get hurt, or do any hurting, if no one leaves the herd—"

"There is one room that we could use," Lucy remarked suddenly.

They looked at her.

"Henry's," she explained. "Only you have a key to his room now, Emily. We could lock someone in there."

"First we have to figure out who," Daisy replied grimly.

"But I have my doubts about trying to keeping everyone together," Lucy went on. "I'm not sure that it will work like we want it to. Won't people keep wandering off? And won't that just put them in more danger?" She shook her head. "Or maybe that's not right. Maybe it's my judgment that's off."

"That's why I want Daisy to talk to Rick," Aunt Emily said. "We've all been cooped up in this house like a bunch of stale anchovies in a tin for too long. I'm worried that we're not seeing what we should. We're too close to it—and to everybody else here. Rick's smart. He knows us and the inn, and he's got a good handle on people."

"Particularly criminals," Daisy couldn't help murmuring.

"Exactly!" Aunt Emily exclaimed. Then her voice softened. "I realize that it's not going to be pleasant for you to tell Rick about Drew, Ducky, but—"

"It's fine. I'll talk to him."

She knew that Aunt Emily was right. They were hemmed in like anchovies, and they were too close to the deaths, so much so that they could very easily be missing something of importance. In her case, that was especially true with Drew. Even after seeing his lifeless body at the bottom of the cellar stairs, it didn't seem entirely real to her that he was gone. She felt a strange sense of detachment mixed with bitterness.

Daisy rose from her seat on the bed.

"Please, *please* be careful, honey," her mama said anxiously.

"I will." She walked over and kissed her on the forehead. "And I'll make sure that Beulah doesn't come to the inn."

Lucy pressed her hand encouragingly.

"You need to lock the door after us, Mama."

"Don't let anybody in," Aunt Emily warned her. "No matter what they say or how they try to convince you."

"Not even Georgia with your tea," Daisy added.

"No one," Lucy promised. "Except you and Emily."

"And Sheriff Lowell."

It was Daisy who said it, but they were all silent afterward, because each of them understood that if Sheriff Lowell came knocking on Lucy's door, it meant something bad had happened to the others.

CHAPTER 22

After waiting for her mama's lock to click behind her, Daisy headed across the hall to her own room. She and Aunt Emily had decided that while she called Rick and Beulah, Aunt Emily would go downstairs and check on the group in the parlor. Coffee and breakfast would keep everybody occupied and in one place for a while. Hopefully Rick would be able to offer some helpful input they could use after that, assuming he—and Beulah—were still at the roadhouse.

With some trepidation, she picked up the phone and dialed. Beulah answered almost immediately.

"Hey, Daisy! I was just about to call you. The boys have been working on digging us out since first light, and they're making pretty good progress."

Daisy breathed a sigh of relief. She had caught her in time.

"The whole thing would go much faster if they had actual shovels, but there aren't any. So they've been making do with a couple of plastic buckets and some beer pitchers." Beulah laughed. "I wish you could have seen what Bobby Balsam did a little while ago . . ."

Daisy sighed again. Bobby was Rick's younger brother by two years and had the exact opposite personality. He was harmless, clueless, and frequently bamboozled by anyone who talked too fast or too smoothly, especially if that person happened to be an attractive female. But the important point from Daisy's perspective at that moment was if Bobby hadn't yet left the General, then in all likelihood, neither had Rick.

". . . He thought that he could somehow save time and effort by jumping from the roof of one pickup to the next. It didn't work, of course, and he ended up headfirst in a snowbank." Beulah laughed harder. "He was stuck upside down like a Popsicle, buried to his middle, with his legs kicking furiously in the air. It was one of the funniest things I ever saw in my life."

Well familiar with many of Bobby's ill-fated schemes, Daisy could easily picture the scene and almost laughed herself. It was also extremely nice to hear such a cheerful voice from the outside world, particularly one not connected with the growing number of dead bodies at the inn.

"And then they had to get him out," Beulah continued, still chortling. "That was a hoot, too, with everybody slipping and sliding and sinking into the snow themselves. It could have been a circus act. I was almost in tears, it was so hysterical."

"But Bobby's okay?" Daisy asked, grateful for the temporary distraction.

"Oh, he's fine. As soon as they got him free, Rick handed him a beer, and Wade gave him a blanket. Bobby was as right as rain a minute later. Speaking of Wade," Beulah dropped her voice discreetly, "he's great, Daisy. I don't want to jump the gun or jinx myself, but I really like him. Mind you, it's been the weirdest first date in the history of blind first dates, considering that it's gone on for two days straight, and we've been stuck here the whole time—"

"Is that Daisy?" It was Rick's voice in the background. "Will you find out if she—"

"Wait." Beulah stopped him. "It'll be easier if I put the phone on speaker. Then I won't have to repeat everything back and forth like a parrot."

A click followed.

"Hello, darlin'," Rick drawled. "How is it at the inn?"

"Hey, Rick . . ." Daisy hesitated, not sure where to begin.

"What did Sheriff Lowell end up saying about Henry Brent?" he asked her.

"Sheriff Lowell hasn't come yet," she answered, a bit unsteadily. "But we're hoping that he can get through before the end of the day."

"The end of the day?" Beulah scoffed. "I'll be back much earlier than that."

"No!" Daisy exclaimed. "You can't come here, Beulah!"

There was a startled silence.

"What's going on, Daisy?" Rick said sharply, his instinct showing.

Her throat tightened, and for a moment, she couldn't respond. Then her words came out dull and disconnected, as though somebody else were speaking them. "Drew. He's dead."

Beulah let out a strangled gasp. "Good God, did you just say . . ."

Her voice faded away, and a second later, there was a thud.

"Whoa! Don't fall down on me, sweetheart."

Rick was talking, but Daisy could hardly hear him.

"Sit on that chair. There you go. And drink this. It'll help."

After a minute, there was some clattering with the phone, and Rick's voice grew louder.

"Daisy? Are you still with me?"

"Yes. What happened?"

"Beulah started to faint and dropped the phone."

"Is she all right?"

He gave an affirmative grunt. "Don't worry about her. I caught her before she hit the floor. And now she's sucking on a glass of whiskey. That'll bring her round."

Daisy drew a shaky breath.

"Don't worry about Beulah," Rick repeated. "We need to worry about you. Tell me what the hell is going on over there. From the beginning, and don't leave anything out."

With some fits and starts, Daisy explained it all as well as she could, trying to include as many potentially pertinent details as possible. It wasn't easy, especially when she had to describe the scene with Drew at the bottom of the cellar stairs. Rick didn't interrupt and let her talk at her own pace, even when she faltered at the difficult portions. She concluded by telling him that Aunt Emily had wanted his advice.

"Get out," Rick responded, without the slightest hesitation. "That's my advice to you. Get out now."

"I can't," Daisy said. "It isn't physically possible. The parking lot is buried. There's no way for me to get to a car, let alone drive anywhere with it."

"What about one of the barns or Beulah's salon?"

"My salon," Beulah murmured somewhat incoherently in the background. "Daisy should go to my salon."

"I can't," she said again. "I can't leave my mama."

"Take your mama with you."

"The snow is awfully deep around the inn, Rick. I'm not sure how far I could get through it, but I'm positive that my mama wouldn't make it past the porch. She's too weak. And she's just beginning to get over her cold and cough. If I take her outside in the icy air now, I have no idea what will happen to her lungs. I can't take that chance."

"But you can take the chance of her staying there?" he retorted.

"Her door is locked, and she's got Aunt Emily's Remington."

"Excellent. So at least she's taken care of. What about your gun?"

Daisy winced, knowing that Rick was not going to like her answer. She owned a small Colt—a .380. Her daddy had given it to her mama the Christmas before he passed, but it belonged to Daisy now. Previously she had kept it at the inn, but several months earlier there had been a robbery at the bakery, which had left her and especially Brenda shaken. As a result, she had taken the gun there.

"The Colt is at Sweetie Pies," she told him.

"For criminy sake, Daisy! Why isn't it at the inn?"

"Because I thought we needed it at the bakery more. We already had Aunt Emily's shotgun. Normally the inn doesn't require an arsenal."

Rick replied with an agitated snort.

"Well, the gun isn't here, so there's no use getting mad at me over it," Daisy continued defensively. "And it's not like I could go waving it around now anyway. May Fowler is already on the verge of a breakdown, and Edna probably isn't far behind. We're trying to keep them calm, not have them think that there's about to be a shoot-out."

"Does anybody else there have a gun? What about that fellow whose car went into the ditch and suggested calling the sheriff in relation to Henry?"

Even though Rick couldn't see it, she shook her head. "I have no idea what Bud might have. I haven't seen a gun, and he hasn't mentioned one. But I doubt that we could trust whatever he said, regardless."

"What about Parker?" Beulah asked, still in the background but more coherent.

Daisy shook her head again. "Parker doesn't like firearms. I think he had a bad experience with Lillian once."

Rick gave another snort. "Every experience with Lillian is bad. If he doesn't keep a gun, it's because he's afraid that one day he might not be able to control the temptation to use it on her."

"No," Beulah corrected them, her voice growing stronger as she dragged her chair closer to the phone. "I'm not talking about Parker having a gun. I mean, what about Parker doing the killing?"

It took Daisy a moment to process the words. Beulah thought Parker was the murderer? "Are you sure that she didn't hit her head on the floor, Rick?"

"My head is perfectly fine," Beulah rejoined.

"I told you that whiskey would do the trick," Rick said.

"Yes, but how much did you drink, Beulah? Because thinking that Parker—"

"Why not him?" she argued. "He could have snapped. Lillian might have finally broken the poor man. We all know what a tyrant she can be, and nobody knows it better than her long-suffering husband. The two people who died were both ones that Lillian held a specific grudge against. Maybe Parker thought he was helping them."

"Helping them by killing them?"

"I didn't say it was rational. I said that he might have snapped."

"But Parker loved Henry," Daisy protested. "They'd known each other since Parker was a wee shaver." She smiled, remembering how annoyed Lillian had gotten whenever Henry woofed and called him "Dog" Barker. "He never would have pushed a secretary on top of him. And Parker liked Drew, too, even though he'd only met him a couple of times before."

"Exactly," Beulah said. "Parker was fond of both of them—especially Henry—and he was tired of Lillian being so nasty toward them. He wanted to set 'em free."

Daisy frowned at the phone. Even for Beulah, that seemed to be going to the extreme. Henry and Drew weren't captive birds. They didn't need to be set free. And they had both held their own against Lillian quite well, particularly Henry, who had given just as good as he had gotten from her, if not better, even.

If they were going to look at every possibility—which at this point, they clearly needed to do—Lillian could certainly be considered a suspect. Henry's teasing had vexed her to no end, and Drew had interfered with the potential happiness of her darling nephew. But putting Parker on the list was really a stretch.

"I don't know," Rick remarked doubtfully.

"You don't know?" Beulah echoed in amazement. "You don't know if Lillian could push Parker far enough to make him snap?"

"Oh, I'm sure she could. There's no question Lillian could nag and criticize a man until he exploded like a tinderbox. But that's just it. He would snap and—as you said—act irrationally. But neither of the deaths was like that. At least Henry's wasn't. It's harder to know with Drew's. The second could be a result of the first. It might not have been intended at the outset, but it became necessary in the end."

"That's what I think," Daisy said. "Drew was getting too close, and the killer got nervous. They were worried about being exposed, and they probably panicked. With Henry, it seems more planned. Not brilliantly planned, mind you. Because then it wouldn't have been done with a piece of furniture during a snowstorm and a party at the inn. But it still seems calculated to me. And Henry must have had some inkling, as well, considering that he took the Remington and hid it."

"You do realize, Daisy," Rick replied, "that if someone got nervous enough to kill Drew, you're in serious danger."

"Everybody here is, Rick."

"Except everybody hasn't been sharing their bed with Drew."

For a second, Daisy flushed with resentment at his presumptuous tone. Then it occurred to her that he was right. She hadn't actually been sharing her bed with Drew, but that wasn't what mattered. They had been spending time together, and the entire inn knew it. If the murderer had indeed thought that Drew was getting too close, then it was only logical for the murderer to also assume that she wasn't far behind. That was not good.

"Was Drew getting too close?" Rick asked her. "Did he know—or did he suspect—who the killer was?"

"No. At least not the last time I spoke with him. But he was trying to remember a voice that he heard arguing with Henry in the parlor. We both thought it was the voice of the murderer. Drew might have figured it out during the night and—"

"I still think it could be Parker," Beulah interjected. "He's such a nice guy. Nice guys tend to be the ones who have meltdowns."

"But it doesn't seem like a meltdown—" This time Daisy cut herself off. There was a strange noise coming from somewhere. "Do you hear that? Is it on my end or yours?"

"I don't hear anything," Beulah said.

"Me, either," Rick agreed. "What does it sound like?"

Daisy listened. "Like a cat crying."

"Brenda didn't bring Blot, did she?" Beulah asked.

"No. Brenda isn't here. She was worried about driving in the storm, and I suggested that she stay home."

"At least that's one person we don't have to worry about," Rick said.

"Small favors." Daisy sighed.

She listened again. The noise was definitely on her end. It pitched high, then low, and then went high again. It could have been the television, but with the power out, that didn't make sense.

"I think it's coming from downstairs," she told them.

"Ignore it," Beulah said.

"I can't ignore it." Daisy rose and walked toward the door of her room.

"Yes, you can," Beulah countered. "Your mama's safe, so let them sort it out for themselves."

"Except I don't know what *it* is. And what about Aunt Emily?"

"Oh, Aunt Emily's scrappy. There's no need to fret about her. In the end, she'll outlive all of us. Guaranteed."

Rick chuckled. Under different circumstances, Beulah's boundless confidence in Aunt Emily's indestructibility would have amused Daisy, too. But Drew had been nearly forty years younger and a lot more fit than Aunt Emily—and he was dead.

She turned the knob, planning on starting with a cautious little crack until she got a better handle on what was happening. But the instant the door opened, it was obvious that the noise was neither a cat nor a television. It was a person wailing.

"Is that somebody screeching?" Rick said.

"I think it might be May." Daisy moved into the hall, trying to identify the voice. "Or maybe Sarah Lunt."

"Beulah's right," Rick informed her sternly. "Ignore it and stay in your room."

"Of course I'm right . . . ," Beulah began.

Not listening to them, Daisy took several steps in the direction of the stairs. The voice became clearer. It was Aunt Emily. A moment later, her words became clear also.

"No, Parker! No!" she shouted. "Don't kill him!"

CHAPTER
23

For a minute, Daisy stood motionless in the hall, wondering if her ears might have deceived her. Did Aunt Emily just yell something about Parker killing someone? Could Beulah indeed be right—not about her ignoring it and staying in her room—but about Parker being the murderer?

There were more noises downstairs. They seemed to be coming from the parlor, and it sounded like a struggle. Arms and legs scuffling. Furniture getting knocked to the ground. A shriek. And then Aunt Emily again.

"Please, Parker!" she implored. "Don't do it!"

Daisy dashed toward the steps. She had already reached the landing before she remembered that she was still on the phone.

"I'll have to call you back," she told Rick and Beulah hastily.

In unison they protested and demanded to know what was going on, but Daisy was too busy thinking about Aunt Emily and Parker.

"I'll call you back," she said again, and then promptly hung up without waiting for a response.

She raced down the stairs and through the front entry. Her feet came to an abrupt halt at the edge of the parlor. Although she had expected some sort of an altercation based on the shouts and noises, what she saw still managed to startle her.

The normally sedate and stately parlor was in a complete uproar. It almost looked like the room had been flooded again—just as it had four months earlier, resulting in the renovations and the supposed party—only with significantly less water and more people.

The gold-brocaded settee usually occupied by Lillian and Parker was empty, its matching throw pillows scattered across the floor. Huddled into the corner of the emerald-brocaded settee was May Fowler, her lace handkerchief pressed to her face, half covering her eyes. The potted dwarf Meyer lemon tree lay at her feet, broken branches and soil spilling over the carpet. The candle stand that had been next to the plant was on top of it instead, one of its cabriole legs cracked and detached from the rest.

Lillian stood pressed against the wall in between the windows and the longcase clock, looking like she was tempted to burst through the glass and sprint outside, if there hadn't been massive drifts of snow blocking her way. Kenneth Lunt was also on his feet, his cheeks florid and his fingers clutching the back of one of the damask armchairs. His wife stood partially concealed behind him. Her chair was tipped over.

Also tipped over was the chair that Bud Foster typically occupied, along with the neighboring tea table. Bud was in the scuffed leather smoking chair, with Aunt Emily standing on one side of him and Edna Fowler on the other. And in the center of it all was Parker. He was positioned in front of the smoking chair, leaning over Bud, his hands wrapped around Bud's neck.

Aunt Emily and Edna were both trying to grab Parker's arms, alternately scolding and pleading with him. Sarah Lunt was shrieking. May was weeping. Every few seconds, Lillian would shout her husband's name. And Kenneth kept barking advice and instructions that no one was heeding.

Based on the condition of the room, the battle had apparently been going on for some time. It must have taken a good deal of effort to move Bud from his original seat across the parlor into the smoking chair and then keep him there. Bud was by no means a feeble man or unwilling to defend himself, as evidenced by his misshapen boxing knuckles and corresponding chipped teeth. But Parker had somehow succeeded, proof of the strength and mettle developed through a country lifestyle.

Parker was also succeeding in choking Bud. Even with Aunt Emily and Edna each pulling on one of his arms, he was still able to maintain his hold and was slowly, gradually squeezing the life out of Bud. For his part, Bud was occasionally gasping a syllable and still struggling a bit, but his energy was visibly failing him. If nobody stopped Parker, it was clear that in a short while, Bud Foster would be dead—the third body in three days at the Tosh Inn.

Daisy stared at the scene with a mixture of shock and disbelief, as though what she was witnessing couldn't actually be happening. Parker was in the process of killing Bud. Did that mean Parker had killed Henry and Drew? Then she heard Parker's angry words, and the truth of the situation hit her. Beulah was wrong. Parker didn't kill Henry and Drew. On the contrary, he was trying to kill Bud because he believed that Bud was the murderer.

"Henry was my friend!" Parker hollered at him. "He was my friend and an old man! How could you do that to a helpless old man?"

"I—" Bud croaked.

"What did he ever do to you?" Parker continued, bellowing even louder. "And Drew, too! What could they have done to justify you killing them!"

"I—" Bud croaked again.

If he wanted to respond further, he couldn't. Parker was simultaneously strangling and shaking him.

"This isn't the way, Parker!" Aunt Emily exclaimed.

"It isn't right!" Edna concurred.

Parker took no notice of them and shook Bud harder.

"Let the law handle it!" Aunt Emily entreated.

"It isn't right!" Edna cried once more.

From her perspective, Daisy was disinclined to have much sympathy for Bud. If he had killed Drew and Henry, then he should certainly be made to pay. Aunt Emily wanted Sheriff Lowell to do it, while Edna was no doubt thinking of a higher power. But what gave Daisy pause at that moment was neither legal nor spiritual. It was the fact that it didn't make any sense. What possible motive could Bud have for murdering them? Had he ever even met Henry Brent? And Bud had been the first one to recommend calling the sheriff. He was also the first one to suggest that Henry's death wasn't an accident. A murderer didn't point the finger at himself and then want law enforcement to be notified of it.

All of which meant that Parker was making a mistake, and she had to tell him. Although she didn't trust Bud, she also couldn't allow him to be strangled in error. Daisy started to join Aunt Emily and Edna in their protest, but stopped again almost immediately. It was futile. She could see that. With everybody yelling and in a general panic, no one was listening. And if she didn't act soon, Bud was going to be unconscious—or worse.

Daisy glanced hurriedly around the room, looking for a
way to attract universal attention. Throwing a book or pil-
low? That wouldn't work. It was too calm and quiet under
the circumstances. She needed something loud and startling. Her eyes paused at the liquor cart. *Perfect.* With quick
steps, she grabbed the nearest bottle, turned toward the
hearth with its polite little fire, and hurled the bottle into it.

The glass shattered with a violent crash, followed a split
second later by a fireball that inflated like a red-hot balloon,
then disappeared up the chimney with a tremendous *whoosh.*
There was instantaneous silence amongst the group. No more
screeching, weeping, or bellowing from anyone. They were
all too busy gaping at Daisy in astonishment. Even Parker
was stunned enough to loosen—but not release—his hold
on Bud's neck. The only sounds in the parlor came from the
now merrily crackling fire in the hearth, and more important, Bud Foster coughing and sucking in oxygen.

Finally, Aunt Emily spoke.

"Was that the applejack?" she said.

Daisy could only shrug. She had taken the first bottle
within her reach and had noticed nothing more about it
than that its contents were an amber hue.

"But there was still perfectly good likker in there, Ducky.
Couldn't you have picked an empty one?"

Although Daisy was tempted to reply that without the
likker, there wouldn't have been such an impressive fireball, she held her tongue and answered only with a slight
smile. Aunt Emily winked at her, and Daisy had to restrain
a chuckle. Leave it to Aunt Emily to be worried about the
inventory of her decanters during such a crisis, and then
be shrewd enough to use it as a jocular opportunity to
defuse the tension of a near-strangulation.

"Now that you mention it," Aunt Emily went on, even though no one had mentioned anything, "I could use a nip in my coffee. Anybody else?"

Her gaze traveled around the group with a cheerful insouciance, as though there wasn't a dead body lying in the dining room, another on the floor of the cellar, and almost a third in the leather smoking chair next to her. They all gazed back at her in mute bewilderment, still dazed by the explosion in the fireplace.

"Parker?" Aunt Emily prodded gently, slipping into one of her more soothing tones—a blend of the gracious hostess and concerned friend. "Why don't you sit down, and Daisy will get you a fresh cup?"

"I'd be happy to," Daisy said, taking the cue. "How about over there on the gold settee, Parker?"

He frowned at her.

"And maybe something to eat," she proposed. In her experience, Parker rarely turned down food, and even more rarely turned down liquor, so hopefully the combination—mixed with the cumulative effects of stress and exhaustion—would be enough to lure him away from Bud Foster's neck.

The frown deepened, and Parker directed it toward Bud. "What about him?" he asked gruffly. "If I move, he'll run."

Bud's mouth began to open in response, but Daisy was quick to cut him off, not sure whether he would more help or hinder his own cause.

"He won't run," she told Parker. "And even if he tried, there's nowhere for him to go. We'd catch him before he made it two feet into the snow."

"Don't let him fool you, Daisy," Parker replied, anger

once again rising in his voice. "He can make it through the snow just fine."

It was her turn to frown. "You mean when he walked here after his car went into the ditch?"

"It's all a lie," Parker spat, glaring at Bud.

She nodded. "I thought it might be. That story never sounded quite right."

"And his name," Aunt Emily chimed in.

"His name is a lie, too?" Parker exclaimed. His fingers twitched, as though this time he was thinking about snapping Bud's neck instead of squeezing it.

"We're pretty sure that it's fake," Daisy said.

Bud's eyes met hers. They were questioning, but less afraid than she expected. This was clearly not the first time that he had landed in a difficult situation. He couldn't be the law, because by now, he would have identified himself. But he was definitely something other than a door-to-door life insurance salesman.

"That newspaper in your coat," Daisy asked him. "You took the name from there, didn't you?"

He inclined his head as far as Parker would allow.

Daisy looked at Parker. "What made you suspicious of his story?"

"I'm not just suspicious," he corrected her. "I'm positive. I *saw* them."

"Saw them? Saw who?"

"Not *who*! The footprints!"

A confused murmur spread throughout the group. They didn't understand any more than Daisy or Aunt Emily.

"Where are footprints?" Aunt Emily demanded. She took considerable pride in the cleanliness of her inn and was loath to hear of footprints, even if they also happened to be important clues in the case of two murders. "I haven't seen any."

Parker gave the same sort of exasperated sigh that he often bestowed on Lillian. "I'll show you. Follow me."

He dropped his arms, straightened up, and proceeded to turn toward the entryway, then abruptly halted, realizing that he had inadvertently released his captive in the process. Bud was on his feet the next second. The two men stared at each other fiercely, like a pair of warring elks about to charge. There was an ominous pause as the entire group held its breath, waiting for the battle to begin again. Daisy, with a swift glance at Aunt Emily, didn't give it the chance.

"Good," she said briskly. "Parker, you can show me the footprints. Bud will come with us. And everybody else can stay here, where it's warm and cozy from the fire, and Aunt Emily can provide drinks."

To Daisy's surprise, no one argued or offered an alternate proposal. Even Bud agreed. He started to walk out of the parlor, with Parker glued to his shoulder, warning him not to do anything stupid. Daisy followed them, passing close to Aunt Emily.

"Henry's room," she whispered. "Where's the key?"

Aunt Emily's blue eyes widened, immediately comprehending the plan. "Brilliant, Ducky. It's in the lower linen closet. Under the washcloths."

Daisy nodded.

"Brilliant," Aunt Emily complimented her again, then she promptly spun around and began organizing the troops for tidying. "If you'll be so kind as to lift that chair, Edna. Lillian can collect those stray cushions. And perhaps someone could help me with the other end of this table . . ."

Her voice faded away as Daisy hurried to catch up with

Parker and Bud. *Brilliant* may have been a bit too high praise, especially since the plan had yet to be completed, but it was working so far. Of prime importance, Parker was no longer choking Bud. In addition, Daisy now had a possible way of getting information from Bud. There was no doubt in her mind that he knew something, was interested in someone, or had some sort of an agenda by being at the inn. At the very least, she intended to learn his real name, along with the truth about how and why he had arrived there. And she was going to do it—with the help of Parker, even though he didn't know it yet—in the privacy of Henry Brent's room. If need be, she would lock him inside. But first, she was supposed to look at footprints.

"Where are we going?" Daisy called to Parker, hoping that their path would take them by the lower linen closet.

"The kitchen," he answered.

Daisy smiled to herself, and a moment later, they were in the hall, passing in between the Windsor bench and the linen closet. She stopped, pulled opened the closet door, and flipped on the light switch. When nothing happened, she remembered that the power was still out. With a grumble, Daisy began digging around the shelves in the dark, searching blindly through the towels. She knew that she was causing a mighty mess, but was rewarded after a minute when her hand found the brass key as promised under the washcloths. Ordinarily Aunt Emily didn't hide room keys, but in this case, she had chosen the location wisely. No one would have thought to look for Henry Brent's key in the depths of the linen closet.

Tucking the clunky key as well as she could into her pocket, Daisy shut the door and hurried after Parker and Bud once more. When she reached them, they were already in the kitchen. The same as Aunt Emily, Daisy had assumed that the footprints in question were dirty shoe marks, although she had no clue how shoe marks could prove or disprove anything about Bud Foster and his story. So it surprised her when Parker—with his fingers clamped tightly around Bud's arm—went straight through the kitchen without pausing and headed out onto the back porch.

"Parker—" she began, but the sudden surge of fresh air silenced her.

The air was cool—rather than cold—and almost sweet. Daisy hadn't been outside since the storm had ended, and she found herself dazzled by a frozen land of glistening white that reached to the edge of her vision. It looked like luminous mounds of sugar undulating into the distance, with faint electric-blue frosting along the ridge.

Parker didn't have to worry about Bud trying to escape, because short of taking a flying leap into the snow and sinking down like Bobby Balsam at the roadhouse, there was no place to go. The inn was a veritable island, floating above and seemingly untethered to the rest of the snowy world. The steps leading down from the porch to the garden were so completely blanketed that not a trace of them was visible. A person unfamiliar with the inn wouldn't have even known that there were any steps at all. The porch itself had varying amounts of snow, based on the direction of the wind. The rocking chairs resembled a line of hulking polar bears, while the potting stand on the opposite end had only a light dusting of flakes.

It was beginning to thaw. Icicles on the railing were dripping. The top layer of snow was mushy and wet, not powdery. But with as much of it as there was, it was going to take a long time to melt—too long for comfort, with a murderer on the premises.

"You see?" Parker said to Daisy, pointing toward the porch floor. "Footprints."

She followed his outstretched finger. There were boot prints in the snow. They weren't fresh. The exact dimensions and tread were obscured, from a combination of subsequent accumulation and drifting. But someone had plainly walked on the porch at some point during the storm, more likely early on rather than later, based on the poor condition of the prints. Regardless, it wasn't difficult to discern the person's path. They had come around the corner from the side of the inn and proceeded along the back porch; there was a muddle of prints at the kitchen door; and then they had returned the same way and disappeared around the corner once more.

"They go to the front porch and the front door," Parker told her. "Although they're harder to see in the deeper spots. Do you want me to show you?"

Daisy shook her head. She had no doubt that he was right. Tracking footprints from one door of the inn to another wasn't particularly tricky. It didn't require any great skills in bushcraft. She looked at a second set of shoe prints. They were scattered around the woodpile not far from the kitchen door.

"Those are mine," Parker explained. "I wanted to help Emily by bringing in some more logs. That's how I saw the other prints. *His* prints."

Her eyes went from one set of prints to the other, then from Parker's shoes to Bud's boots. Even with the drifting and the melting and the prints crisscrossing each other, Daisy could see that the boots presently on Bud's feet looked remarkably similar both in size and shape to the boot prints marching around the porch. She raised her gaze to him.

"Well?" she asked Bud.

When he didn't immediately provide a confirmation or denial, Parker's fingers dug into Bud's arm, and his voice rose in fury.

"They're his prints, Daisy! And I'll tell you what happened! He didn't go to the front door first that night. Instead he came around here and snuck in through the kitchen while we were all in bed. He went into the dining room and pushed the secretary on top of Henry. Then he snuck back out this way and circled around to the front, banging on the door and pretending like he was just arriving. He made up that whole cock-and-bull story about getting lost and being stranded in the storm. His plan was always to kill Henry!"

Daisy waited for Bud to respond. There was a short pause, as though he was carefully considering his words. Then in one swift movement, Bud wrenched free from Parker, jumped toward the woodpile, and grabbed the hatchet that was sitting on top of the stack. The next second, he was holding it to Parker's neck.

CHAPTER 24

She knew exactly how sharp that hatchet was. Daisy had held the hickory handle and swung the steel blade more times than she could count. Over the years, she had chopped an awful lot of kindling for the inn during the winters and various power outages. So had Beulah and Aunt Emily. Had they been there, they all could have told Parker not to move an inch. One good thwack, and his neck would split just like a log.

There was a strange sort of irony in the fact that half an hour earlier, Bud's neck had been at the mercy of Parker, and now the roles were suddenly reversed. But Daisy found herself less startled and also less alarmed standing on the back porch than she had been in the parlor when Parker was strangling Bud. That was because in the parlor, Parker had been completely out of control. His rage and horror at the discovery of the boot prints and how he assumed they related to Henry Brent's death had overwhelmed all his reason. Bud, on the other hand, was entirely rational, or at least so he appeared. He didn't shout, swear, or shake with fury. Instead he remained as still as the icicles dripping from the railing, no twitching or shifting, only his eyes moving, alternately glancing at Parker and then at Daisy.

Daisy remained still as well, taking a deep, slow breath. As calm and clearheaded as Bud seemed, she also didn't want to do anything to alarm him. He truly held Parker's life in his hands. Under the circumstances, even an accidental slip of the hatchet blade could be fatal. No one at the inn could stop that kind of bleeding, and with the condition of the roads, an ambulance wouldn't be able to reach them quickly enough.

For a long minute, they all stared at each other. Parker looked more stunned than terrified, as though he couldn't quite fathom how he had gotten where he was. Bud had a watchful and almost weary expression. Daisy felt weary, too, and also slightly impatient, like they were wasting valuable energy on useless threats and counterthreats when they could be getting down to serious business. She was no closer to learning anything pertinent about Bud or figuring out who had murdered Drew and Henry. It was time to cut to the chase.

"I know it wasn't you," she told Bud. "I know you didn't kill them."

Parker let out a squeak of protest, but Daisy interrupted him brusquely.

"The man is holding an ax to your throat, Parker. It's probably best not to antagonize him."

Bud respond with a snort of laughter. "Well said! I always thought you were the smart one in the group."

Daisy didn't laugh back. Smart or not, she didn't find it the least bit funny that Bud was an inch away from slicing open Parker's jugular.

"It was the way you looked at me when you first opened the door that night I came here," Bud went on. "You saw something not right, and you automatically didn't trust me. That makes you smart."

"It makes me a girl who's had a lying, good-for-nothing husband and lived in the hinterlands long enough to realize that strangers who come knocking on the door always want something, and it's usually trouble."

Bud gave another amused snort, but he added a nod of acknowledgment. "I'll grant you that. So what now?"

"Now you put down the hatchet, and you tell us who you really are and what you're really doing at the inn."

"And if I don't?" he retorted.

There was a moment when Daisy wondered in a panic if she had gone too far and played it too cool. If she was wrong about Bud not being the murderer, then she might have just sentenced Parker—as well as possibly herself—to death. Bud obviously had no difficulties or qualms about using a hatchet, considering how deftly he had grabbed it from the woodpile and turned the tables on Parker. He could cut Parker and fling the blade at her in the same instant, before she could do anything to stop him or even try to move out of the way. But the surge of fear subsided just as swiftly as it had arisen when Daisy remembered that Bud had absolutely no reason to kill Henry or Drew, and if he wanted her and Parker dead, he would have done it already.

"I think that it would be in all of our best interests," she replied tactfully, hoping to sound more confident than she actually was, "if you told us the truth. Then we could help you, you could help us, and when the sheriff arrives, there's no need for him to hear about any of this." Daisy gestured toward the hatchet and Parker's neck.

"Smart," Bud complimented her once more. "And I like you. I like anyone who knows when to keep his—or her—mouth shut with the law."

"Another thing I learned from my husband," she remarked dryly.

"He sounds like my kind of chap." Bud chortled. "I wouldn't mind meeting him."

Daisy shot him a dark look. "So are you going to put down the hatchet? Because otherwise, I think Parker's about to pass out."

It wasn't an exaggeration. Parker had overcome his initial shock and was now beginning to look seasick with fear. His face was puce, his nostrils were stretched wide, and his breathing was fast and shallow. If that hatchet remained at his neck, one way or another he wasn't going to be standing much longer.

Bud glanced at Parker, then at her, and then at Parker again. He seemed to be weighing his options. "All right," he responded at last. He released his hold on Parker and tossed the hatchet back on the woodpile. The blade landed on a log with a loud thump, cracking off a thick piece of bark in the process.

"Thank you," Daisy said, trying not to show how immensely relieved she was.

She reached out a hand to help support Parker as he took several wobbly steps away from Bud and toward her. He was visibly shaken, understandably enough. But to his credit, Parker recovered quickly. By the time he was standing next to Daisy and sufficiently distanced from any immediate further threat by Bud or the hatchet, his normal color had started to return and his bearing strengthened. A moment later, he was glaring at Bud with vehemence.

"Sorry about that," Bud apologized, offering a half-hearted shrug. "But you didn't give me much of a choice. You wouldn't listen."

Parker glared harder.

Unfazed, Bud shrugged once more. "You can accuse me all you want. It doesn't change the facts. I didn't kill anybody."

"What about the footprints?" Parker countered, jerking his head toward the boot prints in the snow.

"What about them?" Bud rolled his eyes. "They don't prove anything. They don't even imply anything."

"They prove you lied! They prove you—"

"Don't be stupid," Bud snapped. "They're melted boot prints on a porch, not bloody fingerprints on a murder weapon."

Parker's face was beginning to go puce again, this time from rage rather than fright. Not wanting another installment with the hatchet—one that might not end as peacefully as the first—Daisy put her hand on Parker's arm in an attempt to calm him.

"Bud's right," she said. "The boot prints don't prove anything in regard to Henry."

"But, Daisy—"

"He didn't kill Henry, Parker. He couldn't have. He wasn't in the inn when it happened. I know you think that he snuck in through the kitchen door before coming around to the front, but he didn't. The kitchen door is always locked at night. I check it myself."

Parker couldn't argue with that.

"You're right, too, though," Daisy continued. "They are his boot prints, and they do prove that he lied." She turned to Bud expectantly. "I assume that since no one is accusing you of murder anymore, you can now explain to us why you were marching around the inn in the middle of the night, in the middle of a storm, before you came to the front door."

"If you can keep your lips zipped," Bud answered, pointedly directing the remark at Parker. "That sourpuss wife of yours is a talker."

Again, Parker couldn't argue. Lillian was incapable of keeping even a mere thought to herself, let alone an actual secret.

"So long as it isn't anything bad about her," Parker said, in loyal defense of the sourpuss.

"Of course it's not about her," Bud replied tetchily. "I didn't come all the way from Charlotte because of that silly woman."

Daisy looked at him with interest. It was the first real piece of information that he had given about himself. Bud Foster was from North Carolina.

"Yes," he finally confirmed, "they're my boot prints. And yes, I went around the back before going to the front. But it certainly wasn't to kill someone. It was to—" Bud stopped and glanced at the kitchen door. "Can anybody in there hear us?"

"The whole place has thin walls," Daisy told him, "so it's always possible. But they would have to be listening from the kitchen, and I can see from here that there's no one in the kitchen."

Bud gave a dissatisfied grunt.

"What about upstairs?" Parker suggested, shivering. "One of the bedrooms. They're private—and warmer."

Daisy would have responded that generally speaking the porch was more private than most of the inn, especially the upstairs bedrooms, but she understood Bud's concern about unwanted eavesdropping, and she was starting to get cold, too. None of them was wearing coats. She thought of the key tucked into her pocket.

"Henry's room—the Jubal Early—would be best," she said. "No one will be in the dining room, and that's the only spot where somebody could try to listen in."

"That'll work," Bud agreed, looking chilly himself.

As they all turned toward the door, Daisy deliberately held back, so that the men would enter first. This was not an occasion for social niceties. She wanted to be last because she wanted to take the hatchet. It was sitting too openly on the woodpile for her comfort. With the weather now clear, anyone could step outside, notice the hatchet, and pick it up. She still didn't know who the murderer was, but she knew better than to leave such an obvious weapon lying around on the porch.

Once inside, Parker immediately began leading the way through the kitchen in the direction of the Jubal Early. Daisy paused by the hearth and listened. There was a mix of voices coming from the parlor. None sounded heated or hostile. She breathed a sigh of relief. At least that part of the plan was working. Aunt Emily was keeping everyone together and seemed to have succeeded in getting them chatting. Early in the day or not, she was probably serving strong drinks.

"It's on the other side of the dining room?" Parker called to Daisy.

"Not so loud!" Bud chastised him.

Parker flinched and hushed.

"Through the archway," Daisy replied in a low tone. "End of the hall."

There was only one archway and one door at the end of the short, narrow hall, so the Jubal Early was impossible to miss. As she had told Bud on the porch, there was nobody— aside from Henry Brent's body under the secretary and blanket at the far end—in the dining room. But just as Daisy was about to follow the men into the hall, she felt something move behind her. Spinning around, she caught a glimpse of a shadow darting through the kitchen.

Her mind went instantly to Georgia. It must have been her. She was the only one in the inn who would scurry like that, and besides, everybody else was in the parlor. But why was Georgia racing around the kitchen? It had almost looked as though she had been digging in the cookie jars on the shelf above the old farm sink. That was where Georgia had put her mama's tea bags. But surely she wasn't making tea? The kettle hadn't been on, and Lucy had faithfully promised not to let anyone into her room. Turning back toward the hall, Daisy shook her head. Of course Georgia wasn't making tea for her mama. She had probably been grabbing some food or a beverage for herself, before resuming her hiding place.

Although Daisy pulled the key from her pocket as she approached Henry Brent's room, she found that she didn't need it. The door was still unlocked from when she and Drew had been there the day before. The lamps had been working then, but once she stepped to the windows and drew back the heavy draperies, there was actually more light in the room now, without electricity. Similar to the view from the back porch, the side lawn was a glittering world of white, capped by an almost blindingly vivid blue sky. The drifts against the windows were high.

Bud joined her as she looked outside. "It's an attractive

spot," he observed. "And very isolated. I can understand why the Lunts are so eager to buy it."

Daisy turned to him in surprise. His description of the inn wasn't what startled her. In that regard, he was correct. The property was attractive and in a rural sense, isolated. But his reference to the Lunts reminded her of their continued and aggressive interest in purchasing the place, and most notably, of Kenneth's appalling remark—*Murder always lowers the asking price.* It had put the couple at the top of the suspect list.

With a large, patronizing smile of chipped and yellowed teeth, Bud said, "You haven't figured it out, have you?"

She frowned at him. Figured what out? Did he know who the murderer was? A thick lump swelled in her throat as a sudden sickening realization hit her. Bud wasn't the killer, but that didn't mean he couldn't be in league with the killer. She and her mama and Aunt Emily had all agreed that two people could have been working together. What about three? Bud Foster and the Lunts.

"Are you . . ." Daisy's gaze narrowed warily, and her fingers tightened around the handle of the hatchet. "Are you working with the Lunts?"

"I'm not *working* with them. I'm *following* them." Bud smiled once more. "I'm a private investigator, sweetheart."

CHAPTER
25

Parker let out a whistle of astonishment. Daisy, on the other hand, was less amazed and more annoyed. Bud Foster's patronizing smile was beginning to irritate her, and she was also irritated with herself. Bud was right. She hadn't figured it out, but she felt that she should have. No doubt Rick—particularly with his knack for seeing through rough and unsavory types—would have discerned that the man was a private investigator within five minutes of meeting him.

It seemed so patently obvious now. The fake name; not sharing any personal details; his ability to disappear into the background; the quick and watchful eye. And it made perfect sense why he had been the first one to think that Henry Brent's death wasn't an accident and also why he was the first one to suggest contacting the sheriff. In his line of work, Bud surely had plenty of experience with criminals, probably even murderers.

"Door-to-door life insurance sales," Daisy muttered.

Bud responded with a hearty laugh. "That was a good

one, wasn't it? I knew you'd caught me when you asked
for a business card and informational pamphlet up in my
room. I thought that you might chuck me out right then
and there, except you got distracted by that newspaper.
Now I understand why. You realized the name wasn't
right."

Daisy was about to ask him what his real name was,
but she stopped herself with a shrug. Under the circumstances, what the man chose to call himself didn't much
matter.

"Fascinating," Parker said, almost reverently. He was
staring at Bud with an enthralled expression, like a small
child mesmerized by a firefighter in all his gear.

Bud turned to him. "So I suppose I should go back to
explaining the boot prints?"

Parker didn't answer. He was apparently so riveted by
the man's profession—or at least some fanciful version of it
in his mind—that he seemed to have forgotten about the
troublesome boot prints.

"As I told you earlier," Bud turned back to Daisy, "they're
my prints. I circled once around the porch before going to
the front door. I knew the Lunts were staying here. I'd had
my eye on them for a few days already. But I wanted to take
a look around the place first. In my business, I've learned
that it's always a good idea to know the layout and potential exits in advance."

"And did you see anything?" Daisy questioned him,
with some impatience.

He shook his head. "I know what you're thinking. I've
thought it, too. I was probably walking around just as the
old man was getting killed. But I'm sorry to say that I didn't
see anybody. It was all dark—inside and out. By that time,

the storm was starting to hit full steam. The windows were frosted, and as far as I can remember, the draperies were closed in the parlor and this bedroom."

Although disappointed, Daisy nodded. Even if the draperies had been wide open and every light inside blazing, it would have been difficult to get a clear view through the howling wind and blowing snow.

"I should thank you," Bud went on, "for letting me in to begin with. It would have been an awfully cold couple of days and nights stuck in the car."

"You didn't actually drive into a ditch?" she remarked dubiously.

"No, but I was honestly stranded. The roads were already so bad at that point, I couldn't go anywhere else, whether I wanted to or not. My only option was to come here—or be buried alive, so to speak. I can understand why your sheriff is having such a hard time getting through, even now."

Daisy nodded again. That explained why his story had always seemed slightly off, but not entirely off. Bud had indeed been staying in his car, and with the bad weather, he had realized that it was going to be extremely unpleasant—if he didn't freeze to death in the interim—so he had taken the chance of coming to the inn, even with the Lunts there.

"But the Lunts don't know who you are, or that you're following them?" she asked him.

Bud grinned. "They don't have a clue."

"You're sure?"

"I'm positive. Obviously they couldn't make a break for it with the conditions outside, but even so, if they had the remotest inkling that I was on their trail, they would have shut up tighter than a pair of clams. And they haven't been careful at all. They keep talking about wanting to buy this place."

"You've heard them, too?" Daisy said in surprise, thinking once more of what her mama had overheard, particularly from Kenneth.

"How else would I know about their plans?" Bud replied. "Granted, I've had to do a lot of sneaking around to listen to them. It would have been so much easier if you had put me on their floor, like I originally asked. Even down here," he gestured at the room they were standing in, "would have been better. Those stairs, especially around the third-floor landing, are ridiculously creaky."

Daisy almost smiled. The stairs were ridiculously creaky, but that wasn't what pleased her. She had finally learned why Bud had been so keen to know exactly who was on which floor. It was for optimal spying. He had wanted to switch rooms to get closer to the Lunts.

"Why are you investigating them?" Parker said eagerly, leaning against the edge of the pecan desk.

Bud pulled out the chair from the desk and sat down on it. Daisy, in turn, took a seat on the bed. This time there was no shotgun under the mattress.

"I don't have to investigate them," Bud told Parker. "I already know what they did. I was hired to find them, and that's what I've done."

"What did they do?" Parker immediately prodded. "I assume they're from Charlotte, like you?"

"They are. Well, one of the outlying suburbs, if you want me to be precise."

Parker waited with rapt attention for him to continue. Daisy was curious, as well, but she was also a bit apprehensive. Private investigators were employed for a great variety of things, some of which could be really bad.

As though he could sense her concern, Bud clucked his tongue and said, "It's nothing too horrifying. Kenneth and Sarah were directors on the board of a church. It happens to be one of those megachurches, with thousands upon thousands of members, so there's gobs of money pouring in. The Lunts decided to take some of it out. Unauthorized, of course."

"No kidding!" Parker exclaimed. "How much money are we talking about?"

"I don't have an exact figure. The church doesn't either yet. They're in the process of doing a full accounting. But they told me that it appears to be somewhere between half a million and a million dollars. It may turn out to be more in the end."

Once again, Parker let out a whistle of astonishment. And once again, Daisy was less amazed and more agitated. Beulah had been spot on when she said that something wasn't right with the Lunts. Something really wasn't right. They were a pair of embezzlers—and from a house of worship. That may not have made it worse from a legal standpoint, but it somehow seemed worse to Daisy. Like the Lunts' moral compass wasn't just tilted, it was completely broken.

"So I was sent after them," Bud went on. "Follow the church's money, before it could vanish into a puff of smoke. At first I thought I might have difficulty figuring out the Lunts' plan. In my experience with these sort of cases, when they try to run—especially a couple—they often end up fighting, splitting up and splitting the money, and generally making a gigantic mess out of the whole thing. But not this time. Not with Kenneth and Sarah. They decided what they wanted, and they made it clear from day one."

Daisy's eyes widened as she suddenly realized what he meant. "That's why they want to buy the inn!"

"Exactly. They need a place to park the cash, at least until it all cools down. And there's no question that they chose wisely. As I said before," Bud motioned toward the window, "it's an attractive and isolated spot. One of the best ways to tuck away money is to purchase a quiet property where no one will take much notice of you. Plus, the inn's got plenty of acreage and built-in value to make a later sale relatively easy when the Lunts want—or need—to liquidate again."

"No wonder they've been so adamant about buying it," Daisy mused, more to herself than the others. "But they were telling the truth—to a degree, at any rate—when they said that they were house-hunting in the area."

"Sarah, too?" Parker asked.

Both Daisy and Bud looked at him.

"The embezzlement," he said. "Sarah was part of it? It wasn't just Kenneth?"

"She was definitely part of it," Bud answered. "Sarah was the board treasurer. Kenneth was only a run-of-the-mill member. From all accounts, she played a greater role in the theft than he did."

"But," Parker frowned, "she seems so nice."

Bud chuckled. "You fell for the shy and timid act, didn't you?"

Parker frowned harder.

"It's understandable," Bud said, with a shrug. "Sarah does have that air of helplessness about her. She's so small and vulnerable-looking, particularly when she's hiding behind the hulking husband. That's her strength, really. You don't see her coming."

For a moment, Parker opened his mouth as though he was about to try to defend the woman, but then he closed it again. His cheeks were tinged with embarrassment.

"I fell for it in the beginning, too," Daisy told him, hoping to make him feel less foolish. "But Beulah—always being so cynical like she is—saw through it and warned me that Sarah might be exaggerating the mousiness, at least somewhat. I was never sure either way. Until now, of course. What always made me wonder was how skittish she seemed. I didn't think that was fake."

"That's because it isn't fake," Bud responded. "She is skittish. You'd be skittish, too, if you had stolen a pile of money from your church and were worried about getting caught and spending the next decade of your life in prison."

Daisy couldn't disagree with that, but there was something that still didn't make sense to her. "What about all that bread weirdness?" she asked. "At supper, Sarah couldn't decide whether she should take a dinner roll or not, until Kenneth told her to keep the basket moving. And then again yesterday afternoon with the crackers in the parlor. It seemed like Sarah wanted them, but Kenneth didn't approve. So if she's not under his thumb—which she obviously isn't—then what's going on?"

"It's an allergy," Bud said.

She blinked at him. "What?"

"Sarah Lunt is allergic to gluten. And not just a little allergic, apparently. *Seriously* allergic. The church told me. They gave me a whole file on her. On both of them. Sarah really likes bread, but she can't eat it unless she's absolutely sure of the ingredients. Otherwise she gets ill. And I don't mean an upset stomach or bad headache. I mean critically, go-to-the-hospital-immediately kind of ill. That's why Kenneth always stops her when she gets tempted. He knows that they can't take the chance of having to find a doctor or fill a prescription. It would make them too easy to trace."

There was a long minute of silence as both Daisy and Parker processed the information that Bud had given them. Parker looked disheartened and flat, as though all the wind had gone out of his sails. Daisy felt sorry for him. He was always so cheerful and kind—joking with Henry Brent, helping to soothe May Fowler, listening to Lillian's endless nagging and complaints with the patience of a saint. Parker saw the good in people before any of the bad. And now there was too much bad. The revelation about Sarah and the embezzlement—on top of the two murders—had left him drained and dispirited. Daisy sympathized, but she also realized that this was not the time to be maudlin. The important point at the moment wasn't that Sarah and Kenneth were criminals. What really mattered was, how serious criminals were they?

"Okay," she said, taking a deep breath. "The Lunts are thieves and liars. The question is, are they also murderers?"

Parker stared at her.

"I've considered that possibility myself," Bud replied, "and I'll be honest with you. I don't know, but my best guess is no."

"Would it change your opinion if I told you that Kenneth had been overheard saying to Sarah that murder always lowers the asking price?"

Bud deliberated for a few seconds before answering, "I

would still say no. I can't be certain, of course. I'm only speculating. But it doesn't fit. Kenneth and Sarah both think they're clever. Except they're not, actually. If they were, they would have made it much more difficult for me to follow them. For instance, they would have gone further than one state. They also wouldn't have been so candid about house-hunting in the area. They wouldn't have stayed at the place they were interested in buying, no matter how badly they wanted it. And they would have avoided every other guest—not to mention a weekend party—like the plague."

"So you think the murders were too clever for them?" Daisy said.

"If not too clever, at least too . . ." He searched for the right word. *"Determined.* Crushing the old man that way. Pushing the other fellow down the cellar steps in the middle of the night. It may seem baffling, like it's not at all rational. But make no mistake, there's a reason behind it. And I don't believe that it's got anything to do with purchasing this—or any other—property. It's something much more personal."

Her brow furrowed. "But what could it be? And if not the Lunts, then who?"

"As to the reason, I have no idea. As to the person, your guess is as good as mine. Although," Bud's brow furrowed back at her, "I wouldn't count out that maid, or cook, or whatever she is, who keeps scampering about the place."

"You mean Georgia!" Parker exclaimed. "But she's so—"

"So sweet? So young? So pretty?" Bud supplied, with a smile. "Let me tell you, *sweet* and *young* and *pretty* never stopped anyone from being a cold-blooded killer."

"But . . . ," Parker protested once more, although he didn't finish the sentence.

"Well, this has been entertaining and enlightening." Bud rose from his chair. "Now I need to get back to the parlor."

Daisy rose also. "Maybe you should stay here."

Bud turned to her questioningly.

"We left the parlor with all that commotion about the footprints and everybody suspecting you," she explained. "If we go back and look like it's been straightened out and everything is hunky-dory, then the real murderer is going to get nervous and wonder if we might be on to them. That could be dangerous. Wouldn't it be better if you stayed in this room, and Parker and I went out and acted as though you actually were the culprit, pretending to have you locked up, just waiting for the sheriff to arrive?"

"It probably would be better," Bud agreed, "except I'm not doing it. I'm not staying in here when the Lunts are out there."

"But they aren't going anywhere," Daisy responded, shaking her head. "Especially not before the roads are clear. You said yourself that they don't have a clue who you are or that you're following them."

"The roads will be clear—or clear enough—soon," Bud countered. "The snow is melting. Not fast, I'll grant you, but it's still melting." He gestured toward the slowly shrinking drift outside the window. "I'm not taking the chance that Kenneth and Sarah somehow get spooked and take off when my back is turned. I've been promised a bonus for finding them quickly and before they've disposed of the money. A *big* bonus. And I have no intention of losing it, no matter what the situation. I'm sorry about the two deaths.

Truly I am. But I'm keeping close to the Lunts, and there's nothing you can do to stop me."

Daisy sighed. She knew that even if she argued until she was blue in the face, there was no possibility of changing Bud's mind. Then she had an idea.

"Fine," she acquiesced. "You go back to the parlor. But could we at least make it look like there's still some suspicion surrounding you? That way the real murderer isn't automatically sent into a panic."

"Fine," Bud echoed. "What do you suggest?"

She hesitated. Her idea had been to give Parker the hatchet, so that it appeared as though he was keeping a sharp—and defensive—eye on Bud. Except Daisy wasn't eager to relinquish custody. The hatchet had grown rather comforting in her hand.

"Parker," she said at last, sighing once more because she could think of no other option, "you take the hatchet and go to the parlor with him. But don't sit on the settee next to Lillian. Sit across the tea table from Bud. Make it seem like you don't trust him and that you're watching him. With any luck, that will relax the killer instead of setting off alarm bells."

"What if Emily—or someone else—wants to know what's going on?" Parker asked her, his tone unsteady.

"Try to avoid saying anything. If Aunt Emily presses you privately, tell her that I'll explain it all later."

"Later?" Now Parker also looked unsteady. "Where are you going to be?"

"I'll be in the parlor soon," Daisy promised. "First I have to make a call."

Bud raised an eyebrow, although he didn't comment. He started to walk toward the door. Parker was about to follow, but Daisy stopped him.

"Don't let go of this," she said, dropping her voice to a cautionary whisper as she held out the hatchet. "Don't give it to *anyone*."

Parker nodded, and with some lingering reluctance, Daisy released the hatchet into his hand. She hoped that she hadn't just made a very grave mistake.

CHAPTER
26

It wasn't that she didn't trust Parker, but Daisy would have felt better with the hatchet still in her possession. Unfortunately, she didn't have much choice. Her comfort at the moment was less important than the killer's comfort. And she needed them to feel confident and at ease, believing that their secret of being a murderer remained safe and that no one suspected them. That way they would hopefully stay calm and not attempt to murder anybody else, at least until Sheriff Lowell arrived.

Daisy's own confidence, however, was limited. She had doubts about how clearly Parker was thinking. He had almost strangled Bud because of a few boot prints on the porch, and then he had been defensive of both Sarah and Georgia, even though he barely knew either one. Daisy worried that his nerves were too on edge and that he might somehow be talked into giving up the hatchet. She really didn't want it falling into the wrong hands.

Trying to suppress her apprehension, she watched Bud lead the way through the kitchen and into the main hall, as Parker followed at a close pace. Daisy was tempted to trail after them and listen to the conversation as they entered the parlor, but she returned instead to the archway at the edge of the dining room. It was the most secure spot for her to talk on the phone without going back outside or heading upstairs. No one could sneak up behind her, whether simply to eavesdrop or for a more sinister purpose.

Her phone showed numerous missed calls and several waiting messages. They were all from Beulah, or more accurately, Beulah's phone. But Daisy didn't play the messages. The battery on her phone was starting to get low, and with the power out, she couldn't recharge it, so she had to be careful with what she had left. It wasn't difficult for her to guess that Rick and Beulah were concerned. She had hung up on them rather abruptly, just after they had heard the screeching and shouting that turned out to be Aunt Emily and the rest of the group trying to keep Parker from choking Bud.

Daisy needed to tell them that she—and the others— were all right. But if she was being honest, it wasn't only for Rick and Beulah's benefit that she wanted to call them. She was looking for information, too. The roadhouse where they were stuck was located on Highway 40. Highway 40 was also the main road to get to the inn. The sheriff—along with everybody else—would have to go that way to reach them, so Daisy was eager to find out the road's condition. If it was now passable, then she wouldn't have to wait much longer for help.

Rick picked up the instant that she dialed. He began by scolding her for not answering her phone or calling back sooner. Rather than irritating her, the rebuke made Daisy smile, partially because it was nice to be worried about, and also because there was something tremendously uplifting about his voice. It was like hearing freedom. She had been at the inn since Friday afternoon, and it was now Sunday. That was only three days, less than seventy-two hours. Except it felt closer to a month. Daisy had experienced cabin fever before from nasty weather or a miserable flu. But this was different and much worse. The walls seemed to be closing in around her. The whole place felt as though it were shrinking down into a doll's house. And she was imprisoned inside it, with all the windows closed and every door locked. Rick was like a crack in the bricks that let in a sudden draft of fresh air.

"It's coming along great, Daisy," Beulah hollered in the background. "Wade is the best snow shoveler you ever saw. They've almost got a truck clear."

"And the road?" she asked. "How does Highway Forty look?"

"Not too bad," Rick answered. "One lane is drivable, sort of."

"Oh, good—" Daisy began, encouraged.

"Are you two talking about the road?" Beulah said, still in the background. "It's a slushy, mushy, slippery mess. I just saw a car go by heading east, and it was skidding all over the place. If it doesn't hit a pole first, it'll end up in the gully on the next hill for sure."

"Oh, not good," Daisy corrected herself with a sigh.

"Don't fret, darlin'," Rick drawled. "It's just slow driving, not impossible. You should know by now that I can make it through just about anything if it means—"

He was interrupted on his end by a pair of muffled voices. Daisy couldn't understand them. Something about tires or wheel wells.

"Take the keys," Rick said in response. There was a jangling sound, like he was pulling a key ring from his pocket and tossing it to someone. "See if she'll start, and try it that way."

There was more muffled talking, then Rick returned to her.

"That was Bobby," he explained. "They're having some issues with the truck."

"If he needs your help, you can call me back," Daisy suggested, "or give the phone to Beu—"

"You've been drinking too much of Aunt Emily's gooseberry brandy if you seriously think that I'm hanging up on you," Rick cut her off. "Bobby can handle it, and I could use a break anyway. I only came inside when you called. Before that, I spent the last hour cracking through the ice on the incline from the parking lot up to the road. My fingers aren't fully functional anymore. They have to thaw out."

"He's commandeered my phone, Daisy," Beulah shouted in protest. "And he won't give it back."

"The battery on mine died," Rick replied, unapologetically. "I don't carry around a charger, and no one else has one either. Not much of a surprise, considering that we all only came here for a beer."

"The battery on my phone is getting weak, too," Daisy told him. "But I can't charge it because the power is still out."

"Then we'll talk fast," Rick said. "What's happening there? What was all that commotion earlier?"

In as few words as possible, she gave him an account of Parker accusing and nearly strangling Bud, Bud revealing himself to be a private investigator in pursuit of the Lunts, and Kenneth and Sarah having embezzled a small fortune from their church, which was why they wanted to buy the inn. Beulah kept throwing out questions in the background, but Rick refused to share the phone and only repeated the bare minimum to her. At first, Beulah was vocally annoyed, but when she learned that she had been right to be suspicious of the Lunts, she pronounced herself vindicated and cheerfully declared that she was going outside to check on Wade and Bobby, and would return with a progress report.

"Where are the Lunts now?" Rick asked Daisy.

"In the parlor," she answered, "with Bud and Aunt Emily and the rest of the group."

"And you think that's safe?"

"I gave Parker a hatchet from the woodpile."

"You gave a *hatchet* to *Parker*?" Rick reproached her. "The man has a better chance of accidentally lopping off his own arm than he does protecting you or Aunt Emily."

"That may be true, but we were short on options," Daisy argued. "And Parker won't actually have to use the hatchet. It's more of a prop than anything else."

Rick responded with a dissatisfied snort. "Assuming the Lunts don't just take it from him."

"They have no reason to try to take it. They don't know that Bud is following them, or that any of us are aware of the embezzlement. Besides, Bud doesn't think Kenneth and Sarah are the murderers."

"Who does he suspect?"

"He isn't sure. But," Daisy hesitated, her own doubts coming into play, "he said that he wouldn't count out Georgia."

Rick was momentarily silent.

"I'm having a hard time believing it," Daisy said, musing half to him and half to herself. "I've never thought that it could be her. Georgia had not the slightest connection to Henry Brent, and she seemed to like Drew an awful lot. Maybe a bit too much, even, if you know what I mean."

"You think she and Drew were fooling around?"

"No, of course not. At most, Georgia might have had a schoolgirl crush on him. It's understandable. Drew was a really good guy . . ." She sighed.

There was a brief pause, then Rick said quietly, "Daisy, I am sorry about what happened to him."

"Thank you." She took a deep breath and went on. "At any rate, Georgia trusted Drew. He listened to her. I don't think she's had many people in her life do that."

"Okay, so then why does Bud—"

He was stopped by Beulah. As promised, she had returned with an update from the boys outside.

"Good news," she announced in a loud voice. "They've got the truck started, and it's out of the snow."

Daisy gave a little exclamation of joy.

"Bad news," Beulah continued. "It's now stuck in a giant mud rut."

Rick gave a not-so-little exclamation of exasperation.

"But Wade, being wonderful," Beulah gushed, "thought to dig through the snow and scoop up some of the gravel from the parking lot to spread beneath the tires to help with the traction."

"Cardboard will work better," Rick told her.

"That's what Wade said, too, except they don't have any."

"Check under the bar, Beulah. There's got to be some boxes for all the bottles this place gets delivered."

Beulah apparently did as she was instructed, because Rick returned to the phone and remarked in an amused tone, "She's got it bad for this guy, Daisy."

"How do you know?" Daisy asked in surprise. Rick and Beulah dueled; they were not confidants.

"She didn't bite off my head or give me the look of death for telling her to do something."

Daisy smiled. "You're right. She doesn't usually let you get away with that."

"Found some!" Beulah called.

"Take the ones that can be ripped into squares or long strips," Rick called back.

"Got 'em! I'm sure Wade will be able to use these. He's so good with his hands."

Daisy had to laugh. "You aren't kidding, Rick. I haven't heard Beulah that complimentary about one of her dates . . . uh . . . ever."

"She's also skipping around the room and humming to herself."

"Don't worry, Daisy," Beulah shouted. "Wade will get the truck free, and then we'll be there in a jiffy."

"No!" Daisy exclaimed. "You can't let her come to the inn, Rick! Not before Sheriff Lowell gets here."

"She's made up her mind," he replied. "And I agree with her. You can't spend another night there without help. But don't panic. Beulah isn't going alone."

"How on earth does that help?" Daisy retorted. "Wade being here might even make it worse! If Beulah suddenly appears in the parlor with a strange man standing at her side, the killer could get nervous about who he is and go after the two of them next!"

"Not Wade," Rick corrected her calmly. "Me. *I'll* be with

Beulah. It's my truck that they're clearing. I'm the one who's driving her to the inn."

Startled, Daisy's mouth opened, then closed, and then opened again. "Oh, Rick, that's so risky. I wish you wouldn't."

"Why, darlin', you sound like you're concerned about my well-being."

Although she wanted to deny it—particularly because of the distinct note of laughter in his voice—she didn't. If Beulah was determined to come to the inn, then Daisy knew that she couldn't stop her. Her heart warmed at Beulah's support, but she also feared for her safety. Rick volunteering to come along was a great relief. With him there, the inn wouldn't seem nearly so dangerous.

"Good. Then it's all settled," he said. "You just sit tight. As soon as we can get out of here, Beulah and I will be there."

"I—" Daisy faltered. "I'm awfully grateful—"

Rick promptly switched the subject. "You told me a minute ago that Bud suspected Georgia. Why does he suspect her?"

"He didn't say exactly, other than that she scampers around a lot. But it's probably because of the hiding."

"Hiding?"

"Georgia isn't with the rest of the group," Daisy explained. "She keeps disappearing. I don't know where, except that it's inside the inn, because she also keeps resurfacing."

Rick chuckled. "I bet she's using our old spot. You remember?"

"Of course. I couldn't possibly forget it."

For many years—all long past now—the uppermost floor of the inn had been a favorite haunt for her, Beulah,

Rick, Matt, and sundry other neighborhood children, although neither Daisy nor Beulah was living there then. Having little use for it herself beyond seasonal storage, Aunt Emily had allowed them free rein of the monstrous attic. With its tiny, cobwebby windows and dark, mysterious corners, it was the perfect place to whisper secrets, share tall tales, search through old trunks that were like gleaming treasure troves to their youthful imaginations, and when they reached their teens, sneak a clandestine kiss or two. It was where Daisy had first fallen under Matt's spell.

Shaking away the memories, she returned to the present. "Georgia could be up there. It's easy enough to get in and out, especially since her room is on the third floor, right next to the attic steps."

"When was the last time you saw her?" Rick said.

"Just a little while ago, actually. I had gone into the dining room and caught a glimpse of her darting around the kitchen."

"What was she doing—getting food?"

Daisy's brow furrowed. "It's funny that you should ask, because I wondered the same thing. I didn't see her eating or drinking, but it looked like she was digging through the tea bags."

"Huh?"

"I know it's odd. We all think so. We've all talked about it. Drew and my mama and Aunt Emily—"

"Hold up a second," Rick interjected. "I'm not following you. What have you all talked about?"

"Georgia and her . . ." Daisy paused. "*Fixation*. That's probably the best way to put it. Her fixation on my mama's tea. Georgia set aside my mama's tea bags so that we wouldn't run out with all the people staying here. At first I thought she was just being conscientious, but then she kept mentioning the tea to Drew, over and over again, every time she spoke to him. She wouldn't stop going on about it."

"Is the tea special somehow?"

"Not in the least. That's what makes the whole thing so peculiar. It's regular old tea, nothing exotic or expensive, even. But apparently it's really important to Georgia. Drew said that whenever he tried to find out if she knew anything about what happened to Henry, all she wanted to talk about was the tea."

Rick was thoughtful. "Where exactly is the tea?" he asked after a moment.

"It used to be in a tin on the counter, but Georgia was worried about what she called 'sticky fingers' from some of the guests, and she moved it to a spot that she considered safer. You know how Aunt Emily has all those goofy cookie jars that she keeps getting as gifts lined up on one of the shelves above the sink? Well, that's where Georgia put the tea bags. She hid them in the Rhett Butler cookie jar."

Again Rick was thoughtful. "You said that Georgia was at the cookie jar when you saw her a little while ago?"

"Yes, except I'm pretty sure that she wasn't making tea, so I don't really know what she was doing there. But," Daisy added, "I did think earlier that all the stuff with her and the tea could be a nervous tick. Maybe it crops up when . . ."

She let the sentence trail away, unfinished, as she remembered that Drew had believed there was more to it than a nervous tick, primarily because Georgia had looked at him so intently while she talked about the tea. It occurred to Daisy that Georgia had also looked at someone in the dining room and the parlor with great intensity, and then talked to her about the tea. That struck her as a rather strange coincidence. It seemed stranger still when she recalled that Georgia had confided to Drew some explanation as to why she had been staring at the person in the dining room and the parlor, after which she had once again talked about the tea.

Why always the tea? What was so darn important about her mama's tea bags? Nothing. Absolutely nothing. Yet they seemed to come up in every one of Georgia's conversations, with almost clockwork regularity. And then suddenly Daisy realized that she had been looking at it all wrong. It wasn't about the tea. The tea bags themselves didn't matter one bit. They were a clue. Georgia had meant them as a clue.

"Sweet heaven," Daisy exhaled. "I've been blind. The entire time she's been giving us—giving Drew, really—a clue."

"And I think," Rick said, having unraveled it, too, "you should look in that cookie jar."

CHAPTER
27

Daisy didn't hesitate. She didn't think about anyone seeing or overhearing her if she left the relative safety of the archway. She also didn't consider whether she should first try to track down Georgia or consult Aunt Emily. With a singular purpose, Daisy headed through the dining room, straight into the kitchen, past the stone fireplace, and halted in front of the old farm double sink. Standing on her tiptoes, she reached up to the long shelf—in between the grinning pink hippopotamus and the slightly lewd dancing girl—and lifted down the Clark Gable as Rhett Butler cookie jar that contained her mama's tea bags.

She didn't know quite what she expected to find in the jar, aside from the tea bags, of course. It was, after all, just a cookie jar. That limited the possibilities considerably, both as to size and weight. But there had to be something inside. She was sure of it. Georgia had spent so much time and energy pointing them in the direction of the tea—and thereby the jar—that it couldn't all be for naught.

"Here goes," Daisy said, half to herself and half to Rick.

Holding her breath, she picked up Clark's ceramic head. Her eager gaze went to the contents of his cutaway.

"Well?" Rick asked.

Daisy didn't answer. She was too busy squinting inside the jar.

"So what's in there?" Rick pressed her impatiently.

"A . . ." She reached down and retrieved the object that was nestled into the bed of tea bags. "A candlestick."

"What?"

"A candlestick," she repeated. "A short, round, silver candlestick."

Rick was momentarily silent, no doubt from surprise. Daisy turned the candlestick over in her palm. When she saw the bottom, she was surprised, as well. She had to blink twice to make sure that her eyes weren't deceiving her.

"It's got Lillian's name written underneath," she said.

"Lillian?" Rick echoed. "Why would Lillian's candlestick be in a cookie jar? How would it even be at the inn?"

"It's not Lillian's candlestick," Daisy corrected him. "It's Aunt Emily's."

"Are you sure?"

"I'm positive. It's one of a pair. Aunt Emily's had them for as long as I can remember, although they're usually on the mantel in the parlor."

"Then how did Lillian's name get on it?"

"That's a good question." Daisy took a closer look at the inscription. It was handwritten, and not very neatly. She rubbed it with her finger. Lillian's name smeared beneath her thumb. She smiled. "I think Georgia wrote it."

"Why do you think that?" he asked.

"Because it's written in crayon. Midnight blue crayon, if I recall my colors correctly. The kind, incidentally, that we used to have with all the toys up in the—"

"Attic," Rick finished for her. He sounded like he was smiling, too.

"Of course that raises another question," Daisy continued.

"Why would Georgia put Lillian's name on Aunt Emily's candlestick?"

"And why would she lead us to the cookie jar to find it?"

"Daisy," Rick's tone grew grave, "it's not evidence, is it?"

"What do you mean?"

"The candlestick wasn't used as a weapon, was it? Georgia isn't trying to tell you that Lillian is the one who—"

"No." Daisy stopped him. "It wasn't Lillian with the candlestick. Henry was crushed. And poor Drew was pushed. The candlestick had nothing to do with either death."

"Yes, but were there any signs of . . ." Rick paused, obviously reluctant to conclude the sentence.

"No," she answered again, following his line of thought. "It didn't look like they were hit first. And even if they were, it couldn't have been with this candlestick. It's barely two inches tall and only weighs a couple of ounces. That may be enough to squash an unlucky spider, but otherwise, it's not much of a weapon. Plus, there's no damage done to it. Crayon aside, the candlestick is in perfect condition."

"And its mate? You said there was a pair. Is the other one still in the parlor?"

"I assume so. Aunt Emily kept them on the mantel next to the little clock."

Daisy tried to picture the room from when she was last in it. Parker had been choking Bud in the leather smoking chair. Needing a distraction to stop him, she had thrown one of the bottles from the liquor cart into the hearth. Had there been a candlestick on the mantel above the hearth? No, the clock had stood alone. And as she thought about it, she realized that neither candlestick had been on the mantel all weekend. She hadn't seen them since Friday when the party first started. Someone had taken them. One was now in her hand, courtesy of Georgia and the cookie jar. Did that mean—courtesy of Georgia's crayon—the other was in Lillian's possession? Had Lillian stolen one of Aunt Emily's candlesticks?

"Sticky fingers!" Daisy exclaimed, suddenly putting it together.

"I thought that was in relation to the tea," Rick said.

"It was. But it was also the candlesticks, or at least one candlestick," Daisy amended as she explained. "Georgia kept going on about pilfering guests taking things that didn't belong to them. I knew there had to be more to it than a few tea bags. She was so worked up. Now I finally understand why. Earlier, she had dropped a tray of glasses in the dining room and then stared at somebody hard afterward. Drew told me that it was because Georgia had seen something she wished she hadn't."

"And you think it was Lillian stealing a candlestick?"

"I do. It fits. Everyone was crowding forward from the parlor as Henry unveiled the secretary he was giving to Aunt Emily. Lillian could have easily grabbed one of the candlesticks from the mantel without any of us noticing. We were all turned toward the dining room, except for Georgia. She had come in from the kitchen with the glasses and was facing the parlor. She would have seen Lillian pocket it."

"But why didn't Georgia say anything?"

"She was scared. I know from Drew that she was worried about telling me and Aunt Emily something because she didn't want to lose her job and have to leave the inn. She thought that she was going to get wrongly accused. And I can believe it. You know how spiteful Lillian can be. She wouldn't hesitate to blame someone else, especially someone like Georgia, who's young and quiet and new. It's only natural for Georgia to assume that we would take Lillian's word over hers."

"I can understand that," Rick agreed. "What I can't understand is why Lillian would want to steal the candlestick to begin with."

"I don't know," Daisy said, "but I'm about to go ask her."

"That's a *bad* idea," he replied sharply.

"Why?"

"Because I'm not convinced that this is just about the theft of one of Aunt Emily's candlesticks. From what you've told me, it seems like Georgia put a lot of effort into leading you and Drew to this cookie jar, and she must be really frightened if she keeps hiding up in the attic. There has to be something else."

"And I intend to find out what it is. Lillian doesn't scare me." As she spoke, Daisy set the candlestick back inside the cookie jar. She didn't want Lillian to see it in advance. The more surprised Lillian was, the less she would be able to conjure justifications and excuses.

"Lillian isn't the person that I'm concerned about—" Rick began.

He was interrupted by the sudden return of Beulah.

"It's clear!" Beulah reported excitedly. "Wade and Bobby have the truck out of the mud and up the incline to the road. We can go!"

"Did you hear that, Daisy?" Rick said. "Beulah and I are leaving for the inn right now. Don't do anything. Just wait until I get there."

Their departure was welcome news to her, but Daisy had not the slightest intention of waiting for him—or anybody else—to confront Lillian.

"Drive safely," she responded sweetly, heading out of the kitchen and into the main hall with the cookie jar tucked under her arm. "I'll see you soon."

"Daisy," Rick's voice rose in warning, "I mean it. *Don't do anything.*"

"Drive safely," she said again, then she hung up the phone and stepped into the parlor.

The entire group—with only Georgia missing—turned toward Daisy as she entered the room. They were arranged somewhat differently than usual, drawn closer together as though that were somehow safer. Lillian shared the gold-brocaded settee with the Fowler sisters. Kenneth and Sarah Lunt occupied the emerald-brocaded settee, while Aunt Emily sat in one of the neighboring damask armchairs. As Daisy had instructed, Parker and Bud were stationed across from each other at the tea table. She was pleased to see that Parker was still in possession of the hatchet. The hickory handle lay across his knees.

No one drank, or ate, or spoke. They all looked at Daisy with nervous anticipation, fidgeting in their seats like schoolchildren expecting a fire drill. Parker had apparently succeeded in not explaining anything. There was an uneasy tension in the room—a general wariness and apprehension. Everybody seemed to be waiting for someone to tell them what was happening and what to do next.

Aunt Emily was the first to break the silence.

"Did I hear you talking to somebody on the phone, Ducky?" she asked.

"Rick," Daisy answered, without further elaboration.

"Oh, that's very good." Aunt Emily's tone was hopeful. "Is he . . ."

Daisy didn't listen. Her eyes were fixed on the mantel above the hearth. She had been correct. The clock stood alone. The other candlestick was gone. She walked toward the gold-brocaded settee and stopped directly in front of Lillian.

"I know it was you," Daisy said.

Lillian blinked at her but didn't reply.

"Are you seriously going to pretend that you don't understand me?"

She blinked again, several times in rapid succession, then she bit down on her lips, hard.

"So you're planning on waiting for Sheriff Lowell to arrive?" Daisy continued, deliberately trying to goad her.

Lillian's cheeks flushed, and her shoulders twitched. There was a disconcerted murmur from the group, but Daisy kept her focus firmly on Lillian.

"You want the sheriff to know?" she pressed her. "You want everybody in the neighborhood to find out?"

As Lillian's whole body began to shake, Daisy thrust the final dagger.

"You want Georgia to tell them all what you did?"

No longer able to restrain herself, Lillian shot up from

the settee, wild panic in her eyes and her neck a deep shade of crimson.

"They're lies!" she shrieked. "Nothing but lies! You can't believe Georgia. She's trying to frame me. I didn't kill anybody! I didn't have anything to do with it! All I did was take the candlestick. One stupid candlestick!" Pulling the candlestick from her purse, Lillian flung it to the ground as though it burned her.

A stunned hush followed, with everyone gaping at Lillian. Even Daisy was a bit startled. Having no proof other than the crayon, she had wanted to provoke Lillian into a confession and to return the missing candlestick, but she hadn't expected her to think that anyone was accusing her of murder.

"I—" Aunt Emily rose from her chair and looked in bewilderment at the mantel. "I didn't even notice the candlesticks were gone."

"I didn't, either," Daisy told her. "But Georgia did. She saw Lillian steal the first one. So Georgia took the second one to protect it." She lifted the matching candlestick from the cookie jar and held up the bottom with Lillian's name written on it.

"That girl is such a meddling little twit," Lillian spat.

Aunt Emily spun toward her, no doubt ready to launch into a scathing rebuke, but Parker spoke before she could.

"What in heaven's name were you thinking?" he said to his wife.

Her face contorted in silence.

"Answer me." Parker's voice was quiet, but it wasn't mild. There was a deep rumble beneath it, like something lurking at the bottom of a dark ravine, just waiting to emerge.

"If you must know," Lillian's nostrils flared, "I did it for Matt."

Daisy's mouth opened in astonishment.

"I was going to send the candlestick to Matt!" Lillian shouted.

They all stared at her. After a minute, Parker asked the collective question.

"Why would Matt want a candlestick?"

"He could sell it," Lillian responded matter-of-factly. "It's sterling, so it must be worth something. All pawnshops take silver, don't they? Matt needs the money."

"If he needs money," Daisy retorted with irritation, "then he should get a job and work like the rest of us."

"But he must be desperate!" Instead of angry and defensive, Lillian's expression had become anxious and pleading. "Matt must be desperate and in need of money, or he would have come back by now."

Daisy threw up her hands in frustration. "For criminy sake! It has nothing to do with money, Lillian. The reason Matt hasn't come back is that he doesn't *want* to. *He doesn't want to be with me.*"

"That's not true." Lillian shook her head, and then her whole body started to shake once more. "Matt would have come back if he could. I'm sure of it. He must be in trouble." Her voice rose to a hysterical pitch. "He needs our help! He—"

"Oh, cork it, Lillian!" Parker roared.

She let out a squeak in protest, but he glowered at her with such intensity that she didn't dare make another sound. Parker's fingers curled around the handle of the hatchet in his lap, and for a moment, it looked like he was sorely tempted to use it on his wife, himself, or some combination thereof. But he didn't. He remained in his seat and closed his eyes.

A few seconds later, Parker opened them again and said in a much calmer, almost weary tone, "If you wanted to give money to Matt so badly, Lillian, why didn't you just send him some? Why on earth would you steal—and from Emily?"

"I didn't want you to find out." Lillian sniffled. "You would have told me that I wasn't being rational."

Parker and Daisy exchanged a glance. There was no contradicting it, because Lillian was most definitely not being rational. But then, there was considerable doubt as to whether she had ever been rational.

"All right." Parker sighed. "If you apologize to Emily, perhaps she'll have the kindness not to take this to the law."

"Of course," Aunt Emily agreed, charitable as always. "Sheriff Lowell won't find out about it from me. There's no need for public shaming."

As she said it, Aunt Emily took the candlestick from Daisy's hand with a discreet smile. Daisy had to suppress a chuckle. The public shaming had already been accomplished. Lillian had been mortified in front of friends and strangers alike, and as much as the Fowler sisters enjoyed gossip, word was sure to spread—quickly.

"And I don't want to hear," Parker added sternly, "any more remarks about Matt. Do you understand me, Lillian? No more pestering Daisy. She's had enough."

Struggling not to laugh, Daisy reached down and picked up the other candlestick from the carpet. It was Parker who'd had enough, and now they were both going to benefit. They would be spared from having to listen to

Lillian's copious complaints and criticisms, at least for a while.

With effort, Lillian murmured something that resembled an apology. Aunt Emily accepted it gracefully, at the same time returning the candlesticks to the mantel. Set upright, the crayon underneath wasn't visible, but Aunt Emily made no mention of cleaning it either way. She was far too clever for that, because as long as Lillian's name remained—or Lillian imagined that it remained—it would keep her slightly more humble.

Lillian plopped herself back on the settee, and all at once, the former tension in the room seemed to evaporate. May reached over and patted Lillian's knee. Edna made an appropriately benevolent remark. Kenneth and Sarah Lunt shared a pleased look, presuming that no one suspected they were also thieves, except on a grander scale. It was as though the hullabaloo with the candlesticks had made everybody forget that there had been another crime. Two much more serious crimes. Two murders.

Parker—being an excellent eater and always on the lookout for a tasty snack—turned toward Daisy and the cookie jar that she was still holding. "You wouldn't happen to have any cookies in there?" he asked hopefully.

"No," she started to reply, "just tea bags . . ."

He was leaning forward in his seat so eagerly, trying to catch a glimpse inside the jar, that Daisy held it out to him for his inspection. As she did, her own eyes saw that what she said wasn't true, and her breath caught in her throat.

Rick was right. There was something else. Something that went far beyond a missing candlestick. Something that explained why Georgia was so afraid and had worked so hard to point them toward the cookie jar. It was tucked along the edge and almost under the tea bags, which was why Daisy hadn't noticed it before. But she recognized it instantly. It was the long-lost piece of paper from Henry Brent's hand.

CHAPTER
28

The paper was yellowed and mildly brittle with age. It was folded like a letter in crisp, straight lines, and there were several small pieces of tape on the corners, as though it had at one time been pasted somewhere. Setting down the cookie jar on the table next to Parker, Daisy pushed aside the tea bags and carefully lifted out the paper.

"What is that?" Aunt Emily asked.

Not sure herself what it was, Daisy hesitated. Edna made a gurgling noise. Daisy looked at her. She was sitting tall and rigid on the settee.

"That isn't yours," Edna said.

"I know. It—"

The gurgling repeated itself, and Edna's voice rose slightly. "You shouldn't have that. It *isn't* yours."

"I know," Daisy began again. "It belongs to Henry."

"No, it doesn't."

Daisy frowned. "But I saw it in his hand."

Edna frowned back at her. "It was in his hand?"

She nodded. "Henry was holding it when we first found him on the floor, but after we covered him with the blanket, his hand was empty. I couldn't figure out where the paper had gone. Now I know that Georgia took it."

"Georgia?" Edna's frown deepened.

Aunt Emily looked back and forth between them. "I don't understand. Georgia took that paper from Henry?"

"It isn't his," Edna objected.

"So it's Georgia's?" Aunt Emily said.

Edna shook her head and gurgled once more.

It was Aunt Emily's turn to frown. "Ducky . . ."

Daisy was just as puzzled. She didn't understand how Edna knew about the paper or who it belonged to when she wasn't the one who had taken it. But then it occurred to her that the most important answer was already in her hand. She started to unfold the paper.

"No!" Edna cried, jumping up from the settee.

Everyone turned to her in surprise. May gazed at her sister with concern.

"Are you feeling all right, dear?" she asked.

"Don't you see?" Edna replied in agitation.

"I see that you're terribly pale," May answered, patting the seat next to her. "It's been such a stressful weekend for all of us. Why don't you sit down and—"

"Are you blind!" Edna cut her off severely. "Don't you realize what it is?"

For a moment, May was rendered speechless by the harshness of her sister's tone. She stared at Edna, then at Daisy, and finally at the paper in Daisy's hand. Suddenly her eyes widened, and she gasped.

"Is that . . . That isn't . . . You don't mean—"

"Exactly!" Edna exclaimed.

May appeared dumbfounded. "But I thought that was thrown away years ago . . ."

Edna's cleft chin jutted out.

"Why is it here?" May continued. "Where has it been all this time?"

There was a pause as the sisters looked at each other, and then May gasped again, as though she had somehow read the answer in Edna's expression.

"It was in the secretary?" she said, astounded.

Edna responded with a troubled sigh.

"Oh, Edna," May sighed, too, "why didn't you tell me? I wouldn't have sold the secretary if I had known. Or I would have removed it first. Or—" She stopped, her brow furrowed. "But I'm sure that I checked all the drawers and compartments before the boys loaded it onto the truck with the rest of the furniture. There wasn't anything in the secretary."

"It was taped to the back."

The words came out low and soft. Some in the group might not have even heard them, but Daisy did, and they echoed through her mind. *Taped to the back.* She remembered Henry squeezing behind the secretary, trying to examine some thingamabob, as he had called it. It was the paper. The paper had been taped to the back of the secretary. Henry had obviously retrieved it, because he had been holding it when he died. Georgia had then taken it and put it in the cookie jar. Now Edna—and perhaps also May—was apparently claiming it. But why? What was so interesting about the paper?

Daisy started to unfold it once more. Edna let out an ear-splitting wail, but it was too late. The paper was already open and legible. Based on its age and creases, Daisy had expected a letter or some similar form of correspondence. Instead the paper turned out to be a certificate. More precisely, a certificate of appreciation. It was dated 1915 and presented to Jeremiah Thomas Fowler, in recognition of his "Fraternity, Charity and Loyalty." The certificate was bestowed by an organization of veterans called the Grand Army of the Republic.

It took Daisy a minute to process what she was reading. Jeremiah Thomas Fowler was Edna and May's great-great-grandfather, and he had been commended for his service on the fiftieth anniversary of the conclusion of the Civil War. Perfectly logical. Entirely reasonable. Certainly laudable. And then Daisy realized the problem. The Grand Army of the Republic wasn't for veterans of the South. It was for veterans of the North. That meant Jeremiah Thomas Fowler had fought for the Union, *not* the Confederacy.

Her startled eyes went to Edna. Edna looked back at her with a fevered, swirling gaze.

"Would somebody," Aunt Emily said, exasperation in her tone, "kindly explain to me what that is," she gestured toward the certificate, "and what is going on?"

"Don't," Edna pleaded, clutching her hands together imploringly. "Don't tell them, Daisy. You don't have to tell them. They don't need to know. Henry was going to tell them, but I stopped him. Now he can't tell, not anymore . . ."

An ice-cold wave of horror washed over Daisy. It struck her so hard that she couldn't speak and almost crumpled to the ground. May must have reached the same mortifying conclusion, because she sucked in her breath sharply and gripped her lace handkerchief with white knuckles.

"Good God, Edna," she exhaled. "What have you done?"

"I had to do it," Edna replied tearfully. "I didn't have a choice. Henry discovered the certificate. He said that it was important. Historically important. That the historical society needed to know. But if they found out, then *everyone* would find out, and we would be disgraced. The whole family would be disgraced."

"Lord grant me strength," May whispered, twisting and almost ripping the handkerchief in half.

"I tried to reason with him," Edna went on, her voice slowly steadying. "I tried to make him understand. The certificate belongs to the family. It has to stay with us. But Henry wouldn't give it back. He said that I should wait and think about it. Well, I didn't want to wait and think about it. I just wanted him to keep his mouth shut. And that's when it happened. That's when I did it. It was surprisingly easy, tippy as the secretary was. But it was dreadfully noisy, so I shut off all the lamps as quick as I could, in case someone came down the stairs. Of course, then I couldn't see anything. I assumed the certificate was in Henry's pocket, underneath the secretary somewhere. I was hoping that I could get to it once the sheriff arrived."

"Edna!" Aunt Emily cried, aghast. "Are you saying— you're the one who—"

"I'm sorry for ruining your party, Emily, but it couldn't be helped. And I'm also sorry," Edna turned back toward Daisy, "about Drew. He seemed like such a pleasant young fellow. Awfully good-looking, too. If it's any consolation, I didn't plan on killing him. I went down to the kitchen, not able to sleep, and there he was getting oil for the lanterns. We talked, and sadly, Drew figured out what I had done. It seems that he had heard Henry and me arguing the night before, and he recognized my voice. Obviously I couldn't let him tell you. So I pushed him into the cellar. He fell hard. Everything broke."

Anger boiled up inside Daisy like a blazing inferno, but Edna spoke again before she could explode.

"You mentioned earlier that Georgia took the certifi-cate," Edna said to her. "From the way she knew her Con-federate history and about General Stuart, I have to assume that she understood it. Do you think she's told her friend's meemaw about it? The one in the Daughters?"

Daisy took one look at the acute anxiety on Edna's face, and all of her anger, all of her grief, all of her shock, turned into disgust.

"That's what you're concerned about?" she spat. "You murdered two men—two of the warmest, kindest, dearest people any of us will ever have the good fortune to meet—because you were afraid of getting kicked out of the Daughters of the Confederacy? You didn't want to lose your presidency of a club?"

Edna stiffened with pride. "You don't understand. It's about heritage—"

"Heritage!" Daisy scoffed. "Don't talk to me about heri-tage. My family fought in the American Revolutionary War. And Aunt Emily's family is the oldest in the county."

"Then you must understand—" Edna began again, more beseeching.

"I understand," she retorted, "that I don't have the lux-ury of fretting about who was on which side of what battle a century or two ago. I have to worry about *now*. Whether I'll have customers and food at the bakery tomorrow. Whether my decrepit car will start so I can even get to the bakery. Whether my mama will get better or worse, and whether I'll be able to pay her medical bills."

Having no response to that, Edna dropped her head.

May moaned piteously. "Oh, Edna, how could you ever imagine that this would honor our family—or our friends at the Daughters? You haven't preserved our heritage.

You've perverted it into something horrible. You've taken lives!"

"And those lives are *not* going to be remembered as part of some ghastly story attached to an inane piece of paper that should have been tossed in the waste bin decades ago," Aunt Emily declared with force.

Edna's head sprang back up. Her eyes were filled with fear. "What are you going to do with it?"

"Burn it," Aunt Emily said. "We all know the truth now. It can never be hidden again."

"But you can't!" Edna protested. "It's a family document! It must be maintained!"

"Which is precisely why I'm destroying it. After what you've done—all the misery you've caused because of it—it's the best punishment in my power." With dignity, Aunt Emily turned to Daisy and motioned toward the crackling fire in the hearth. "If you would do the honors, Ducky . . ."

"Gladly." She glared at Edna. "For Drew and Henry."

"No, Daisy! No!" Edna shouted.

Daisy started to move in the direction of the hearth, but she made it only one step before Edna launched herself into the air like a missile. Instinctively Daisy jumped to the side, and instead of landing on top of her, Edna knocked over the tea table. The cookie jar went flying. So did the hatchet from Parker's lap. Daisy and Edna both looked at it, then they looked at each other, and in the same instant, they dove for it.

Edna, who was closer, reached the hickory handle first. Grabbing it, she began flailing it around wildly.

"Give me the certificate!" she screamed. "Give it to me!"

The blade of the hatchet swiped Daisy's forearm, slicing

CHAPTER
29

The cavalry arrived more or less simultaneously, except there was no longer any need of a rescue. Edna had neither the physical nor mental strength to pick herself up from the parlor floor. Bud showed not the least intention of letting Kenneth and Sarah—and the generous reward attached to them—out of his sight. Lillian was purring with conciliatory sweetness to both Parker and May, although it was probably less sweet than it would have been half an hour earlier. No doubt Lillian was feeling considerably less chastened now that her crime appeared so very trivial in comparison to Edna's.

Together Daisy and Aunt Emily walked to the front door and stood outside on the porch, watching the assemblage of plows, law enforcement vehicles, and fire and rescue-squad trucks as they shoveled, maneuvered, and tried to park on the narrow road without ending up in a ditch.

"I should check on my mama," Daisy said after a while.

"I'm sure that she's fine," Aunt Emily replied. "She's probably the most relaxed and rested of all of us."

open the skin. It was more of a graze than a gash, but it still hurt, and a second later, her wrist was covered with blood.

"Son of a—" Daisy growled.

Out of the corner of her eye, she could see Parker, Bud, and Aunt Emily all rushing to her aid, but she didn't need their help. She threw one swift punch at Edna's stomach, and the air went out of the woman's lungs. As Edna sunk to the carpet, Daisy pulled the hatchet from her loosened grip. With blood dripping down her fingers, she walked slowly backward toward the hearth, the hatchet in one hand and the certificate in the other.

"Stop her, May!" Edna sobbed. "Stop her! He may have been a damn Yankee, but he was still our kin."

May didn't even look at her sister. Instead she turned to Daisy and held out her lace handkerchief. "For your arm," she said.

Daisy nodded and dropped the certificate into the fire. No one spoke as the paper curled and blackened. Edna wept, and faint sirens could be heard in the distance while the flames licked the last shreds into ash.

After a respectful moment had passed, Kenneth glanced sideways at Sarah, then—genial and smooth—he said to Aunt Emily, "With all of this tragedy, you must want to sell the inn now."

Wrapping May's handkerchief around her wrist, Daisy almost laughed.

Daisy smiled. "And poor Georgia, who's huddled up in the attic, awaiting her fate. Someone needs to tell her that she still has her job and doesn't have to leave the inn."

"So long as she stops dropping all the dishes and doesn't mention anything related to Jeb Stuart for the next six months." Although Aunt Emily began with a chuckle, she ended with a sigh.

It was echoed by Daisy. "It's been a hundred and fifty years, and I can't help wondering if that war will ever be over."

"Not in these parts. Not any time soon." She patted Daisy's uninjured arm. "That's what you learn when you become an old biddy. It's all a carousel, Ducky. Good and bad—happy and sad—past, present, and future. Everything keeps circling around. We choose to step on or off. And in your case, my dear, you need to choose a different horse."

Daisy raised a questioning eyebrow.

"Will you look at that," Aunt Emily drawled, laughter in her voice. "Here comes a new horse now."

Following her gaze, Daisy saw that Rick's truck had pulled up to the edge of the driveway leading to the inn. Beulah was waving enthusiastically and leaping through the melting snow toward them. Rick walked more slowly after her. His eyes were on Daisy.

Aunt Emily gave her a nudge. "You go talk to him, Ducky. It's only polite, after all. He did bring Beulah home. Don't worry about the others. I'll explain everything to Beulah—and to Sheriff Lowell, if he ever manages to get out of that car of his."

Tugging on a pair of boots, Daisy started down the porch steps. Beulah met her with a monstrous hug, a hundred questions, and a fervent declaration that they were all going to adore Wade Watson Howard III when he visited the inn tomorrow evening for supper. Daisy simply smiled and with great affection hugged her back.

As Aunt Emily began to answer the proliferation of questions, Daisy continued toward Rick. She reached him near the middle of the driveway. His dark gaze went immediately to the blood-soaked handkerchief wrapped around her wrist.

Before he could ask, Daisy said, "It turns out that Parker is perfectly safe with a hatchet. Edna Fowler, however . . ." She gave a light-hearted shrug.

Rick lifted her arm, inspecting it. Daisy didn't know if it was because of the cool air or the sensitivity of the wound, but his fingers felt hot against her skin.

"It looks much worse than it actually is," she assured him. "I've had far nastier cuts at the diner and the bakery."

"I told you not to do anything," he rebuked her gruffly. "I told you to wait."

"Well, you should know by now that I rarely do what anyone tells me, and it annoys everybody."

Although Rick grunted in acknowledgment, his lips curled into a smile.

Daisy smiled in return. "I would invite you into the inn, but even ignoring the fact that the place is currently harboring a wide range of criminals, I can't spend any more time inside. It's so nice to be outdoors." She raised her face to the bright rays of the sun and the topaz blue sky.

"How about a drive?" he suggested. "The roads are rough, but it's mighty pretty with the ice covering the trees and the snow on the hills."

She hesitated for a moment, then Aunt Emily's words about carousels and horses repeated themselves in her head.

Daisy wasn't so sure that the woman wasn't being a bit batty, and Aunt Emily did have an undeniable soft spot for Rick. But either way, it was only a drive. And she really didn't want to deal with Sheriff Lowell or go back to the parlor.

"A drive sounds nice," she agreed.

They turned and started to walk toward Rick's truck. At the end of the driveway, they came to the inn's mailbox. The door was slightly ajar, and Daisy opened it to clean out the accumulated snow. To her surprise, she found an envelope inside.

"How strange," she murmured. "We collected the mail from Friday, and there wasn't any on Saturday because of the storm."

Pulling out the envelope, Daisy discovered that it was red and in the shape of a greeting card. She winced, and her stomach knotted. She didn't want it to be from Drew. Not now. Not when he was gone. He could have put it in the mailbox on Friday when he arrived for the party.

"A little early for a Valentine, isn't it?" Rick said. "That's not for another week." Seeing her pained expression, he added lightly, "It's probably for Aunt Emily. You know how many admirers she has. I can look at it if you don't want to."

"No," Daisy answered, shaking her head. She appreciated the offer, but she had to do it herself.

With reluctance, she tore open the envelope. It was indeed a card. A large crimson heart. When Daisy saw it, her knees quivered, her brain spun, and she almost pitched to the ground. Rick grabbed her before she fell.

"Whoa, darlin'!"

Struggling to breathe, she leaned against his chest. Rick wrapped a sturdy, protective arm around her.

"Daisy?" he asked, gazing at her with concern.

"Matt," she whispered. Her throat was so tight that she could barely get out the words. "It's from Matt."

Rick's eyes turned black, but his arm tightened rather than released her. Daisy handed him the card, and he read it aloud.

Roses are red,
Violets are blue.
Don't worry, baby,
Soon I'll be with you.
—M